CLAIMING HER COUGAR

SHIFTING PINES
BOOK TWO

JENNY FENSHAW

SHIFTING PINES PRESS

Book Cover Designed by Dark Water Covers Premades and Formatting

Editing by Empowered Writing Author Services, HEA Author Services, and Patricia Raine Lam

PROLOGUE

Mallory

"I LOVE THIS SONG!" I YELL OUT TO MY GIRLFRIENDS AS WE GET READY TO take the shots the server just brought us. We're having a bachelorette party for my friend Katie, and we snagged a prime table in the VIP section of the hottest nightclub in Vegas' coolest casino. Our friend and fellow bridesmaid, Melissa, is a host for the high rollers here and got us a suite for the weekend—and the VIP hookup in the club. It's been too long since we've all gotten together and let loose.

"I do too, Mallory! Let's dance!" Katie shouts as we slam our shot glasses on the table with a thunk. Everyone's face is puckering from the limes we've bitten into. Yeah, we're sexy. Katie's penis tiara is listing to the left, so I reach out to straighten it on her head. Then I realize it's *Katie* listing to the left. We probably shouldn't have taken that last shot of Patrón. Oh well.

We aren't the only bachelorette party here tonight, but I know we're the coolest and hottest. Wait, that doesn't make sense —Oh well. I'm buzzed, but not drunk. Maybe I didn't inherit actual shifting from my wolf shifter parents, but I got their ability to metabolize alcohol quickly. By the end of this song, it will be like I never took that last shot. My friends are all regular humans, no shifter blood in them, so the drinks are hitting them faster than me. This party trick served me well at the college we all attended in Pennsylvania. I killed it at beer pong. While everyone else was getting sloshed and clumsy, I'd stay coherent and coordinated.

We're a group of fifteen good-looking ladies, and between the penis tiara, the bride and bride-squad sashes, and our general merriment, it's obvious we're a bachelorette party. They always attract attention. I'm one of the few single girls in our group, so I'm checking out the guys looking us over. YOLO, what happens in Vegas, and all that.

My gaze stops on a hottie at the bar. He's staring at me too. He's tall, probably around six foot three. Dark brown hair, bright blue eyes, and a neatly groomed beard framing lips quirked in a half smile. He's in a black dress shirt with the sleeves rolled up, exposing his powerful forearms. He fills out a pair of black slacks really well. Broad shoulders, trim hips. In a word, yummy. It's been a long time since I've felt such an instant attraction to a man.

Okay, if I'm being honest, I don't think I've ever been this attracted to someone at first glance. As the next song starts, my group lets out a collective whoop, and we continue dancing. It's possible I shake my ass a bit more than usual, knowing it's looking great in my short, tight, royal-blue dress. I'm a curvy girl, and my butt is one of my best curves. I glance over my shoulder to see the dude at the bar watching my ass. I give an extra wiggle, and he bites his bottom lip. Wish I was biting it. I wonder if his beard is soft or scratchy?

His blue-eyed gaze meets mine, and I gasp at the heat I see there, the possessiveness. My core clenches. I'm not one to go all swoony over an alpha male. I've dealt with way too many of them in my life, and, since I'm often related to them, they're usually annoying. But for one night, I can do alpha. More like do *an* alpha.

"Grabbing some water," I call to Ashley over the thumping bass of the song. She lifts her blonde hair off her neck as she sways her hips to the beat.

"Good idea! Let's go!" She turns toward the bar but stops short when she sees the actual cause of my thirst. "Oh. "

"I'll be going to the ladies' room after," I tell her with a wink.

"Uh-huh. If you aren't back in half an hour and haven't texted me, I'm looking for you. Text me if you leave the club."

"Yes, mom." My tone is teasing, but truth is, I appreciate knowing someone has my back. I'd do the same for her. For any of my friends.

I approach the bar and squeeze in a couple of spots down from my quarry.

"What can I get you?" the bartender asks. Her name tag says Teagan. She's a stunning blonde who could probably make more money as a model than as a bartender.

"Hi, Teagan. I'd love ice water with mint if you have it, please." I get a couple of bills from my wristlet.

She places my glass in front of me, and I slide her the money.

"No charge," she informs me.

I smile. "I know. Thanks. This is for you."

She accepts the tip with a grin and a nod before moving on to the next person.

Picking up my glass, I take a sip as I glance to where Hottie McHotterston was. He's no longer there. Damn.

Liam

The redhead is stunning. Her deep auburn locks are in one of those half-up, half-down styles girls do, and it's curled, the long tendrils trailing halfway down her back, and I want to grab it and pull on it while I bury myself in her. Her pale neck is slender and graceful—I want to rain kisses down it and suck on it hard enough to leave my mark. I'm a sexual man, but I don't think I've ever had this kind of instantaneous reaction to a woman.

"Want another, Liam?" Teagan, my best friend, asks from behind the bar.

"Nah, I'm good. Thanks." I turn back to watch the dance floor.

She must be with a bachelorette party if the penis tiara and sashes are anything to go by. Thank goodness she's not the one wearing the bride sash.

My breath catches when she turns to look over at the bar and her gaze lands on me. Her green eyes widen when they meet mine. I don't know how I can tell they're green from across a neon-lit dance floor, but I can, and I don't think it's my extra-sharp shifter eyesight. She turns back to her group and continues to dance to the thumping, sensual beat, her curvy ass swinging more than it was before. If she's trying to entice me, it's working.

She talks to one of her friends and saunters toward the bar but doesn't come to me. Instead, she squeezes in a few spots down. The club is loud with music and chatter, but my superior cougar shifter hearing picks up her order of ice water with mint. Good. She'll taste like mint when we kiss, and we will be kissing tonight, if I have any control over the situation.

I move from my spot at the bar and stand behind her. She accepts her water and tips the bartender. She glances at where I'd been standing, and her shoulders droop slightly. In disappointment?

She sips her water as she turns to face the dance floor again. When she sees me standing behind her, she chokes until she manages to swallow it.

"Hello," I say, taking her in. She's taller than average but still around half a foot shorter than I am, even in her heels. A stretchy, sleeveless royal-blue dress covers her luscious curves. Her breasts are full but not ridiculous-looking. I'd bet my last dollar they're natural. I long to rest my hands on the indented waist of her classic hourglass figure. Her gently curving hips lead to long legs ending in black heels. I'd love to have those legs wrapped around my waist and those heels digging into my ass.

"Hi." Her voice is pleasant. Calm. Yeah, it was just a single word, but I can tell.

"Having a good time?" There are so many things I want to ask—her name, where she's from, does she want to go back to my room, has she ever been with a cougar shifter like me? But I'll start with a good time.

"I am," she answers with a shy smile. "Are you?"

"I am now." Wow, that's cheesy. Sounds like a pickup line. But it's the truth.

She takes another sip of her water, looking up at me through her lashes with her red-painted lips wrapped around the straw. My cock stirs at the thought of her giving me that same look with those lips wrapped around it.

"You're here with friends?"

She nods. "Bachelorette party. Friend from college." She looks around. "Are you here with friends too?"

"No, I'm in town for work and decided to check it out." I look over my shoulder at the dance floor. The song's just switched to something slower and sexier. "Wanna dance?"

"Sure." She places her water on the bar.

I follow her to the dance floor, my hand resting on the small of her back, just above the curve of her delectable ass. She turns and puts her arms around my neck, and I rest my hands on her waist. We move in a natural rhythm with each other.

"I'm Liam," I say.

"Mallory."

"Do you live in Vegas?"

"No, just here for the weekend. You?"

"Leave town tomorrow," I admit. I swear I can smell her arousal, and it's driving me crazy. I think she's feeling the same as she presses closer to me.

"So, just tonight?" Her bright green eyes are heavy-lidded as she looks up at me.

"How much have you had to drink?" I don't care how hot they are, I don't mess with drunk girls.

"I'm sober. Had a couple shots earlier, but I metabolize it quickly and have been drinking water." She smirks. "How about you?"

"Sober. Couple whiskeys, but shifter metabolism. Cougar," I clarify before she asks.

"Rwarrrrrr," she mock-growls as she nips at my jaw, and it's so ridiculous, I laugh.

Her fingers tunnel into my hair, and she tugs to lower my head. All she had to do was ask. My lips meet hers, and forget growling, my cougar wants to purr. Mallory's lips are soft and pliant. They part to allow my tongue to slip between them. The noise of the club fades. I focus all my senses on the woman in my arms. My hands flex on her hips, pulling her even closer to me. My cock is at full mast, my desire obvious.

"Let's go somewhere more private," she says, pulling back from our kiss. Her lips are swollen, and I want to taste them again. I nod because I'll follow wherever she leads me.

Grabbing my hand, she leads me to the VIP section where her party has a table. Her friends are still on the dance floor, so it is just the two of us in the area, but it's not private. She leans over and sifts through stuff strewn on the table, coming up with a foil-wrapped square.

I meet her smile with a grin of my own, looking around the space. "I'm game if you are. Where?" It's not like I'm a virgin, but I've never had a hookup in a club. When in Vegas...

"Back here?" She wanders behind a bunch of big plants that form a private nook away from curious eyes.

"Works for me," I pluck the condom from between her fingers and tuck it into my back pocket. I can't believe we're doing this.

It's dark behind the plants, but the ambient light of the club is enough for me to see her beautiful face. Her eyes are wide, and her chest rises and falls on deep breaths.

"We aren't doing anything you aren't comfortable with, Mallory. You can change your mind or say no at any time," I assure her.

Reaching out to grab my belt loops, she pulls me toward her as she walks backward into the shadows of our private little hideaway. "I want this, Liam. So much. I've just never done it in a club or anywhere public before. Kiss me?"

I position myself so if anyone looks back here, they only see my back. They won't be able to see Mallory. I lean in and press my lips to hers, and we pick up right where we left off on the dance floor. We avail ourselves of the freedom to explore, and I grasp her curvy ass with one hand while using my other hand to fondle one of her full breasts. I was right—they are natural. I strum my thumb over a taut nipple, and she moans into my mouth.

Her hands roam over my shoulders, down my biceps, and around to my ass. I grind my erection against her pelvis, and we both groan. I could get off just dry humping her like a randy teenager, but Mallory slips her hand into my rear pocket to retrieve the condom I stashed there. Holding it up between two fingers, she moans a simple, "Please."

I answer by taking the packet from her grasp and kissing her more firmly, pressing myself against her, and pressing her back against the wall. I run my hand up her thigh, under her skirt. Brushing my fingers along the apex of her thighs, I growl deep in my throat at how hot and wet she is.

"Liam, please, I want this. I want you." Her eager fingers unfasten my belt and undo my pants. All the while, she never lifts her lips from my jawline, where she's busy planting tiny, playful, hot kisses. Before she can pull my cock out of my boxer briefs, I hook my fingers in the sides of her thong and drop to my haunches, lowering the tiny scrap of lace so she can step out of it. I put it in my pocket for safekeeping and, while I'm down there, press kisses along the inside of her thigh and give a lick along her slit. She shudders and grasps my shoulders to steady herself. She tastes so sweet. I wish I could savor her, but this isn't the time or place to do that. Rising, I kiss her again, allowing her to taste herself on my tongue.

"All good?" I ask.

"It will be once you're in me. Please, Liam."

I rip open the condom package and make quick work of sheathing myself. "You sure?"

"Yes, please, Liam. I want you."

I close my eyes for a moment, savoring those words. Then I force them open so I can watch Mallory's face as I wrap her leg around my hip and push into her. She's tight and hot, and I groan. So good. Once I'm fully seated within her, I still for a moment to allow us to adjust to each other. Her walls tighten around my cock, inviting me to start moving. We kiss and moan into each other as we move together to mutual satisfaction. I end up fully supporting Mallory's weight with both of her legs wrapped around my hips as I pound into her.

Her sexy moans and groans make me crazy, and all I want to do is make her feel even better. I shift a hand from her ass, along her hip, so I can use my thumb to massage her clit. That pressure is all it takes to push her over the edge. Her walls tighten around me with pleasure, and her orgasm washes over her. Her eyes are closed, and in the dim light, I think I can just make out a flush along her cheekbones. With two more hard thrusts and a deep groan, I follow her over the precipice of pleasure and empty myself into the condom. I know this is just meant to be a hookup, but it feels like more. Am I romanticizing this because I'm not the guy that has random encounters in dark corners of clubs? Is it something more, or is it just hot—okay, mind-blowing sex?

We catch our breath as we remain wrapped in each other's arms, tucked into our little corner of paradise.

"Wow," Mallory says reverently, stroking the nape of my neck and resting her face against my shoulder.

"So much wow," I agree. "That was incredible."

"Mallory?" A voice calls from the other side of the potted plants forming the wall of our hideaway.

Wide green eyes meet mine.

"I know you're back there. I'm sorry to interrupt," the voice says.

"It's okay, Ashley. Everything all right?" Mallory calls out.

"Katie isn't feeling great, so we're taking her back to the room. Take your time. Just wanted you to know."

Ashley and Katie must be part of the bachelorette party.

Mallory sighs heavily, and I withdraw from her body, lowering her legs so she can stand on her own.

"Thank you, Liam. This was incredible. The best I've ever had." She presses a hard kiss to my lips but pulls back before I can deepen it. "I need to go make sure Katie's okay. They've all been drinking a lot, and I'm the sober one of the group."

She pulls her skirt down and, before I can say anything, slips past me and exits our nook, rejoining her friends. I tuck myself back in and close my fly. I'll clean up when I get to my room. Exiting our nook, I glimpse auburn curls leaving the club. I reach into my pocket and finger the silk of her thong. I hadn't planned on keeping it, but I guess now it's my souvenir from this incredible night with my sexy, naughty Cinderella.

1

SIX MONTHS LATER...

MALLORY

Ugh, why did I decide to increase my water intake this week? This is my third trip to the ladies' room this morning. If my department had laptops, I think I'd just make this stall on the far left my office for the day. The flight to my parents' home in Florida for Thanksgiving is going to suck if I keep having to pee every hour. As I sit here, I run through the checklist of what I need to do to prepare for tomorrow's trip when I'm distracted by a bump on my leg.

"What's this? A dryer sheet?" I poke at the lump in the leg of my favorite pants. The dark-gray-and-black houndstooth pattern is subtle, and the bootleg cut flatters my curvy size-fourteen self. I lift my pant leg to snag the dryer sheet balled up there. Oh crap. It's not a dryer sheet—it's a small gray mouse clinging to my trouser sock and staring up at me with beady black eyes.

"*Aaaghh!*" There's no holding back the shriek that comes from me. It's a final battle cry before certain death. Mine, not Mickey's. No one else is down here, so at least no one's hearing me freak out like a goober.

The outer door to the restroom bangs open, and a masculine voice calls out. "Miss? Are you okay?"

Just my luck. The one time someone's here, I'm having a close encounter of the rodent kind. "No, I'm not okay! There's a mouse!" I'm still peeing. How big is the human bladder? Whatever the size, I think I have an extra-large one.

"Okay, I'll take care of it. Where is it?" The man's calm voice comes from outside the stall door.

"In my pant leg." I close my eyes, partly to avoid looking down at the vermin doing a barnacle impression on my calf and partly to pretend I'm home in my cozy bed and this is all a jacked-up, Dorito-induced dream.

"In your... The pants you're wearing?"

"Yep," I answer, popping the "p" while *still* peeing.

"Did you try shaking it out?" I know he's trying to be helpful, but I don't feel like playing twenty questions right now.

"Well, I'm a bit busy right now," I say drily. "It's clinging to my trouser sock."

"Shake your leg, maybe it will come loose."

My flow has decreased to a trickle. Screw hydration. I'm drinking one glass of water a day from now on. I shake my leg as much as this small stall will allow without ramming my shin into the door and smushing the little critter. The mouse holds on like it's going for eight seconds on the mechanical bull at the Mountain Bar. I swear I heard it go "Wheeeee!"

"It's still there!" A slight edge of hysteria tinges my voice. What if it scampers up the rest of my leg and bites me on the hoo-ha? How would I explain that at the ER? Oh no. Do mice carry rabies? Is this a rabid mouse?

"I'm sure it's not rabid. It's just scared." His voice holds the calm, measured tone of someone trying to talk someone off the ledge or convince them not to cut their bangs.

Oh crap, did I say that out loud?

"Yeah, you did."

"What do I do now?" I ask in the echoing room. My bladder's come to the end of its six-year odyssey to empty itself.

"I'm assuming you don't want to touch it, otherwise you would have already plucked it off?" That's a reasonable assumption on his part.

"No, I don't want to touch it! And I'm sitting here on the toilet with my pants down. What the heck would I do with it once I got it?" I'm not in the mood for reason. I want action.

"If I promise not to look above your knees, can you open the door so I can get it off your leg?" He really has a nice voice. It's deep and soothing. And familiar. I'm assuming it's one of my coworkers, but no one else is usually down here. Oh no. Please don't let this be my boss, Mr. Morgan. I would have to quit and move out of New Jersey. I wonder if they need real estate parale-gals in Florida.

"It's not like I have a choice." I know, I'm so gracious.

I unlock the stall door and ease it open so that my left leg is visible. My little gray hitchhiker is still there, clinging to my sock, trembling. If it wasn't attached to me, maybe I'd think it was cute. Speaking of cute, my rescuer is a big hunk of a man. I can't see his face clearly, but I'm assuming he's in his late twenties, like I am. The fluorescent lights pick up some dark copper tones in his rich brown hair. His eyelashes are so long, they look like they brush his cheeks as he keeps his gaze downcast, reaching out a large hand toward my leg.

"Oh, it's just a baby," he croons, plucking the little critter from my sock. Cradling it gently in his palms, he turns away from the open door of the stall and walks to the main door of the bathroom.

I quickly put myself back to rights and call out over the sound of flushing, "What are you going to do with it?"

"Feed it to the snake in the file room," he replies.

"*What?*" I shriek, wrenching the stall door open all the way.

Chuckling, he opens the main door to the restroom and says, "I'm taking Mickey outside and letting him loose in the tree line."

My rescuer's gone before I have the chance to thank him. After washing my hands, I look for him in the lobby, but don't see him. Maybe he left for the day? He seems familiar. I assume he works for the company that services the building and not Morgan Development directly. I think we have a service company...or do we handle cleaning in-house after-hours? Normally, when there's an issue, my co-worker and friend, Daphne, tells Betty, the sixty-something receptionist upstairs, and it gets handled. I've never had to do anything in the almost- year I've worked here.

I resolve to ask Daphne about it when she's back in the office on Monday. She took off this holiday week to surprise her boyfriend in France. Logan's a travel photographer, and he's visiting a bunch of Christmas markets throughout Europe. I hope she's having a wonderful time—she deserves it.

After my ordeal, I'm embarrassed and want to keep it to myself. However, I need to let the powers that be know we have mice so they can be dealt with before they overrun the office. When I get back to my desk, I call Betty. It doesn't matter who the CEO is, everyone who's ever worked in an office knows that it's usually the receptionist that runs the show.

"Hi, Betty. It's Mallory. We have a little problem downstairs."

I tell Betty about the mouse, then lean back in my chair. Where do I know that guy from? Big guy, good-looking, with pants that fit *real* good. A voice made for whispering in a woman's ear and hands just right for wrapping around a woman's... Oh, no. I sit upright with a gasp. No, no, no, no, no. Not *him*.

Liam, the same day

My mind keeps drifting to the woman I rescued in the bathroom. Mallory. It has to be. I kept my promise and didn't look anywhere other than her shapely calves and her little gray friend when I was helping her, but when I turned away to exit the bathroom, I caught a glimpse in the mirror of auburn curls tumbling down her back, brushing the ivory column of her neck. I know that neck. Know that I've kissed it. Wanted to bite it. Wanted to claim her. But I didn't. I've been hearing her husky voice in my sleep for six months. Has she been here the whole time? Does she recognize me?

I go to my favorite local pizza place to get lunch. My stomach gurgles at the comforting scents of Italian hoagies and cheesesteaks. My takeout plans change when I see Mallory sitting at a table, looking at her phone.

"Pack my sub to go, please, but I see a friend, so it's possible I may sit with her to eat," I tell the guy manning the counter.

He glances over at Mallory, gives me a smirking smile, and nods.

"Good luck, man. I'll bring it over to you."

I grin back. "Thanks."

I approach Mallory's table. All the other tables are taken, so hopefully my plan works. "So we meet again, Mallory."

Her beautiful green eyes widen when she looks up at me. "Um, hi."

"I'm Liam." I hold out my hand.

"I remember." Her creamy skin flushes prettily. "Thank you for coming to my rescue this morning."

"Happy to have helped." I chuckle and look around the restaurant. "Looks like it's a full house. Okay if I join you?"

She glances down at her meal then looks back up. "Sure."

I put down my water bottle and pull out the chair across from her. "Thanks. Ooh, chicken parm. Good choice. I ordered a sub. Please keep eating. Mine will be here in a moment. So, have you worked for Morgan Development long?"

"Almost a year. How about you? I haven't seen you around before. Do you work at multiple locations?" She takes a bite of her meal and closes her eyes in pleasure. I remember that look, and the last time I saw it, some chicken parm didn't put it there. I did. Can't blame her. The sex was exceptional. So is the chicken parm. She opens her eyes and raises a brow at me.

"Yeah, I travel all over for work," I answer.

My sub arrives. I unwrap it and take a bite.

"Are you based here normally?" she asks.

"Uh-huh, I'm from here, but most of my time is on the road. I'm home for the holiday. What are you doing for Thanksgiving?"

"I'm flying down to my parents' in Florida."

"Oh, are you from Florida?"

"No, I'm from here. They moved down there when my younger brother started college. I'm the third out of four kids."

I nod. "Cool. I'm the oldest. I have a younger sister in college. Is your boyfriend going with you to Florida?"

She gives a slight smile. "No. I don't have a boyfriend."

Yes!

"Is your girlfriend going to your family's Thanksgiving?" she asks in what I consider a flirting manner.

"No girlfriend. I'm single."

I know we're technically adhering to the adage 'what happens in Vegas stays in Vegas,' but it is driving me crazy. I never wanted to leave it in Vegas. Once we were together, I knew I didn't want it to be a one-time thing. I've thought about her often in the months since that night in the club. I don't know that I believe in the fated mate nonsense that the romantics of the shifter community try to convince us exists, but I believe sometimes you click with someone unexpectedly.

I'd hoped to run into her again as I traveled the country, going to my family's outlets. Every redhead garnered a second glance, just to leave me disappointed. I'd imagined I'd turn a corner, and she'd be walking out of a store, laden with packages. She'd run into me, drop her bags, and as I helped her pick them up, she'd realize it was me and admit she's been thinking about me and our time together too.

It's like one of those fricking romance movies that my mom and sister make me watch with them, but it would have been cool.

Instead, while I've been traveling coast-to-coast practically nonstop, she's been here. I tried to get info from Teagan since she could access the reservation from the bachelorette party, but she refused, saying to trust in fate. Well, fate is a crazy bitch.

Mallory glances at her phone, I assume to check the time. "I've gotta get back to the office. I'm sorry." She closes the to-go container she had her meal served in. She must have expected leftovers.

"No worries. I need to get going too. Um, any chance I could get your number?" Nothing ventured, nothing gained.

Her jade green eyes widen slightly, and she bites her bottom lip. Is she trying to be seductive, or am I making her uncomfortable?

"Oh, um, okay."

I hand her my phone so she can put in her number. When she hands it back, I shoot her a quick text that says, "Thanks for letting me eat lunch with you."

Mallory smiles slightly as she saves my contact, then rises from her chair, picks up her to-go container, and locks gazes with me. "It was nice having company. Have a happy Thanksgiving, Liam."

I quickly wrap the rest of my sub and stand. She's not wearing sky-high heels this time, so the top of her head reaches my chin. That's a good height.

"You too, Mallory. Safe travels. Maybe we can hang out when we're both here?"

She chuckles. "We'll see. Take care."

"Bye, Mallory. Take care." I watch her walk away, admiring the curves her pants lovingly caress. I smile when she gets in a cute green MINI Cooper, glad she drives something fun and not something boringly practical like a Honda.

I don't know what I was expecting, but having lunch like two strangers was not it. We aren't strangers. Okay, yeah, we don't know each other very well yet, but we have a connection. I felt it in Vegas, and I feel it now. Fate wouldn't have brought us back together, living in the same town and working for the same company, if it didn't mean something.

2

LIAM

I HAVE A COUPLE HOURS BEFORE I NEED TO LEAVE FOR THE NEWARK AIRPORT to pick up my cousin and his girlfriend, so I take the rest of my sub and drive back to the pool house I live in on my parents' property. I travel a lot in my job as a VP for Morgan Development, so it makes sense to crash in the pool house when I'm local rather than waste rent on a place I'm rarely at. It's decent—bedroom, bathroom, kitchen, and living room. I appreciate that there's a separate driveway so I can park my F-150 alongside it. More importantly, I can come and go as I please without being noticed by my parents. They know I'm a twenty-seven-year-old man with my own life, but I'll always be my mom's little boy. I don't bring women back here. It's easier to just get a room at an Atlantic City casino or go to her place if I'm hooking up. I don't need women realizing I'm one of "those" Morgans with the outlet malls and shopping centers. I want to be liked for who I am— as a man, not for my bank account. With my old truck and wardrobe of jeans and work boots, I look more like the maintenance guy I present myself as on site than an heir to one of the biggest retail developers in the United States.

I *am* a maintenance guy. For now. My job is to travel to our properties and make sure they're running smoothly and safely. If things need to be upgraded, I evaluate the options and present the best choices to the board for consideration. Hell, I change light bulbs and empty trash cans if necessary—whatever it takes to keep things moving smoothly. I'm a maintenance guy with an MBA from a prestigious university, a trust fund, and a very healthy bank account.

But I'm going to be more than that. Even though my dreams of playing hockey are over because of a really bad car accident eight years ago, it doesn't mean I can't still be involved in the sport. For years, my involvement with hockey was purely as a spectator. Now, there's talk about the formation of the Paranormal Hockey League, where shifters and other paranormal folk can play hockey on a professional level, and I want in on it. Atlantic City would be a great spot for a franchise, and I'm going to purchase one with my best friends, Teagan and Jake. I want to create something that's just mine, not my family's. At Morgan, I just keep the existing sites going. Sometimes I scout for a new center location, but that hasn't been happening much lately. I don't want to maintain the status quo; I want to be responsible for something new, and I want to help it grow.

The plan is to do a joint venture with Morgan Development and buy an old pier across the boardwalk from the casino Teagan owns and refurbish it to be the home of our hockey team. Teagan will have the largest ownership stake and be the face of the ownership too. Jake will be the general manager, and I'll be the coach.

That needs to be my focus. Now is not the time to pursue any kind of romantic relationship. Get the team going, establish my career outside of Morgan Development, be here enough to make it logical to get my own place and move out of the pool house—those are the things I need to be focusing on, not reacquainting myself with the hottest girl I've ever been with. Trust fate. Yeah, right. Trust her to have rotten timing.

"What the hell? I'm going to kill you," Logan calls out as he approaches me in the Newark Airport. His girlfriend, Daphne, looks confused until she notices me holding a sign that says, "Congratulations! Can I be the godfather?"

"Not funny, dude." Logan says as they walk up to me. With our tall, muscular builds and dark hair, we look like we could be brothers, not just cousins.

I shrug. "Who else should be the godfather of your firstborn?" I wrap Daphne in a hug. "If it wasn't for me, you wouldn't have gone to France, and you wouldn't be home now."

"Thank you for the ride ," she says, "but you realize rental cars and Uber exist, right?" She gives me a quick kiss on the cheek. "If, or when, we have a baby, I'll put you at the top of the list for godfather, no matter what your cousin says."

"Taking you back to Daphne's house?" I ask as we get in my old red-and-tan Bronco. It's a more comfortable ride for three than my pickup truck. Old Fords are my weakness. I restored it so everything's perfect. New vehicles have more bells and whistles but none of the personality.

"Our house," Logan states firmly. "We're going to surprise the family by showing up Thursday."

"Wow. They're going to love that. They still think you need to be in Europe until mid-December for the Christmas markets."

Logan leans against the passenger door so he can face me. "We had a great time and saw some cool stuff, but it turns out we both wanted to be home and with family to start our life together." He opens one of the bottles of water I put in the center console. "Daphne doesn't have family. It's just her. I realized I missed being with all you jerks. I know I'm fortunate to have you, and I want to share that with Daphne."

I wouldn't be in a rush to come home if I finally had my dream girl with me in a romantic location. Not that I have a girl. Not that I have time for any kind of relationship stuff. What was I thinking, giving Mallory my number, pursuing her? I don't have time for that.

But when I'm near her I don't seem to be able to focus on ambition. There's only her curves and her hair and her smile. Argh. I need to stop thinking about her like that. I need to focus on the hockey team, the pier, and my career beyond Morgan Development. I can deal with romantic stuff later. Maybe. If Mallory's still available. I hear a snore from the back seat and see Daphne is already asleep.

"Is Daph a shifter?" Normally I don't ask about personal things like that, but it's just us. Even if she wasn't part of a pack or a flock, she'd still have a shifter community.

"Nope. Human. No pack or anything." He chuckles. "She asked if she'd lay an egg when we had a baby. I guess she thought since I'm an eagle shifter, I was hatched?"

I glance back to make sure she's still asleep. "Seriously? Hasn't she ever known a shifter before?"

"Not really." He shrugs. "Or not knowingly. You know, it's only been the past few years since the shifter community has gone mainstream, and she's a homebody. She doesn't have friends having babies. Until they make *A Very Shifter Christmas* movie or there's a shifter hockey team, she's going to be a bit clueless."

His mention of shifter hockey reminds me of the emails waiting for me at home.

"Is she cool with it all? The shifting?" I wonder if Mallory's a shifter. I didn't sense it or smell anything, but if she was an avian shifter like Logan, there wouldn't be a scent like with a cougar or wolf shifter.

"Yeah, no problem. She'd never seen me in eagle form before, so I was nervous that was going to freak her out the first time I shifted in front of her, but she just wanted to touch my feathers. The fact that I shift into a freaking golden eagle and fly around with my dad on weekends was a nonissue. Or that my mom and brother and your family are cougar shifters. She doesn't care that our kids could be eagle shifters or cougar shifters."

"Or human," I remind him. Me, my dad, and sister, Kendall, are cougar shifters. Mom is human. I wonder if it bothered her, not being included in shifter stuff when we'd go for a run in the woods. Growing up, it was hard. Shifters were still a secret. Then that family of grizzly bears purposely shifted on camera for that *Brides Behaving Badly* reality show, and suddenly the world knew we existed and had been here the whole time. Still, I had to be careful. I not only had to deal with normal puberty, but also all the changes being a shifter wrought on the body.

"Or human," Logan agrees. "Or there could be something in her family tree that she doesn't know about, and we end up with a wolf or a kangaroo or something."

Shifter genetics are unpredictable, that's for sure. I've always assumed if I ever have kids, they'd be cougar cubs like Kennie and I were. I know mixed shifter families are becoming more common now, but when we were growing up, Logan's family of both eagle and cougar shifters was an oddity. Shifters with humans weren't a big deal, but two different shifter species mating and making a family got a lot of whispers. But hey, love is love. I'd be fine with human kids or wolf pups or whatever, as long as they're happy and healthy. My mind drifts to Mallory again, and I yank it back. We had one hookup and a lunch. There will be no happily ever after or babies or anything like that. Still, when I think about Logan and Daphne and what they're starting, there's a pang in my chest. It's probably indigestion from the extra hot peppers on my sub earlier. It's not envy.

Right.

3
LIAM

We hold Thanksgiving at my Uncle Mike and Aunt Holly's house, and I can tell by the full driveway that my parents and both sets of grandparents have already arrived. I don't see my Logan's Jeep, so I'm assuming their eventual arrival at his parents' home will still be a surprise—I didn't tell anyone I picked them up from the airport the other night.

I park at the curb in front of their large brick colonial and walk up the path to the front door. Aunt Holly has a display of pumpkins and hay bales on the porch and a wooden turkey holding up a sign that reads *Gobble 'Til Ya Wobble.* On impulse, I snap a picture of the display and text it to Mallory with a "Happy Thanksgiving" caption.

When I enter, I receive greetings and hugs from my family—blood related and chosen. We're lucky to be part of a family that believes there is plenty of love to go around.

When Logan and Daphne arrive, there's another flurry of excited greetings. Everyone's shocked Logan came home for the holiday, since he rarely does. He announces his plan to travel less frequently and focus more on expanding his photography business closer to home, and you'd think he just cured cancer or something. I understand that everyone is happy he'll be home more often, but I'm here for almost every holiday, and no one welcomes me with tears and cries of joy like he's getting. I'm being ridiculous. I know that. But sometimes it feels like I'm taken for granted, like everyone assumes I'm always going to be here.

My cousin Andy is in the family room next to the kitchen. He's a senior at a university in Pennsylvania and captain of the baseball team. He introduces me to the guys playing a card game with him, all teammates who didn't go home for the holiday weekend.

"Kennie here yet?" I ask Andy. When they're both home, they're joined at the hip. I'm six and a half years older than my sister. We're close, but since she and Andy are both twenty-one, they relate to each other in ways that she and I don't. Logan and I have a similar relationship and friendship.

"Not yet. She stayed after the football game to talk to some of the cheerleaders," Andy replies. Kennie was a competitive cheerleader for years, so I'm not surprised. She probably knows a bunch of them from the cheer gym where she works when she's home.

As we grab sandwiches, chips, and drinks from the spread set out for lunch—we *are* shifters, and eating is an all-day event—the front door opens, and Kennie walks in with a couple I haven't met before. They're probably the friends from school she brought home with her.

"Daphne!" Kennie calls out, giving her a big hug.

I rescue Daphne's plate before she drops it. She wasn't expecting the Kendall tsunami to come her way first. My sister is barely five feet tall and looks delicate, but she's solid muscle. Daphne stumbles back a step when Kennie hugs her. Logan accepts his hug and the barrage of questions. I wonder if everyone's surprise that he's here and their expectation that he wouldn't be makes him feel guilty for the years that he chose not to come home.

"Meet my friends." Kennie gestures to a guy a little taller than me with short, dark auburn hair and bright blue eyes. He's muscular without being bulky. "Trevor."

Trevor smiles and reaches out for a handshake. He has a strong, sure grip.

"And Randi." Kennie gestures to the lovely girl at Trevor's side. "Guys, this is my cousin Logan and his girlfriend Daphne." She puts her arm through mine. "This is my big brother, Liam."

"Do you attend school together?" Daphne asks.

"We do," Randi answers. "Kennie and I are roommates, and Trev is my teammate."

Kennie adds, "Randi and Trev are on the cheerleading squad at school. They're stunt partners and are so good. We stayed after the game to help some of the high school squad with their stunts."

After everyone eats, I play a game of soccer with my cousins and guests. Andy and his teammates are one team, while I play with the girls, Logan, and Trevor. Our team wins.

As we sit down for dinner later in the afternoon, I look around at everyone gathered and give my own private thanks for having my family and our friends to share the day with. I'm blessed. Someday, I want to have these times with my own family. I wonder if Mallory's having a good day with her family. I hope so. Unbidden, I imagine future holidays with her here. *Stop it, Liam. Team first.* It's going to be a few years before I can start thinking about anything more than a hockey team and remodeling old piers. I need to get back some of what I lost in the accident first. Then I can think about stuff like relationships and feelings. And Mallory.

We've finished the savory portion of the meal and cleared the tables to make room for the desserts when Trevor excuses himself to take a phone call out on the patio. The sun is still slanting through the trees, and I figure it must be a FaceTime call because he's looking at the screen and talking. Probably his family. It's nice that they're connecting today. Family is so important.

Kennie and Randi go out to join him, and they all gather around the phone, laughing and waving. I guess he's introducing them to whoever he's talking to.

"Liam, can you let the kids know we're going to start dessert, please?" Aunt Holly asks as she and Mom pull things from the butler's pantry and freezer to set up a dessert buffet on the breakfast bar.

I stick my head out the patio door to tell the threesome huddled around Trevor's phone about dessert when I hear a feminine voice over the speaker. I can't hear what she's saying, but something's familiar. I can't put my finger on it though. The hairs on the back of my neck prickle. All thoughts about the voice on Trevor's phone disappear when my phone buzzes. I pull it from my pocket and see Mallory's sent a selfie. She's wearing mouse ears, and there's a theme park in the background.

> Me: I thought you were afraid of mice?

Trevor comes back in with my sister and Randi.

> Mallory: In my pants, yes. Walking upright in a theme park, also yes. LOL. But when in Rome...

> Me: Having fun?

> Mallory: Yeah. Flights got delayed, so we're having family Thanksgiving tomorrow instead. My parents are theme park fanatics, and we have tickets for everything, so came here to walk around. They'll be running in the Shifter Sprint on Saturday.

I didn't know she was from a shifter family.

> Me: Don't want to run?

> Mallory: I love to run, but not thirty miles at a time, and I'm not a shifter. My family is. Wolf shifters. But it skipped me. So I'm the babysitter. :smiley face emoji:

So she comes from a shifter family. That's good. She knows I'm a cougar shifter.

> Mallory: I don't want to keep you. Have a great weekend.

> Me: You too.

While our grandmothers and mothers are discussing their upcoming epic Black Friday shopping trip and roping in Daphne, Kennie, and Randi to shop with them, I prepare brownie sundaes alongside Logan and Trevor.

Logan looks at the ladies and, satisfied they aren't paying attention to us, leans toward me. "Can you help me with a project at my house tomorrow?"

"Sure, what do you need?"

"I want to hang Christmas lights, and it'll be easier with an extra set of hands. It's a surprise for Daph. Her dad always used to hang them when she was growing up. She loves them."

"Yeah, no problem. Do you have them already?"

"No. I'm going to run to Home Depot once they leave to go shopping in the morning."

Trevor speaks in a low tone. "Do you guys want an extra hand? With the girls shopping, I'm just going to be hanging out at my house. I'm happy to help."

"Your house?" I shoot him a questioning glance.

"Yeah," he replies. "My family lives in Shifting Pines. I'm staying there this weekend so I can get in a run and do some skating drills. My parents moved down south when I started college, but my sister still lives here. She's with them and my siblings for Thanksgiving, so the house is empty. It's only twenty minutes from your place, so I figured I'd stay there instead of imposing on your parents."

"For decorating, the more the merrier," Logan says. "I'd appreciate the help. Just please don't tell the girls. I want it to be a surprise for Daphne. Did you want to go to Home Depot with us or just meet at my house?"

"I love Home Depot. I'll take any excuse I can find to go. With Kennie and Randi, I get dragged to Sephora more often than any man should have to suffer through. It'll be nice to recharge my testosterone with some power tools. What time were you planning on going?"

I like this guy. He's down-to-earth and funny. We arrange to meet at Logan's house at nine the next morning.

"Skating drills?" I ask Trevor as we sit and enjoy our sundaes. "Do you play hockey?"

"Yeah. I started when I was younger," he replies. "We have a synthetic rink set up. Nothing beats real ice, but it's good enough to do some skating and shooting drills for fun. Mercer doesn't have a team, and with law school, I couldn't devote time to even a club team. If I could find one that took shifters. So I rarely get to lace up my skates anymore." He shoots me a glance. "Do you play?"

"I used to when I was younger, but I can't anymore."

"Oh, man, I'm sorry." Trevor looks slightly abashed.

"No worries," I assure him. "Bad car accident. I healed up, but I can't risk the hits."

"Can you still skate?"

"I guess so? I haven't tried."

Logan looks at me. "You haven't skated at all since the accident? You practically lived on the ice."

I shrug. "No point if I'm not playing."

Trevor nods. "Well, if you want to skate and shoot some pucks, come on over. You too, Logan, if you skate."

Logan holds out his fist for Trevor to bump. "Thanks, man. Rugby was my sport, but I can stay upright well enough to not completely embarrass myself."

The house Logan shares with Daphne isn't that big, so even with the thousands of lights Logan used to festoon the place, it didn't take that long to decorate. She's going to be shocked when she sees it lit up tonight. So will the folks on the International Space Station. Good thing Daphne's grandfather was an electrician who installed a heavy-duty electrical panel. They're going to use every bit of it with this display.

After stringing up the lights, we head out to Trevor's rink. It's full-size, and if I'd had this available to me as a kid, I would've been thrilled. We hit the ice hard.

"How are you feeling? Getting your legs back?" Logan asks as we sit to take off our skates and guzzle some water.

"I'm doing well. I'm probably going to feel it tomorrow, but it was good to be skating again and shooting some pucks. At least when I fell, I didn't get wet like I would have on real ice."

We're packing up to take Logan back home to meet Daphne and show off our work when Trevor pulls out his phone.

"Oh, let me text Lory that I'm ordering light bulbs. I see some are burned out. I'll change them when I'm home for Christmas. She'll wonder what the boxes are when they arrive."

I pull out my phone to see if Mallory has texted anything else. I smile, looking at her selfie. She's adorable.

I catch Logan looking at my phone and tilting his head in a bird-like manner. Great. I don't need his eagle eyes seeing Mallory's picture and bugging me. I put my phone away.

"Is your sister single?" Logan asks Trevor.

What the hell? I do not need him playing matchmaker. Anyway, Mallory's the only woman sparking my interest now.

"Yeah, very. She's had some bad relationships and sworn off men, especially shifters. I think she wants a nice human accountant when she settles down. Maybe a schoolteacher. Someone quiet. Not alpha. The opposite of us." He laughs.

That clinches it. I'm definitely not his sister's type.

4

MALLORY

THE DAY AFTER THANKSGIVING...

My flight from Atlantic City to Orlando was uneventful, thank goodness. I had a lot to think about. It turns out the department Daphne and I work in is going to close after the beginning of the year, and we'll move upstairs with the rest of the legal department. We'd been handling collection matters for condo associations, a holdover from the start of Morgan Development, before they changed their focus to commercial properties. I'm excited by the move. My dream career is to be part of the development team—have input in the location of new projects, work on getting them approved, the building process, and ultimately the mix of tenants and amenities when it opens. I want to help create something, not just manage its existence.

I'm at the airport waiting for my siblings to arrive. The flights my brother and his family were on and my sister's flight both ended up delayed, so they're all arriving this morning. We're going to do the traditional meal today instead. I'm betting Thanksgiving with my family won't be as calm as my flight was. We love each other, but we don't understand each other. Or they don't understand me.

Everyone is a high achiever, type A personality, and I'm...not. At least, not to the extent they are. My dad is a patent attorney, and my mom is a chemical engineer. They're so successful and ambitious, they don't understand why I'm content being a paralegal when I could've gone to law school and been an attorney. At least they recognize my choice not to go to law school and don't think I was incapable of getting in. In a way, I think that confuses them more—that I could be more, but am choosing not to be. They don't understand I have career goals, but those goals won't get my name on the door or the letterhead.

I enjoy being behind the scenes, making plans and watching them come to fruition through the efforts of a team. You'd think my family would understand since my parents are both in professions based on methodology and step-by-step planning, but they don't see the similarities in my methodical nature and their own. They only see that I'm not in charge.

There's no point in telling them my goals and dreams.

They won't get it.

They don't get me.

"Mallory!" I turn and see my older brother, Ethan, waving to me across the baggage claim area. He's an architect and lives in Maryland with his wife Aurelia and their two sons.

"Hey, Ethan," I say, giving him a hug. I don't see anyone with him. "Where are the boys? And Aurelia?" Not that I care where his wife is. I can't stand her, but I love Matt and EJ.

"She took an Uber to our hotel."

"Hotel? You're not staying at Mom and Dad's?"

"*Oof!*" Ethan lets out a grunt as our sister, Valerie, leaps on his back. Ethan is a big guy, but Valerie's a strong wolf shifter female, and when she's coming at speed, she packs quite a wallop. If Ethan was a regular human and not a wolf shifter as well, she probably would've tackled him.

"Hey, Val." Ethan groans the greeting as Valerie slides off his back and steps around him for a hug.

"I've missed you guys!" she gushes as she hugs first Ethan and then me.

I'm five foot seven, not a short woman, but standing next to these two, I feel tiny. Ethan is about six foot five, and Valerie is close to six feet tall. Our parents joke that I'm the runt of the litter since our younger brother is as tall as Ethan. The height disparity always made family portraits tricky, much to my mother's annoyance.

"Where's Aurelia and the boys?" Valerie asks, looking around the baggage claim area. With her height, it's easy for her to see over the crowd.

"They took an Uber to the hotel," Ethan answers.

"Hotel? You're not staying with Mom and Dad?"

He sighs. "It's complicated, Valerie." Since they have their bags, we make our way to the garage.

"Complicated how?" I ask. I've never liked Aurelia. She's a bitch —literally and figuratively. She comes from a pack in Maryland, and her people run in high society circles and dabble in government. She's always acted as if she's too good for everyone except for those in her snobby circle. I'm pretty sure the only reason she and Ethan married was because she got pregnant with EJ, and there was no way Ethan wasn't going to raise his child. I may not shift, but I understand the mate bond with wolves, and that's not what they have.

I hand Ethan the keys for Mom's SUV, and we make our way to the parking lot.

When he gets there, Ethan opens the rear liftgate, and they put their bags in. "We're separating. Our marriage has been over for years, and we're both finally miserable enough to admit it and go our separate ways."

This, my brother and his wife, is why I've got my rule, why I'm determined to avoid relationships. They rarely end well. I know that, and now so does he. Maybe, even if all Liam wants is a second night, it's better to say no. He's too tempting, and I won't face that pain again.

"Wow." It would be funny how Valerie and I both say that in

unison, but there's nothing funny about this situation. I open the back door and climb in. Valerie will be more comfortable being up front, since her legs are so much longer than mine. Ethan hates being a passenger, so he always drives when we're together.

"Yeah. Wow about sums it. Aurelia doesn't want to stay with Mom and Dad. She doesn't want to be here at all, but it's important to her to keep up appearances. Her brother is running for political office, and she doesn't want any negative publicity to affect his campaign. Like anyone is going to care about our marriage." He maneuvers out of the parking complex and starts the drive toward the condo our parents call home. "I'm staying at the condo with the boys the first couple of nights because being with family is important, and Aurelia will enjoy some alone time in the spa at the hotel she chose. They'll be with her a night or two. We traveled down here together for appearances and will fly home together, but it's a sham."

"Wow." I know I'm repeating myself, but it's all I can say. "How are the boys?"

EJ is eight and Matt is six, old enough to know something's going on but not old enough to understand all the grown-up issues.

He sighs. "I think they're okay. I hope they're okay. We don't fight in front of them, but the house is just so...cold." He checks the mirrors as he switches lanes. "Aurelia isn't a bad mother. She takes care of the kids, but she isn't a mom, you know? Now that they're older and have opinions, she's not interested. They're boys, so not fun to dress up."

I can practically see Valerie vibrating with anger at his admission. I put my hand on her tense shoulder to try to ground her. I love my sister, but she's scary when she's angry. She's a she-wolf through and through. Matt and EJ aren't her pups, but she loves them fiercely, and the thought of them not being loved as they deserve guts her. I feel the same way, but I'm able to control it better.

"What the fuck is wrong with her?" Valerie grounds out through clenched teeth.

Ethan shakes his head. "I don't think she can help it. She wasn't raised as we were. She didn't have the strong pack dynamic we did." He glances at me in the rearview mirror. "We've decided I'm going to have primary physical custody of the boys. She'll have ample visitation and communication, but they'll be best with me."

Valerie snorts. "How on Earth did that happen? I can't imagine her father being okay with that. Even if he has nothing to do with them, he'll want everyone in his orbit under his control."

"He doesn't want the world knowing he has shifter grandsons." His clenched jaw is the only sign of the anger he feels. "Aurelia's bloodline has been diluted enough through the generations of breeding with humans that the other grandkids don't shift. Won't shift. Me being a full-blooded wolf shifter threw a wrench into his plans. Obviously, the boys are too young to shift, but the signs are there that they will when they hit puberty. Now that shifting is no longer a secret, they won't have to hide things like we had to." He glances at Valerie. No reason to look at me. I can't shift, so I had nothing to hide.

"Because they're precious little wolf shifters, he's just going to throw them aside?" Valerie's voice cracks. "They are his grandchildren, his flesh and blood! What is wrong with him?"

"They aren't like us, Val. Appearances matter to them, and they want to appear 'normal,' especially with Byron running for office. The constituency will accept shifters in the family tree, but moving forward, that type of voter wants humans only. It's disgusting, and it's scary, and frankly, I'm happy to get my boys away from that. Why would I want them around people who think their wolf side is something to be ashamed of?"

We pull up to Mom and Dad's building, and Ethan turns off the engine. Turning in his seat, he reaches out a hand to each of us. "I'm telling Mom and Dad what's going on before I get the boys. Please, just be cool about this and don't talk shit about Aurelia. She's their mother, and they love her. Hell, once upon a time, I loved her, and she loved me too. I know that. This is best for all of us. We tried to keep it together. She tried to feel more, but she can't, and it eats her up inside. We don't want the boys to grow up like she did. She wants to break the cycle, and this is how we're doing it. She's brave."

Swallowing the lump in my throat, I squeeze his hand. "You're a good man, Ethan Carter." I hope I can find a man like my big brother someday. Okay, that sounded creepy. I mentally spritz some brain bleach.

My parents take the news of the split much better than expected. Maybe they saw things I didn't, or just their greater life experience served them well. I'm relieved when there's no drama in that quadrant and they move on to focusing on other things wrong in the universe, like my career choices and single status.

I guess Valerie gets a free pass on being single since she's a marketing diva up in New York City. It's okay to be single if you have a career to fulfill you. At least for a while. Once she hits thirty, then they'll start in on her finding a nice man and starting a family. If he's a shifter from a good pack, even better. I don't even think they care if I'm with a man. A woman would be fine too, as long as she was a shifter from a good pack. They just want us paired up and settled and happy.

"So, Mallory," Mom begins while I chop up celery for the stuffing we'll have with the turkey tomorrow. "How is work going?"

At least she didn't call it my "little job." That's progress. "It's going okay. They're going to close the department I'm in, so I'll be moving over to the main legal department. I don't know if I'll work on leasing or something else under the legal umbrella, but we'll discuss that in the coming weeks."

"Why are they closing it down? Is the business in trouble? Maybe you should start looking for something more stable. Law school is still an option."

I put down my knife, mostly so I don't get distracted and cut myself, but also because I talk with my hands when I'm agitated, and that's just a potential felony waiting to happen.

"They're moving in another direction. I'm excited by the

change," I assure her. "I much prefer working with contracts and leases than court pleadings. Litigation isn't really my thing."

"As long as you're happy, Mallory. That's what matters most."

If I didn't know better, I'd swear aliens abducted my mother and replaced her with a pod person.

She sighs. "I guess it's good that there are followers. Not everyone is a leader." Yep, there it is. Genuine Mom, no pod person there, and she's just going through her checklist for preparing dinner. She's made close to thirty years' worth of holiday dinners, but she insists on having a checklist to make sure she doesn't miss anything. One of her favorite sayings is, "Failing to plan is planning to fail."

I love my family, but I wish I had stayed home and done a Friendsgiving meal or gotten some Chinese food and binge-watched something mindless on Netflix. My younger brother Trevor had the right idea of going over to his friend Kennie's for the holiday weekend.

"Will you be okay with the boys while we do the Shifter Sprint tomorrow?" Mom asks. Part of the reason my parents moved to Florida is their weird love of theme parks, which the Orlando area has in abundance. All the parks host events catering to the shifter community throughout the year, and the event my family loves most is a race through the park in their wolf forms. Shifters of all shapes and sizes come to take part, and tomorrow is the predator class. They learned to have separate races for predators and prey after that grisly scene in 2013. Emphasis on *grizzly*? I snort to myself and then realize Mom is waiting for an answer. Since I don't shift, nor do I think running thirty miles at one time sounds like a fun little jog, I happily babysit my nephews.

"Yeah, it's no problem. We'll have fun. You'll catch up with us when you're done, and then we'll come back here to have leftover dinner." I love spending time with my nephews, and we'll have a blast in the park, riding rides and watching the racers. My favorite part is when some of the more goofball shifters wear tutus and mouse ears. There's something so whimsical about a giant grizzly bear in a pink tutu racing past the castle. I know my nephews are eager to be old enough to shift and take part in the race. I guess then I'll be riding the rides by myself. Oh well.

Being alone is nothing new. My asshole exes have taught me it's better to be alone than to be with the wrong person. I'm not making that mistake again. I'll find a fuck buddy when necessary, but never again am I risking my heart in a relationship.

My mind drifts to Liam. I know he's an awesome hookup, but if I went back for seconds—who am kidding, thirds and fourths at least —would that give him the wrong idea? My plan moving forward is one-and-done when my need is greater than my vibrator and a fresh pack of batteries can satisfy.

No feelings, no risking my heart. Just some mutual pleasure. Keep it casual.

Of course my family all received medals in age, gender, and animal divisions in the Shifter Sprint. Again.

Dinner after was quiet. Well, as quiet as it could be with two little boys that I filled up with sugar at the park. Shifter kids are more energetic, but when you sugar them up, it's a whole new level of hyper. Turns out the boys are going back to the hotel to spend the night with Aurelia. Oops.

"Promise me you'll never date a coworker, Mal," Valerie says over her mimosa as we enjoy our pedicures. It's Sunday morning, and while everyone else is at the parks again, my sister and I treated ourselves to mani/pedis.

My thoughts drift to Liam, the hunky maintenance man who rescued me in the ladies' room —and banged my brains out in Vegas. Since he works for the building maintenance company and not Morgan Development, we aren't coworkers, and although I'd love another opportunity to do dirty, sexy things with him, I wouldn't consider that dating. "Okay, I promise. But there's a story, and I need to hear it."

We're soaking our feet, so there's no one to hear what we discuss, but Valerie still leans in close to say, "I'd been seeing this guy when we worked in the same place for the past year. He works in the Chicago office. They were hookups—no promises, no commitments. We were both single."

I nod and look over at her. She's chewing on her bottom lip, which is her tell for when she's reluctant to say something. It doesn't show itself often because it's rare Val doesn't let whatever she's thinking or feeling fly.

"Turns out we weren't both single. He has a wife and child."

"Ouch," I say. "Maybe they're separated?"

"A pregnant wife. And from what I saw, they have a very affectionate relationship. I was in Chicago earlier in the week. I arrived Sunday."

She stops speaking, and I wait for her to continue. I'm uncertain if she's trying to hold back tears or control her anger. Maybe both?

"Apparently her family was visiting and staying in the same hotel I was because when I arrived to check in, they were all in the lobby, being obnoxiously cheerful, discussing where they were going for dinner." She takes in a deep, shaky breath. Holds it for a moment and lets it out in a whoosh. "He had his arm around her and was resting his hand on her stomach. There was so much love and adoration in the look he was giving her. Their little girl is around five and looks just like him. She was holding her mother's hand and gazing up at him like he was her hero."

I take Valerie's hand to lend her strength. It's ice cold and trembling slightly.

"He didn't see me. I made it to my room before I vomited." She turns stricken eyes to mine. "I was the other woman, Mallory. I was sleeping with someone's husband."

I squeeze her hand and wait until she meets my gaze.

"No. This is not your fault. *He* is the cheater here, not you. He knows he made a commitment to someone and chose to break it. That's *not* on you."

Her gray eyes swim with tears, and it breaks my heart to see my strong, wonderful, big sister hurting like this.

"What did he say when you confronted him? I'm assuming you confronted him and told him what a sleaze he is?"

"When I saw him in the office on Monday, he acted like he normally did and tried to arrange for us to meet after work like we usually do. The other times we've hooked up, we've both been traveling, or he's been in New York. This is the first time we were in Chicago. He was ready to meet up, fuck me, and then go home to his wife and child."

She's shaking with rage now, and I worry about the champagne flute she's holding.

"Here, let me take this." I slip the flute she just drained from her grasp and set it next to my partially full one. I'm sure our soak has gone on longer than normal, but I think the staff recognizes we're having a moment and is giving us our privacy. I make a mental note to add extra to the tip in gratitude for their discretion.

"I didn't confront him," she confesses. "Just said I couldn't meet him and walked away. I was afraid I'd cry or shift or scream at him. That's what I'm most ashamed of—that I said nothing. I just walked away. Logically, I know it's not my fault he's a lying, cheating scumbag. He's the one being unfaithful, but I didn't say anything. I slunk away like an omega with her tail between her legs."

That is so unlike Valerie. She's always been fearless and outspoken, not one to let an injustice—real or perceived—go without remarking on it.

"Do you love him?" I ask gently.

"No, but I think I could have, and that scares me. That my judgment could be so off to not recognize a lying scumbag at fifty paces. How can I trust myself to find a good one when the one I thought I found is a deceitful sack of shit?"

I signal for a refill of our mimosas and that we're ready for the rest of our pedicure. I know Valerie, and she's told me all she's going to about this subject for now. Maybe it's the curse of the Carter siblings to not have lasting success in romance. So far, it hasn't happened for any of us, no matter how hard we try.

I'm so glad to be home. I'm excited to hear about Daphne's trip to France to spend time with her boyfriend, Logan. Fingers crossed it was everything she hoped it would be.

Waving my badge to enter our downstairs office area, I'm eager to start packing so we can move upstairs once the desks arrive and are assembled. Hopefully, Daphne likes the furniture I picked out for our new office.

"Hey, Mallory!" Daphne calls out from her desk, where she's packing a box.

"Hi, Daphne. Welcome back!" I walk over and hug her. I'm not usually a hugger, but Daphne Foster is my girl. We just click.

"So, how was France? Did you have a great time?" I put my purse down and grab my red plaid mug to get my morning hot cocoa. Daphne follows me into the kitchenette area.

"It was wonderful," she replies with a happy sigh. "Oh! We got you a present, but I'll give it to you after we move upstairs." She finally stops to take a breath.

"You know about the move?" I ask, surprised.

"Uh-huh, Will and Mike told me at Thanksgiving dinner. Oh, yeah, we ended up coming home Tuesday so we could spend Thanksgiving with Logan's family. The furniture arrived, and the guys put it together yesterday, so we only need to pack up our desks and set up."

"Wow, everyone's been busy."

"Well, I know I don't want to stay down here with critters. You had a mouse run up your pant leg? That's insane!"

I shudder. "How about we don't discuss it and get the heck out of here? The sooner we're upstairs, the happier I'll be."

Daphne hands me a box. "Get packing, then. The sooner our stuff is packed, the sooner we're out of here."

"Are we boxing the files we're taking upstairs or putting them on carts or what?"

"Ooh, good question," Daphne responds. "I don't know. Wanna run upstairs with me, check out the space, and ask?"

"Yeah, okay." I sip my cocoa. "Let me finish this"—I heft my mug —"and pack up. When I left Wednesday, we were caught up, so unless Miller went crazy dictating stuff over the weekend, we're good."

I put my clip-on fan, blue stapler, and rose gold unicorn tape dispenser—a prize from a favorite romance author—in my box. Wow, I hardly have any personal items here. When I worked with Steve, my late boss, the bulletin boards around my desk were full of leftover pages from old calendars that had pictures I liked and printouts of motivational quotes. I had knickknacks, framed pictures of my family, and a candy dish full of the peppermints Steve and some of my favorite real estate agents liked. My desk here at Morgan looks like I'm ready to leave at a moment's notice. I don't even fill half a paper box. If it wasn't for the fan, I could put everything in my purse and call it a day.

I didn't realize I was treating this as temporary before now. Is it possible that after Steve's sudden death and losing the job I loved and thought I'd be at for years, I've been afraid to get attached and settled in? I hate having deep thoughts on Monday mornings. Mondays are hard enough, especially after a holiday, without the added layer of introspection.

Daphne looks at my box and then at her box, laughing. She tilts it so I can see, and there's hardly anything in hers either. "Should we just combine them and sort? Or will we look pathetic going up there with only one box between the two of us?"

I open my drawers and grab the folders of labels and forms and the pad I keep notes on and pile them on my desk. "How about we combine our boxes of personal items, and then the second box could be the folders of labels and forms? That will clear out all the stuff we'll need and use in one trip."

"Good plan!" Daphne grabs some folders out of her drawer and adds it to my pile, and then puts the whole thing in her box. She gives me her few personal items to add to mine and, with her box in her arms, asks, "Ready to go?"

"Sure am!" I swallow my last sip of cocoa, wipe my mug with a tissue, and tuck it into my box.

We take the elevator up to the third floor and go to our new office, saying hello to everyone calling out to welcome us.

"Here we are! Office sweet office." Daphne leads the way into our new space.

"Wow, they got so much done over the weekend. It even has a new office smell!"

I'm amazed; they not only cleared out all the boxes from when this was used for storage but assembled the desks I selected. The desks look great in the space.

"They really did. I got us a plug-in air freshener because it was musty in here." Daphne looks around, clearly satisfied. "Okay if I take this desk?" She puts her box on the desk in the middle of the room, leaving the corner desk for me. I was hoping for the corner desk, so I'm great with it.

"Sure! I got to pick the furniture. You get to pick the space you want."

A knock echoes on the wall outside our door. We look toward the sound, where Will is standing in the doorway, one shoulder propped on the frame.

"Moving in?" Will enters our office and looks at me. "Setup okay?"

"Yes, it looks great. I wasn't expecting it to be done for today," I reply.

"They were able to deliver everything Saturday, so we made it a family project, putting it together while our wives shopped."

"They had races. If your desk falls apart, blame Will. Mike and Logan did my desk," Daphne explains.

I laugh. "I'm sure it's fine."

"If it's not, blame my son," Will answers.

"How are we moving our working files up here? Do you want them boxed, or are we going to use file carts?" Daphne asks.

"How about we use the carts as much as we can," Will suggests. "Are you ready for your computers to be moved up here? Mallory said you'd just need a laptop with the file management system on it so you can close out files down there."

"Whatever Mallory says. She handles the opening and closing of files in the system for us. I'm ready to be up here for day-to-day work as soon as our computers and working files are up here." Daphne looks at me for confirmation, and I nod in agreement.

"All right, I'll tell IT to move them." Will leaves our office, so Daphne and I are alone again.

I turn to Daphne. "Did they tell you they're closing our department in the new year? Pretty sure they were going to tell us today, but Miller accidentally spilled the tea last week. I told Mike I wanted to continue in the legal department. I assume they'll talk with you about what you want to do."

Daphne chews on her lower lip. She's nervous, and that makes *me* nervous. "I have stuff to tell you, but I don't want to go into it here. I have errands to run at lunch, but do you want to come over for dinner? I'll order something. Want Chinese?"

"Sure, okay. Logan won't mind? I know you guys just got home." I worry about what she has to tell me. She had Thanksgiving dinner with the bosses. Maybe she knows more about the department closing than I do.

"No! He won't mind at all. I think he was going to hang out with his cousin, but even if he's home, he'll be working on picture stuff. Won't be in our way in the least. Do you want to come right from the office? I know you live out in the boonies, so it would be silly to drive all the way home just to turn around and drive to our house."

"Yeah, thanks. I need to swing by the library to pick up some DVDs I requested, but then I'll come by?"

My phone vibrates, signaling a text. I pull it out to check, hoping it's not family drama.

> Liam: Hi, survived the weekend?

> Me: Hi, I did. How about you?

> Liam: It was good. Crazy. Big family, plus people brought guests. It was good though.

> Me: Happy to hear it. What's up?

> Liam: I was wondering if you wanted to grab lunch today or dinner sometime this week? I'm out of town later in the week, but I'd like to see you before I go.

Wow. I wasn't expecting that. I think about my conversation with Valerie, but Liam technically isn't a coworker, and even if it turns out he works for Morgan Development and not the building service company, he works in maintenance, not the legal department. Our paths won't cross professionally.

> Me: Sure. Want lunch today? Francisco's again or somewhere else? I'm going at noon.

> Liam: Francisco's works for me. I'll meet you there. I'm at a property in Atlantic City now.

> Me: Sounds good. See you then. Bye, Liam.

> Liam: Looking forward to it, Mallory.

"What has you smiling like that?" Daphne asks.

Crap. I don't want to say anything about Liam yet. There's nothing to talk about.

"Something stupid my sister sent me. It's nothing." I give Daphne her belongings and unpack my few things. Maybe I'll bring in some pictures tomorrow. I'm finally ready to put down some roots here. Morgan Development is where I want my future to be. I need to remember that's my priority. Not cute guys who gently carry little gray mice to the woods so they'll be safe. The messes with Ethan's and Valerie's love lives are great reminders that the Carter siblings are cursed when it comes to love. I can't forget that and sacrifice what I can have in my career here for a crush.

Keep it casual, Mallory. Liam can be a fling, not a forever.

5
LIAM

I wish I had more time this morning for my meeting with Teagan and Jake, but I don't want to be late for lunch with Mallory. When I texted to see if she'd agree to meet me before I had to travel down to Maryland and Virginia to check our centers there, I didn't think she'd suggest today. That was a wonderfully pleasant surprise. If lunch goes well, maybe we can meet for dinner one night before I go.

I need to get to know her better. She's gorgeous, and she seems funny and down-to-earth. Daphne and my family all have positive things to say about her, so that's a plus. Not that they knew many of the women I've hooked up with in the past, but that's because I knew they wouldn't like them. Hell, I didn't necessarily like them all that much either. They were hookups, not relationships. My last attempt at a relationship was in college, and that was enough to make me shy away from anything more than mutually satisfying hookups.

Mallory doesn't seem like a hookup girl though. She's so connected to the company and Daphne that we couldn't just hook up—it would be too messy.

Vegas was a fantasy. This is real life.

So, I'll get to know her and see what could work. Keep it casual, get together when we can, but nothing serious. No expectations, no demands. She'll have to understand I have other things in my life that take priority over a serious relationship. Not that I can tell her about those other things until the Paranormal Hockey League is announced and it's confirmed we've been awarded a franchise. I'm still a hockey player at heart, and we're a superstitious lot. I'm not going to risk anything by talking about it too soon. If it can work at that level, that's good. If not, well, I guess I'll travel a lot more and stay out of the office for the next year to avoid any awkwardness before I leave the company.

I don't see Mallory's MINI Cooper when I pull into the parking lot. I made better time than I expected, so I'm a couple minutes early. Should I go in and wait for her? Get a table? Wait here in the parking lot so we can go in together? Drive around the block until she arrives?

I don't know why this is so difficult. It's not like this is the first time I've gone on a date with a girl. Not that this is a date-date. It's just a friendly lunch. Maybe that's why it's trickier. I know how to act on a date, but how do I act with a friend that's a girl? Daphne is my friend, but I'm not trying to date her. Okay, if she would've given me the time of day and taken my flirting seriously, I would've tried dating her, but she was always so hung up on my cousin, I knew there was no chance, so no pressure.

I've second-guessed myself so long that Mallory pulls in, takes the spot next to my truck, and solves my dilemma. I get out and approach her driver's side door as she exits her car.

"Hi. Been here long?" she asks, leading me toward the restaurant.

"No, just got here. I was trying to decide whether to wait in my truck or go inside and wait." I hold open the door for her.

"I'm so glad you were here first because I was stressing over the same thing," she confesses with a laugh as she walks inside.

I chuckle as we approach the counter. I'm relieved she's struggling with the awkwardness too.

"Next awkward moment. I'm paying this time. You can get next time. Deal?" I hope there will be a next time.

"Okay, but I'll cover the tip." She freezes and flushes.

"Just the tip," I tease with a smirk. We both burst out laughing. I like that her humor matches my inner twelve-year-old boy.

"What do you want?" I ask as we look up at the menu board posted on the wall. The air is redolent with the scent of garlic as a fresh order of garlic knots is removed from the oven. Mallory's stomach rumbles, and I wipe my chin to make sure I don't have drool in my beard.

We look at each other. "Garlic knots," we agree in unison.

"After all the holiday food, I should eat something healthy like salad," she says, "but that's no fun. Any interest in splitting an appetizer sampler and an order of garlic knots?"

Her green eyes are so pretty.

Oh, wait...she asked a question and is waiting for me to answer.

"Yeah, that sounds good." I hope that was an appropriate response.

She smiles, so I guess it was. She turns her smile to the guy working the counter today. He gives her a big grin back, and I have the irrational urge to punch him.

"Hi, we'd like to split an appetizer sampler, an order of those delicious garlic knots and...two sodas?" She glances at me for confirmation on what I'd like to drink.

I nod in agreement and add, "A basket of fries too, please."

I take out my wallet and hand over some cash while Mallory takes some bills from her purse to put in the tip jar on the counter. She's a generous tipper. I like that. She grabs our cups and approaches the soda machine while the cashier counts out my change.

"What do you want to drink?" she asks, glancing over her shoulder.

"Coke is fine," I reply, thanking the cashier when he hands me my change and says our order will be out in a few minutes.

We choose a booth by the window and settle in on either side and look at each other awkwardly. I decide to break the silence.

"So you had a nice Thanksgiving?" Wow, way to go with the scintillating conversation, Liam.

"I did. My family all won their divisions in the Shifter Sprint, so they were happy. They're very competitive, so if one of them hadn't won, they would've been grumpy."

"You said you enjoy running. Do you race too?" It's obvious she works out. Her figure is deliciously curvy, and she's fit. She's wearing black trousers with a subtle pinstripe and a dark green V-neck sweater that looks great with her dark red locks. Makes her eyes appear a deeper green too, and the entire outfit showcases her curves. I can see a hint of cleavage even though she's wearing a white open-collared shirt under her sweater. Nothing inappropriate for the office. She looks professional yet approachable. I don't know when I started paying attention to women's fashion other than how easy it would be to get off and if it'll wrinkle when I toss it to the floor, but I'm noticing details with Mallory.

"I ran cross-country in high school and college, but I prefer to run for my mental and physical health, not for medals. I just go out my back door and run the trails through the forest. I don't need to beat anyone. I'm the odd one in my family. I'm not competitive, and I don't shift. Whole family of wolf shifters. I mean the *whole* family. Parents, siblings, aunts, uncles, cousins—they all shift. They have to go back a couple of generations to find another non-shifter, my grandmother's cousin Marilyn."

I almost spit out my soda. "Cousin Marilyn? Like from that old TV show with the monsters?"

She grins. "Yes! A great uncle was a writer on the show and based that character on his cousin Marilyn. Obviously, a lot of the characters were exaggerated for TV, but Marilyn was based on family. I'm betting Thanksgiving was awkward for years after that."

"Yeah, probably. How does your family handle you not shifting? We're cougar shifters, but my mom is human."

Mallory sighs. "I always felt like a burden when I was younger. Everyone would shift, but someone would have to stay behind with me. They'd try to make it seem like it was a special time we got to share, but I know they drew the short straw and missed out because they were stuck with me."

Our food is brought to our table along with plates so we can share, and we take a selection of everything.

"Oh, my goodness. These garlic knots are incredible." Mallory moans in delight as she takes a bite. My cock stirs slightly at the sound.

"The mozzarella sticks are good too," I say after swallowing my first taste. "I'm sure you weren't a burden." She probably wants to focus on eating, but I can't let our conversation go. Her nonchalant tone hides something else, some other feeling, I want to figure out.

"Oh, I was. My parents never said so, but my older siblings and cousins made sure I knew having to babysit me was a dreaded chore for the whole family. They weren't trying to be cruel. They can just be very...forthright. I'm the runt of the litter, shorter than everyone except for my nephews. Everyone's been trying to fix me up with a nice shifter man for years. Marilyn married a human, and her branch of the family tree drifted away. None of them shift. I think they want to hope I'm a fluke, and I can give birth to shifter kids and raise them in the pack." A rosy pink stains her cheeks. "Sorry to be talking about kids. We've only just met. Well, met again after Vegas. It's weird to talk about kids on a first date." The rose shade turns to scarlet. "Not that this is a date." She's stammering now. "It's just lunch. That's it."

I reach out and touch her hand. "It's not weird. We're getting to know each other. Cougars aren't pack animals, but I have a close human family. We don't have a pack dynamic to complicate things. We do that well enough just being ourselves."

That brings a smile to her lips, and my heart gives a funny little thump.

Do I ask? What the hell. "So your family tries to fix you up with shifter men. Is that what you want? To date a shifter?"

"Um, it depends on the man. Not that I want to date anyone. I'm focusing on my career from now on." She grimaces. "I've dated shifters and humans, and both have cheated on me, so I want someone loyal. I'll probably end up with a Bernese mountain dog." She laughs. "As a pet!"

We share a smile over the plates. I like that we're sharing a meal. It feels...intimate. I'm really liking Mallory and am glad we're getting to know each other better.

Dunking a fry in a puddle of honey mustard on her plate, Mallory looks at me through her lashes, feigning nonchalance. "How about you? Are you looking to date a shifter woman?"

"Not particularly. Like you, I'm focusing on my career for now. Also like you, I've dated both human and shifter, and there were issues unrelated to their shifter status in each relationship. I want loyalty, to be liked for who I am, compatibility. All the usual stuff. If they're human, I want someone that's okay with the shifter side of my family. That would accept our child if they were a shifter. You know as well as I do how funky shifter genetics can be. If there are shifters in the family tree, then a shifter baby can pop up to parents with dormant shifter genes. She'd have to be okay with that."

If neither of us is looking to date, then what are we doing here? Why can't I stay away?

The air around us becomes thick, awkward. She dips more fries into sauce, and I gnaw on a garlic knot, looking for a less sensitive topic of conversation.

"Did you want to go the Flyers game tomorrow night?"

Her head shoots up, and her eyes go wide.

Damn. It must have sounded like I was asking for a date. Way to make an awkward silence more awkward, Liam. Wait...was I asking her on a date?

"Morgan Development has a box, and we can sit in there. The Flyers are playing Dallas."

Not a date. I'm inviting her to a coworker thing with other coworkers. Unless she thinks it's a date. I'm okay with her thinking it's a date.

"Do you work for Morgan Development?" Mallory asks. "I thought maybe you worked for the company that helps care for the building."

I freeze with a chicken finger halfway to my lips, dripping honey mustard back on my plate. She doesn't know who I am? She's having lunch with me, thinking I'm a maintenance worker? Not that there's anything wrong with working in building maintenance, but my title of Vice President of Operations is usually considered more impressive.

"I work for Morgan Development. I'm in outlet operations. That's why I'm going out of town. I'm checking out the centers in Delaware, Maryland, and Virginia to make sure things are running smoothly. The seasonal decorations are how they're supposed to be. That everything looks good, making sure the centers are operating as they should be."

"Oh," Mallory says, "like maintenance but for the outlets, not just the corporate office."

"Sure." I need to tell her who I am, but it's so nice to be with someone who likes me for myself, not because I'm a Morgan. Not because I'm wealthy, or because I could get us a table at any restaurant in any casino in Atlantic City just by requesting a reservation for William James Morgan III. She wants to get to know the Liam who changes light bulbs and drives an old pickup truck and will share an appetizer platter at a pizza place. I don't want to give this up yet. I'll tell her soon. Maybe when I get back from my trip.

"Anyway, did you want to go to the game? We don't have to sit in the box. I can get tickets for regular seats if you'd rather."

"No, that's silly. I've never watched a game from a box. I'm usually in the upper nosebleed section. It won't be weird having me there?"

"Why would it be weird? I have an extra ticket, an invitation to sit in the box, and can bring a guest. I'd like to bring you. You're a fan. We'll have fun."

"Do they give out tickets often? I was new during last year's hockey season, and being downstairs, I never knew what was going on upstairs."

"Now that you're upstairs, you'll be in the thick of things. When there are extra tickets, they'll offer them to the different departments. We'll have to make sure you're on the distribution list so you know about them."

"I'd really like to go, thank you." Mallory's smile is sweet and shy. "Since I live out in the boonies, it would probably make sense to meet somewhere and ride together. Want to meet at the mall? We can jump on the expressway."

I'd rather pick her up from her home, but I don't want to push it. "That works."

"I gotta get back to the office. This was nice. Thank you," Mallory says as she checks the time on her phone. We've somehow eaten almost everything as we talked, leaving an onion ring, a chicken tender, and a few fries. The garlic knots are long gone.

I gather our plates and carry them to the trash can, dumping the leftovers in the bin.

"I'll follow you back. I have a few things to do there." I hold the door for her to exit, then walk Mallory to her car and stand by her door as she opens it and gets in.

"I'm looking forward to going to the game tomorrow. See you at the office." She pulls her door closed, and I head over to my truck and get in. She gives me a wave and backs out of her space before exiting the parking lot.

I start my engine and sit there. I should have told her the whole truth. She's going to find out who I am, and she'll wonder why I didn't just tell her. How do I explain I assumed she knew who I was without sounding like a pompous jerk? Is she going to accept that I was enjoying the anonymity and didn't want to give it up yet? Or is she going to think I was trying to make a fool of her? I'll tell her on the way to the game. That way, she knows before we're with everyone else and has time to process it. We'll have a good time, and she'll see it doesn't matter what my last name is. Yeah, that's a plan. Putting my truck in gear, I back out of my spot and drive back to the office.

6

MALLORY

Oh boy. Lunch with Liam went better than I expected. He's funny and sweet. Goodness knows he's hot. I already know all those muscles he has aren't just for show. I flush, remembering him pounding into me against that wall in Vegas. He supported my weight like I was a feather. Neither of us wants to date, so maybe we could just do a casual thing. It's not like he's a guy I can take home to my parents. He's a cougar shifter and a maintenance guy. I'm not a snob, but if my parents have a hard time with me being a paralegal, I doubt they're going to be impressed with me dating someone who changes light bulbs and makes sure signs are properly placed as a career. I know I promised Valerie not to date a coworker, but we are in completely different departments. The situation is nothing like hers. A guy from the operations department isn't going to impact my job in the legal department.

I take my purse up to the new office. They've delivered our computers, so I sit down and log in to make sure there isn't anything pressing to deal with. Daphne returns from lunch as I'm logging out. We need the files up here so we can do the few new things that Miller, the attorney we work with on collection matters, has dictated, so I tell her I'm going back downstairs to finish loading the carts.

"I'll come with you. There isn't anything to do up here until we have the files. We could each take a different section of shelves and load a cart," she suggests.

I rise and grab my phone. "Sounds good."

We take the stairs down to the lobby. We're crossing to the door for our former area when the elevator dings, and the doors open to reveal Will and Mike.

"Were your computers set up okay?" Mike asks as they step out.

Daphne nods. "Yep, all good. Going to finish loading the carts to get the files upstairs and get back to work."

"Hey, Liam, I didn't know you'd be by today," Will says, looking over my shoulder.

"Hey, Dad, yeah, I finished checking out the AC site. Figured I'd help with moving the files if they needed me," Liam answers.

Dad? Dad? Why the fuck is Liam calling Will "*Dad*"? I struggle to keep my face expressionless, but I feel the blood drain from it. I hope no one notices.

"Oh, hi, Liam," Daphne says. "We're not going to turn down muscles. Have you officially met Mallory? I know you rescued her, but I didn't know if you knew each other."

Well, the blood is rushing back to my cheeks now with Daphne's reminder that this man has seen me using the toilet. My boss's son. I'm betting he's not just a maintenance man. His job title must include more than changing light bulbs.

Liam looks at me. I can't read the expression in his blue eyes, but they aren't the light blue they were during lunch. They're darker, like the sky before a summer storm.

"We've met. Hi, Mallory."

"H—hi, Liam," I choke out.

He gives me a brief smile, but it's more guarded than the grins he flashed me at lunch. I wonder if he realizes our relationship has just changed. Not that it was a relationship. It was a lunch...and hot sex six months ago. But not a relationship. Not even a hint of one. Nope. I guess I came out ahead since I was going to buy lunch next time, and now there won't be a next time. My heart aches at the thought of there not being a next time. I'm sure it's just the garlic knots. It's heartburn, not heartbreak. I'll buy him a pretzel at the game tomorrow night. Wait. The game. How can we go now? It was one thing when I thought I was going with a random coworker, but I know Liam isn't just a coworker now. I don't know his title, but it's somewhere above mine. I hate it when my sister is right.

"Have a good lunch," I say to Will and Mike, then turn to the file room. I need to get away and regroup. I swipe my badge to enter the room and go into the back area, snagging a file cart as I walk by. Daphne can work in the main space. I realize my miscalculation when Liam follows me in.

This room feels way too small with Liam's oversized presence. I didn't realize how tall and broad he was until we were in this space together. I recognize he's not trying to intimidate me with his size. My brothers are both tall, powerful men, and even though they're wolf shifters, they're big teddy bears.

I'm not intimidated, but I am so aware of him. I can smell him. I don't know if it's cologne, his soap, or just *him,* but I smell pine trees, sunshine, and a hint of sea air. The heat coming off his body is making me sweat. I crack open a window to get some cool air coming in. I close my eyes and take a few deep breaths to try to clear my head. When I open my eyes, I find Liam's eyes trained on my chest. I cross my arms.

Liam closes the distance between us, stopping a mere two feet away. My head is spinning from his nearness. It's like I'm getting drunk on pheromones or something. His blue eyes are no longer cloudy. They're bright blue, and I swear they're flashing. Oh no, it was the fluorescent bulb overhead flickering before burning out.

"Do you need to go change that?" I point up at the burned-out bulb. Such a bitchy thing to say, I know, but I need room to breathe, to think, and I can't do that while he's so close to me. My fingers itch to trace the line of his jaw and read the stubble like it's a sonnet written in braille. I keep my arms firmly crossed over my chest.

"I didn't realize until lunch that you didn't know who I am. I didn't know how to tell you. I decided to tell you tomorrow night on the way to the game," Liam says.

"Wait until I'm stuck in a vehicle with you to tell me something major like, hey, I'm the son of your boss?"

He at least has the grace to blush at my whisper-shout. I start a playlist on my phone in hopes it disguises our conversation.

My country love song playlist starts. Bzz. Wrong answer. I switch it to my "Men are Scumbags" playlist and smile. Okay, really, it's my girl power playlist, but it's multipurpose.

I lean against the file cabinet I should be emptying and cross my arms over my chest again. Liam glances down again. I hope he enjoys the view because he has no chance of anything else now.

"What do you really do for the company?" I ask. "You're not a maintenance man."

"Well, I kinda am. My title is Vice President of Operations, so part of my job is making sure things are running smoothly. If necessary, I change light bulbs and empty trash cans."

I roll my eyes. I just can't with him right now. I turn and open the top drawer and start pulling out files.

"If you're going to be here, you may as well be useful. I'm going to pull our working files first. You can put them on the cart. Once we pull all of them, they'll go upstairs." I load him up, wondering how many he'll accept before he unloads them. Will he be stubborn and try to prove how strong he is, or will he be logical and accept fewer files at a time so he's able to load them on the cart without dumping them? I'm begrudgingly impressed when he goes with logic.

We work in silence for a couple minutes, songs about telling Earl goodbye and boots under beds providing the soundtrack to our efforts.

"I'm sorry," he says softly. "I wasn't trying to deceive you. I'm used to everyone here knowing who I am, and since you work with Daphne, I just assumed you knew."

"Well, we never exchanged last names, so I guess it's fair." I wipe my hand on my trousers and stick it out. "Mallory Carter."

His large hand engulfs mine, and a wave of memory washes over me—the way his hands brought pleasure to my body that night months ago. Why do we have to work together?

"Liam Morgan. Officially I'm William James Morgan III, but I've always gone by Liam."

"Nice to meet you, Liam. You have a nice name." I pull my hand from his reluctantly.

"Thanks. Sometimes it would be a lot easier if it was something different." He rolls his eyes and sighs. "I know I'm not a Kennedy or whatever, but people in certain circles hear the Morgan name and expect things. Makes it hard to meet people. It was nice realizing you liked me without knowing who I am."

It's my turn to sigh. "I'm sorry. You seem like a nice man."

"Do you still want to go to the game tomorrow night?"

"I don't know…"

"Hey, Daphne!" Liam calls out.

She pokes her head in and takes out her earbud. "What?"

"Were you and Logan going to the Flyers game tomorrow night?" he asks.

"Yeah," she replies. "Are you? Ooh, did you want to go, Mallory? We're sitting in the Morgan Development box. Free food and drinks. You could ride with us and stay over if you wanted so you don't have to schlep home after."

"We could all ride together," Liam suggests.

I shoot him a glance. I know he's making it difficult for me to bow out and explain to Daphne why I don't want to go.

"Let's talk about it tonight, okay?" I try to change the subject, hoping Daphne will go back to her shelves and not notice the tension between me and Liam. The less she sees us together, the better. I don't want her trying to play matchmaker or asking questions about why I'm always so tense around him.

"What's happening tonight?" Liam asks with faux innocence. If it wouldn't be an HR issue, I swear I'd punch him. I satisfy myself by shooting him a 'Why are you being so nosy?' look.

"Mallory is coming over after work for dinner and to hang out. We have stuff to talk about. I think Logan was going to see about hanging out with you," Daphne says.

Oh, crap. Liam and Logan are cousins. That didn't occur to me. Well, this just got more awkward.

Liam pulls out his phone to check for a text from his cousin. "Haven't heard from him yet. What were you having for dinner?"

Oh no. He better not be inviting himself over.

"Chinese," Daphne answers. "I can order extra if you guys want to join us."

Sweet, naive Daphne. She walked right into that. I huff out a deep breath as I turn back to the file cabinet and start pulling more files to hand to Liam.

I enjoyed lunch, but I'm betting dinner won't be as comfortable.

7

LIAM

Mallory turns back to the file cabinet with a huff, and Daphne winks at me. I try to hold back my grin—I think she's trying to fix us up.

"I'll text Logan and let him know we're doing Chinese for dinner, and then you guys can do whatever you want while Mal and I hang out and catch up." Daphne flashes a self-satisfied smile and returns to the main office.

"I don't appreciate being manipulated, Liam. Don't use my friendship with Daphne against me." Mallory snarls as she shoves a pile of files at my chest with enough force to knock me back on my heels. I wasn't expecting her strength. I should have.

"You were looking forward to going to the game. This way, it still works out without being awkward."

"Oh no. It's still awkward. Now it will be awkward with an audience. Thanks."

I chuckle, thankful she doesn't punch me. I feel safe in assuming she wants to. She sits on the floor to go through the bottom drawer without having to bend over. She gives a sudden yelp and rears back.

"What? Are you okay?" I squat next to her. I barely resist the urge to pull her into my arms. To comfort her. To protect her. I just want to hold her. I'll probably never get the chance to feel her soft curves against mine. Feel her breath against my neck. Her lips against mine again. Add it to the list of missed opportunities in my life.

"Yeah, the cricket carcass startled me. At least it's not alive. I don't know why I'm surprised anymore, but I always am. I hate crickets."

"How about I go through this drawer? You tell me what to pull to take upstairs, and I'll hand it to you to put on the cart. Do you only get crickets in the bottom drawers?"

She stands and brushes off the rear of her trousers. "The bottom two drawers or shelves. I've never seen them higher than that. I've only seen a live one twice. It's always dead ones. I don't know how we get them, but they creep me out."

"Hopefully this is the last you encounter them," I say, an attempt to reassure her. "Once the new files are upstairs, I'll unload what remains in the bottom drawers and stack them on the desks so you can close them out."

Mallory sighs. "You don't have to do that. But thank you. It's just startling. I know that even if it was alive, it wouldn't hurt me." She shoots me a grin. "It's enough you rescued me once. You don't have to keep being my hero."

I wouldn't mind being her hero.

Whoa, slow your roll, Morgan. You've had lunch with her twice. You can't go slaying dragons for her. Not that I'd slay a dragon. The ones I know are nice guys. Okay, I only know one—Teagan's cousin, Rhys. But he's a cool dude. Well, not *cool*. He's a fire-breathing dragon. He actually runs hot. Why am I going off on this tangent? Oh, yeah, being her hero.

"I don't know if I want to be privy to your thoughts or if it's a good thing I have no clue what you were just thinking about." Mallory's green eyes sparkle, and her cherry red lips tip up.

I quirk a half smile. "If you knew the twists and turns my mind took, you'd never give me the time of day. It was just a random thought."

"If you say so. Okay. From that drawer, the files we'll need are..."

Mallory leans over me so she can read the labels and calls out the files destined for upstairs. She smells like apples. Must be her shampoo or body wash. Apples are my favorite fruit, but I've never been turned on by the scent of them before. I close my eyes and breathe deeply; my cougar wants to purr in happiness. He must like apples too. I know he likes Mallory.

"That does it for in here," she says. "Let's finish loading the cart with files out there and then take them upstairs." She grimaces. "I'm sorry. I'm being presumptuous. If you have other stuff to do, we're fine without your help."

I stand, appreciating Mallory's height. The top of her head comes up to my chin. She'd be easy to kiss without having to break my back bending to reach her. I can't be thinking about kissing her, especially not in the office. Not that she wants to date me any more than I want to date her. We've each admitted we want to focus on our careers for now, not date or have a relationship. Now that she knows I'm not just a maintenance guy, that's another strike against me. Figures, I finally find a woman who likes me for me, and it's my job and my family that are objectionable. Not my old truck, not my jeans and work boots. My last name and executive position have tanked it for me.

But does it matter what her objections are? I mean, of course they matter, but I keep telling myself I need to focus on the team and what needs to be done to make that a success. I don't want to date anyone. I don't want to be in a relationship. But then my thoughts drift to Mallory and a clear desire to be with her.

Does my heart know something my head doesn't? Is my cougar trying to tell me something? Is my cock trying to get some action? All the above?

What was so simple in Vegas is infinitely more complicated in New Jersey. I wish she'd give me a chance. I like her. Not just because she's fricking gorgeous but because she's smart and funny. I wish we had spoken more in Vegas instead of just hooking up. I had planned to go someplace quieter where we could talk and get to know each other some more, maybe agree to stay in touch. Unfortunately, we didn't get that chance.

It looks like I have Daphne willing to play matchmaker though, and I'll gladly accept her help. Maybe if we hang out together enough, Mallory will start seeing me differently. Our good friends are dating, so we'll run into each other sometimes. My travel schedule will mess things up, but this time of year, my trips are shorter and not as frequent, so maybe that will help her miss me a bit. We'll see how dinner goes tonight. Hopefully, Mallory agrees to go to the game so we can hang out. I doubt we'll have lunch together anymore.

I push the file cart into the main area and fish my phone out of my pocket to shoot a text to my cousin.

> Me: Having Chinese at your house tonight.

> Logan: You are? I think Daphne is having her friend over.

> Me: Mallory. I know.

> Logan: Is there something going on?

> Me: Hopefully we're all going to the game tomorrow night.

> Logan: Uh-huh. Pick up beer.

> Me: Okay.

Daphne's phone chimes. I assume it's a text from Logan. Judging by her smirk, he's telling her about our exchange. Whatever.

"Do you get crickets in here too?" I ask Mallory, looking around the main office. We really need to get a pest management company in here and figure out what's going on.

"Sometimes."

"Okay, I'll do the bottom shelves again, and you take the upper shelves. I'll read off the names?"

"That works. Thank you for helping us."

The three of us work well together, and after filling the carts twice, we get all the files upstairs where they belong. I leave Daphne and Mallory to do the organizing and go down to Dad's office.

"Hi, Allison."

Dad's assistant smiles and waves. "Hey, Liam."

"Is he available?"

"I think he's getting coffee."

"Are you looking for me?" Dad calls out.

"Yeah. Checking in before I head out," I reply.

"Okay, come on in."

I follow him into his office, closing the door behind me. He raises his brow at that but doesn't say anything as he takes a seat behind his desk.

I sit in a chair in front of his desk.

"Daphne and Mallory have moved their current files upstairs."

"That's good," Dad says. "It'll be nice having them up there."

"Did you know they have crickets down there?" I don't know why that bothers me so much, but it angers me they had to deal with bugs, especially when it scares them. No one should have to work where they're afraid.

"Liam, what is going on?" Dad leans forward and rests his forearms on his desk, lacing his fingers together.

"We have employees dealing with mice and crickets, and that's unacceptable!"

"Yes, it is, and we're handling it. I wasn't aware of the situation until recently, or I would have done something. This isn't about a mouse or crickets. I repeat, what is going on?"

"I...I don't know." How do I explain all this to him and not sound ungrateful?

"Is it the time of year?" Dad asks.

"What?" I look at my watch to check the date. Oh.

"I know the first couple of years, you would get anxious as the anniversary approached. So would your mother. The past few years have seemed better for both of you."

He's talking about the car accident that took my hockey dream away. It's been eight years today.

Teagan, Jake, and I were on our way home from college for the weekend. We had just been home the weekend before for Thanksgiving, but my girlfriend at the time wanted me to take her to a party since I had a rare Friday night free, and I wanted to make Tiffany happy. Our university was only ninety minutes away, so coming home wasn't a big deal. I was driving my truck down a rural stretch of highway when a farmer driving a tractor-trailer full of whatever pulled out from a side street without looking and slammed into my driver's side, seriously injuring me and Teagan, who was sitting behind me. Jake was uninjured, other than some bruising from his seatbelt. Thank goodness he was okay. He was able to get us out before the engine fire did more than give me a couple of superficial burns on my leg. Teagan and I both recovered but my injuries ended my hockey career.

"No, I didn't even realize the date." I shrug. "Nothing's going on. Is the box full tomorrow night? Daphne and Mallory were planning on going. Me and Logan. I'm assuming you and Uncle Mike."

"Mallory is going? I didn't know she was a hockey fan. She's never gone before."

I don't mention she didn't go because she never knew tickets were available.

"Yeah, Daphne invited her. If there was room, I figured I'd offer tickets to Teagan and Jake too." If I have my friends there, it won't seem as much like a double date, and maybe Mallory will be more comfortable.

"There's always room for those two. Invite them. Your mom and Aunt Holly are coming too. They crush on that player from Dallas."

I roll my eyes. The guy is my age, a fact they choose to ignore because it's "icky."

"I'm here if you need to talk, Liam. About anything," Dad says earnestly.

"I know, Dad. Thanks." I really am fortunate in so many ways. I adjust my position in my chair. "I went to the Atlantic City property. It's interesting, but it would need an overhaul. They've tried doing retail before, and it didn't work as well as they hoped. I really think it needs to be a mixed-use property."

"Do you think we should pass?"

"No. I think it's going to be perfect for a rink and some supporting retail, but without confirmation that we're getting the hockey franchise, it's too risky to commit to purchasing it yet. Our regular retail model won't work there. It needs another element to drive traffic."

"The property isn't even for sale yet, so we have time. It's just when it is listed for sale, I think it would be best to move quickly. My source says we have about six months." Dad leans back in his chair.

"Six months is a good timeline. We should know about the franchise way before that. When I know something, I'll tell you."

"Fair enough. When do you leave? Wednesday?"

"Yeah, I'll be hitting the Delaware, Maryland, and Virginia properties and be back a week from Thursday. Barring anything goofy, I'll be in Jersey through year's end. I'll check out the New Jersey properties and get ready for my property tours in the new year."

I check my watch. It's almost 5:00 p.m. Rising, I give Dad the half grin that I know I inherited from him.

"I don't know if I'll be in here tomorrow, but I'll see you at the game."

"Have a good night, Liam."

I take my leave and say goodbye to Allison and Betty as I pass their desks. Climbing into my truck, I decide to swing by home to change before going over to Daphne and Logan's. I don't want to look like I'm too eager to spend time with Mallory. I *am* extremely eager to spend time with her. I just don't want to make it obvious. Yet. My cougar, the universe, whatever, won't leave the idea of Mallory and me alone. And maybe this feeling or message is right. It's not about never. It's about when. Maybe I'm not avoiding. I'm waiting.

I use voice-to-text to ask Daphne if she wants me to pick up anything for her and Mallory while I'm getting the beer.

> Daphne: Nope, we're good. Beef and broccoli as usual?

> > Me: Yep.

> Daphne: Are you trying to pick up Mallory?

> > Me: I thought she was driving to your place herself. I can pick her up from wherever though if she needs a ride.

> Daphne: You know what I mean.

> > Me: Why do you ask?

> Daphne: Because she's my friend, and I guess you are too.

> > Me: Ouch.

> Daphne: Shut up. You flirt with everyone. I want to make sure you aren't just playing around. If you're hitting on her for fun, knock it off.

> > Me: Simmer down. Want to get to know her, that's all. No games.

Do I ask for her help or not? Daphne's going to torture me with the knowledge of my burgeoning crush on Mallory, but if it advances my cause, it'll be worth it.

> Me: I'd be happy for your help. I think she likes me, but since I work for Morgan and am an executive, it's a no-go.

> Daphne: Well, that complicates things. You could quit...

> Me: Ha. Seriously. Neither one of us wants a relationship now, but no reason we can't be friends and lay some groundwork, right?

> Daphne: I guess. But don't make things weird.

> Me: Probably too late for that...

> Daphne: Ugh. Bye.

I enter my pool house, thinking about Daphne's comment. I could quit my job at Morgan Development now and maybe remove an impediment to a relationship with Mallory, but that seems rather drastic. Plus it would leave a hole in the company until my cousin Andy graduates in the spring and is ready to step into my role.

Maybe I'm not the one who has to leave though. She's a paralegal. She could find a job at any of the law firms around here. Maybe one of the casinos.

No. I can't even consider that seriously for a second. I'm not so much of an asshole that I'd ever suggest that her career is less important than mine. If Morgan Development is where she wants to be, then that's where she'll be.

I have to hope that if we're meant to be together, we will be. I guess I'm a bit of a romantic, just like Dad. He knew from the first time he met Mom in Grammy Morgan's classroom that she was the woman for him. Mom was Grammy's student teacher and was reluctant to get to know Dad because of the conflict, but he convinced her. Hmm. The parallels aren't lost on me. I'll have to chat up my parents on their history to see if I can pick up some tips. I don't have to use anything I learn from my parents, but it's good to have information.

My brain keeps telling me now is not the time, that I need to focus on my career and the team. I don't need a relationship complicating things. But I think that's fear talking. I'm not going to let fear rule me. My heart and my cougar and yeah, my cock, keep reacting to Mallory. I can't stop thinking about her. Why should I? Would dating her really make me less successful? Do I really think being with her would ruin my chances with the team? No, I don't. I'm going for it. I'm not giving up on Mallory yet.

I debate whether I should shower before going to Logan and Daphne's, but no one else will have, and I don't want to look like I'm trying too hard. I'll just change my shirt. I put on a black T-shirt and a gray heather sweater and decide to change into clean jeans since I was poking around some dusty places in the Atlantic City property. I wash my face, brush my teeth, and run a comb through my hair. I think I look pretty good. I hope Mallory does too.

I pick up the IPA Logan and I currently favor from the liquor store and park at the curb in front of my cousin's home. The ranch house looks cute, dripping with all the Christmas lights I helped hang. Headlights appear in my rearview, and Mallory's MINI Cooper parks behind my truck. I get out and wait on the sidewalk for Mallory to exit her vehicle.

"Did you just get here too?" she asks.

"I did. Just pulled up a moment before you. I was admiring the lights."

"They're beautiful," she says wistfully. "I love the old-fashioned multicolor lights the most. My family favors the white lights, so they always outvoted me."

As we walk up the walkway to the front door, we hear a whir, and the inflatables on the lawn start to grow.

"Oh, my goodness. They have a Gritty!" Mallory enthuses.

"Are you a Gritty fan too? Daphne is obsessed with him. When we saw this at Home Depot, Logan knew he had to get him as a surprise for her."

"I *love* Gritty. He's my boo thang. Best mascot in sports. I still love the Phillie Phanatic, but Gritty is next-level awesome. If I ever got a tattoo, it would be to commemorate my Gritty love."

I'm distracted by thoughts of where Mallory would put a tattoo of the Flyers mascot and that all her beautiful skin is unmarked.

"You're here!" Daphne calls from the porch. I didn't realize she'd come outside.

"OMG, you have a Gritty! I am so jelly!" Mallory squeals, hugging Daphne like they didn't just spend eight hours together.

Laughing, Daphne hugs me as Logan relieves me of the six-pack. "Logan scored major points getting him. We got the Snoopy yesterday. I think we're going to end up being that house." She makes air quote fingers when saying *that*. No doubt they will indeed be *that* house in the neighborhood, and I'm glad. Daphne has suffered a lot of loss, and she deserves to be happy and have all the holiday celebrations life offers.

"I kinda want a blow- up Gritty," Mallory says as she enters the house, "but I'm out in the woods. No one will see him but me, so that seems silly."

I cross the threshold behind her. "If it makes you happy, it's not silly. Life is short. Take joy where you can find it."

Three pairs of eyes look at me with various degrees of surprise.

I shrug.

"You're absolutely right, Liam," Daphne says, with a sheen in her big brown eyes. She knows as well as I do how fragile life is. She lost her parents in a car accident when she was a teenager. I thankfully survived my accident, but it reinforced the truth that tomorrow is not guaranteed. If you have a chance for happiness, you should embrace it. If happiness is a curvy redhead with gorgeous green eyes, then I'm all for embracing her too. Now to convince her that her happiness can be found in a six-foot-three, bearded, broken, former hockey player.

8

MALLORY

I LOVE THE CHANGE LOGAN'S BROUGHT NOT JUST TO DAPHNE'S LIFE, BUT TO their home as well. When I've hung out here with her before, it was like entering a time capsule from when her grandmother owned the house. Daphne kept most of the furniture and knickknacks the same as her grandmother had it. Daphne inhabited the home she inherited, but she wasn't *living* in it. Logan stayed here between trips as a travel photographer, but he hadn't really made a mark on the home, either. Now that they're a couple, his place in her life and home is more apparent.

There are pictures from his travels on the walls that weren't there a few weeks ago. They've ripped up the old carpet to show off the beautiful hardwood floors underneath. Brighter colors are splashed around with throw pillows and a patterned area rug under the coffee table. It looks like somewhere a couple in their twenties live. The Christmas lights and inflatables bring joy to the exterior, and it looks like they're decorating the bay window in the living room.

"What are you putting in the window?" I ask.

"We have a collection of ceramic houses that Gran and I used to put in the window. I didn't bother the last few years, but this year, we're setting them up again," Daphne says.

"Did you show her the addition to the village, Logan?" Liam asks.

Logan glares at his cousin. I guess he didn't show her.

"Is the food being delivered, or were one of you going to pick it up?" I try to change the subject.

"Delivered," Daphne states. "What did you do, Logan?"

Well, I tried.

"I may have gotten a new building for the village, Sunshine," Logan says with a charming grin.

My heart melts when he calls her Sunshine. I've never had a pet name from a boyfriend. I get called Mal sometimes, but that's not cute or sweet. That's just being too lazy to say a couple extra syllables.

"If you got a strip club for my Christmas village, I will hurt you, Logan Morris," Daphne promises.

"Ooh, stripper elves dancing on a candy cane pole!" I bounce on my toes in excitement at the thought. "That would be so awesome!"

"Marry me," Liam says.

I know he's joking, but my heart skips a beat at his words. I wish. Wait. No, I don't. No marriage. Casual, Mallory. Remember, you want casual.

Daphne and Logan look at me, her in horror, him in admiration.

Logan takes his phone out of his pocket. "I didn't get a strip club for the Christmas village, but I really want one now."

"You better not be googling a paint-your-own-ceramics shop, Logan," Daphne warns.

"That sounds fun. Let me know if you find one," I say.

"There's one across from the Municipal Complex," he informs me.

"Text me the link, please?" My phone buzzes in my pocket. "Thanks!"

Logan leaves and comes back carrying a box.

Daphne opens it and pulls out a ceramic Home Depot store for their Christmas village. I love it. Apparently, Daphne does too because she's clapping and bouncing, and appears to be about two seconds from squeeing.

A car pulls in the driveway, and the driver grabs a collection of bags before hustling to the door. Logan is there waiting, ready to accept our food.

"Where do you want to sit?" Daphne asks. "Island, table, living room?"

"I'm good with living room," Liam says. "That good with you, Mallory?"

"Yeah, that works," I say.

"What do you want to drink, Mallory?" Logan asks after he sets the bags on the coffee table. He hands Liam a beer.

"Diet Pepsi, please."

We end up sharing our entrees. Taking bites from Liam's beef and broccoli feels so personal. Couples share food. When we shared lunch today, it felt like we were maybe building something. Now I know the only thing I should be building is a wall around my heart.

"We've done lunch and dinner together," I blurt out. "All that's left is breakfast." I wish I could call back my words because it sounds way more suggestive than I meant it to.

"I just mean to...to complete the set. I...I wasn't propositioning you," I stammer. Where's a sinkhole opening beneath you when you need it? I'm probably as red as the Christmas lights lining Daphne's roofline.

Liam laughs kindly. "I know what you meant. I'd be happy to have breakfast with you in whatever context." He winks.

It's a mix of playful and flirtatious, and I wish I could just plant a kiss on his full lips and remind myself if his well-groomed brown beard is soft or scratchy. I don't remember from Vegas, and that makes me sad. I was so caught up in the moment and the thrill of it, I didn't note the details.

Stop it, Mallory. You can't be thinking those kinds of thoughts about a man you can't have. You work with him. He's the son of your boss, the nephew of your supervisor, the cousin of your good friend's boyfriend, and probably your future boss if he takes over for his father one day. In no way is getting involved with this man a good idea, and fantasizing about him is an even worse one.

Liam turns to Logan and Daphne, who are sitting on the living room floor across from us, around the coffee table. "We ran into each other at Francisco's and had lunch together the other day and then again today. Now we're having dinner. All that's left is breakfast."

"Uh-huh." Daphne looks at us wide-eyed. I don't know what she's thinking, but she needs to stop.

"So, Daphne, you said you had stuff you wanted to talk about, but not in the office. That's why I'm here. What's up?" Yeah, it's tacky to ask in front of the guys, but I need to get out of the hot seat somehow.

"Oh, yeah! I forgot about that. I picked up a little present for you. I'll give it to you after we're done eating."

"You didn't have to get me anything!" I protest.

"Hush. I saw it and thought you'd like it. As for what I wanted to talk about... Liam, you're here as a friend, not as a VP of Morgan Development."

"Okay," Liam agrees.

"Before I left for France, I spoke with Will about cutting back my hours. I didn't know at the time that our department was closing, Mallory." Daphne's brown eyes meet mine. "Will knew they were closing collections, so that wasn't a big deal. We got talking about the tours we did and how I minored in marketing in college."

I nod to show I'm following.

"Long story short, we're going to test drive doing and posting video tours of nearby centers along with some of the local sights to see if they create interest, and maybe do some more cross-promotion with area attractions. Once they close collections, provided these practice promos don't bomb, I'm going to shift to the marketing department and do tours at centers around the country."

"Wow, that's great! But does that mean we aren't going to share an office soon?" I'm so happy for Daphne. She started doing recorded tours and posting them online to achieve her childhood dream of being a tour guide. But I enjoy sharing an office with her. I was excited to get out of our dungeon downstairs and enjoy our windows with the view of the woods. I don't want to share that with someone else.

Daphne frowns slightly. "I don't know. I'll hopefully be traveling, so I won't be in the office all the time. I don't know if they'll let me keep that desk or not." She shrugs. "We have a few months to figure it out."

Liam looks at me. "You worked on the tours Daphne posted?"

"Yeah," I say.

"I couldn't have done them without her!" Daphne reaches out to squeeze my arm, her brown eyes shining with gratitude. "She was my tourist that I spoke to, so I didn't look like a crazy woman talking to myself. And she brought the wine when I uploaded them. She's my emotional support buddy."

Logan stands and starts clearing our plates. We've made a big dent in the meal, an impressive feat considering how huge the portions were. The restaurant must be used to feeding shifters.

Daphne rises as well. "Let me get your present, Mallory!"

Liam and I remain seated at the coffee table. He swipes a finger along the edge of the coffee table right in front of me. I'm unable to suppress the shiver that runs through me when I imagine that finger running down my arm. Up my leg. Along my breast.

"I know a cute breakfast place on Route 9," Liam says.

"What?" I hope it's not obvious how distracted I am by the turn my thoughts took.

"Somewhere to have breakfast after I come back so we can complete our meal set."

"We're not going out for breakfast." I'm picking at the colorful throw rug nervously. I pull my knees up to my chest and wrap my other arm around my shins. Let the wall building begin. I slant a glance at him and quickly refocus on the rug.

"Okay, then we can cook it together. I'm good at eggs. Do you have a waffle iron, or would you rather have pancakes?" He asks like my answer matters.

I can't imagine a situation where we'd be cooking breakfast together. Okay, that's a lie. I can imagine half a dozen mornings spent cooking breakfast together. They're all after nights we spent doing all sorts of hot and naughty things.

It's been way too long since I've had sex. Our encounter in Vegas was the last time. I'm just horny. I'd be reacting like this to any attractive man. It's not a Liam-specific reaction. Please, don't let it be a Liam-specific reaction because it will remain unsatisfied.

"Here you go! I hope you like it because I can't return it," Daphne says with a laugh, setting a small box in front of me and settling across the coffee table again.

"Hey, where's my present? You wouldn't have gotten to France without me," Liam whines.

"Really?" I ask.

"Really. I drove her to the Newark Airport so she'd get to Paris early in the morning. Good thing I did because Logan had tickets to fly home that afternoon. If she flew out of Philly, she would have landed right as he took off, and they'd still be on separate continents. I'm a hero."

Rolling my eyes, I pick up the small white cardboard box and open the lid. I grab a thin gold cord and pull out an intricately designed model wooden house. It's small, just about three inches square, but the detail is incredible. So many precise cuts in the thinnest natural wood. It's lovely.

"Oh, Daphne, I love it. It's so intricate and delicate!"

"Yay! I was hoping you'd like it. There was a stall at one of the Christmas markets in Strasbourg full of them, and I know how you love houses, so I thought you'd like a little model of the style of building we saw in Strasbourg. The town is full of old timber buildings. You can feel the history. Here." She hands me a little battery-operated tea light. "Put that in the house."

As I do so, Liam gets up and turns off the ceiling fan light so the living room is darker. I gasp at the warm, golden glow shining in the house.

I hold it up so I can appreciate it. "It's beautiful."

"Yeah, beautiful," Liam agrees.

I glance up at him. He's looking at me, not the house. I look at Daphne and find her looking at Liam with a matchmaking gleam in her eye and a small smirk. Oh no.

I put the house on the table and walk on my knees over to Daphne's side of the coffee table to thank her.

"Not going to happen," I whisper in her ear as I hug her.

"We'll see," is her whispered response.

9
LIAM

I'M LIVING DANGEROUSLY, GETTING DAPHNE INVOLVED IN MY PURSUIT OF Mallory, but I'm betting I'll need all the help I can get. I'm under no illusions that I am so irresistible that every woman wants me. I'll respect that Mallory doesn't want to date me, but I can't know that for sure if we don't hang out as friends first. If Daphne can help with this, I'm going to accept it. Who knows? Maybe when Mallory gets to know me better, her resistance to dating me will fade.

I don't need to know her better to want her more. My interest in her is growing every moment. I don't believe in fated mates. You choose who you end up with. It's not fate. It's not magic. It's simply hormones and logic. We obviously have compatible hormones based on Vegas. Logic is showing we have things in common—we know the same people, like the same things, and for now, we work for the same company. She liked me before she knew I was a Morgan. Ironically, the thing that often draws women to me is a major point pushing her away. Fate. Ha.

"Did you still need us to leave so you two can talk?" Logan asks Daphne.

I try to stifle my snort-laugh at his bluntness.

Daphne looks to Mallory, who shakes her head.

"No, we're good. Do you need to get home early, Mallory, or do you have time to play a game? We could play something simple like Uno or Phase 10."

Mallory glances at the grandfather clock in the corner. "It's only seven. I can stay a while longer. I just need to leave around eight thirty, so I'm home by nine-ish."

Daphne pulls out a deck of Phase 10 cards when we all agree that sounds more fun than Uno. Logan shuffles and deals, starting an hour of the most cutthroat game of Phase 10 I've ever played. Daphne seems so sweet, but she's ruthless.

Mallory looks at me with wide eyes. "Did you have any idea she was like this?"

Daphne dances around the living room, celebrating her victory, yelling out, "Booyah!" and "Suck it!"

"Only when she has more than one beer at Flyers' games. I didn't know she was like this in general. Popcorn?" I offer her the bowl sitting at my elbow. She takes a handful and eats it kernel by kernel as she watches Daphne's antics.

Daphne finally stops dancing and drops to her knees next to Mallory. "Oh, yeah, the game! Mallory, did you want to sleep over tomorrow night? I figured Logan could drive me to work tomorrow, you could drive me home, and then we'd go to the game together. It'll be close to midnight when we return, and then you'd have to drive home. Just stay here and go to work with me."

"I don't know..." Mallory starts.

"You're welcome to stay at my place, Mallory," I offer.

She shoots me a glare and turns back to Daphne. "If you're sure I won't be in the way, I'd appreciate staying over. Thanks."

I'm impressed. She accepted gracefully. Considering she was trying to get out of going to the game once she found out who I was, this is amazing.

"You won't be in the way at all," Logan assures her. "We'd worry about you driving home that late, so you're doing us a favor."

"Wow." Mallory laughs, smiling at Daphne. "He is charming. You weren't exaggerating!"

"I told you! And he's not even the most charming one. This one" Daphne gestures to me "is the real charmer."

Mallory glances my way. "Thanks for the warning." She stands up and says, "Well, let me head home. Thank you for dinner. I had fun. I'll see you all tomorrow."

I stand as well. "Thanks, guys. I'll walk Mallory to her car and head out myself. See you tomorrow."

I don't miss the glance my cousin and Daphne share as Logan snags our jackets. I want to be a gentleman and help Mallory into hers, but I think that would be pushing it. Instead, I open the door for her to leave after we say our goodnights.

"You didn't have to leave early just because I am." Mallory gives Gritty a high five as we walk past him on the way to our vehicles at the curb.

"I know, but I have emails to catch up on and some reports to read before I leave town. I wasn't planning on having a late night tonight, anyway."

We stop next to the driver's side door of Mallory's car. The streetlight is like a spotlight, and Logan and Daphne are probably peeking through the curtains. I don't dare glance to check. I don't want to break this moment with Mallory. The fog of our breath mingles in the crisp fall air. I wish our bodies were mingling. Mallory shivers slightly, and I long to pull her into my arms to share my heat. She'd feel how fast my heart is beating from being near her. It's hard to resist the urge to lean down and kiss her, but that isn't a great idea. I can be patient. The MINI Cooper's lock disengages when Mallory hits the button on her key fob. I reach for the door handle and open it for her. She sits in the driver's seat and looks up at me as I stand in the open doorway of her car.

"I'll see you for the game tomorrow night. Drive safely, Mallory." I tap the roof of her car and back away so she can close her door.

"See you tomorrow. Have a good night, Liam."

Before the door shuts, I rush to say, "Hey, could you please text me when you get home? Just so I know you got home safely?"

I hope she doesn't think I'm trying to keep tabs on her. I'm not. This time of year, there are deer and other critters about, and she lives alone. I know she's been driving these roads for a decade, but I didn't know her then. I know her now, and I worry.

Looking at me appraisingly, Mallory seems to consider my request. "Okay, I will. Drive safely too. Goodnight, Liam." She gives me a quick smile that I feel like a kick to the chest and closes her door. I get in my truck and watch her drive away. I can't wait for tomorrow night.

The atmosphere inside the arena is electric, like it always is before a home game. It's a sea of orange and black jerseys with a rare green Dallas jersey spotted now and then. The Philly/Dallas hatred doesn't really carry over to hockey the way it does with football, but it's still brave to wear anything Dallas-related in the City of Brotherly Love.

"They're here!" Mom cries out as we enter the box. She's seen three of us in the past week, so I know her excitement is for the fourth member of our party—Mallory. Dad and Uncle Mike glance over and do the chin-lift acknowledgment thing, then resume their conversation in the back of the room.

Teagan and Jake aren't here yet, and no one else from the office is here. I was hoping there would be a larger group of people so Mallory would feel like part of the crowd. Nothing to do but approach my mother and aunt.

"Hi, Mom, hi, Aunt Holly. What's up?" I lean in to kiss each of their cheeks. Logan does the same, and the moms hug Daphne. When that's all done, their attention falls to Mallory, who's standing there with a polite smile on her lips and a deer-in-the-headlights look in her eyes.

"Hello," Mom says, holding her hand out to Mallory. "I'm Faith Morgan."

"Nice to meet you, Mrs. Morgan. I'm Mallory Carter." Mallory shakes her hand and smiles.

"Call me Faith, please!"

"And I'm Holly Morris," Aunt Holly says. "You work at Morgan with Daphne and Mike?"

"I do," Mallory affirms.

The teams skate out for pregame warm-ups, catching Daphne's attention.

"Ooh, want to go down to watch, Mal? We can see your captain up close!"

"Your captain?" Mom asks.

"She has a crush on the Dallas captain," Daphne says, ignoring Mallory's glare. "She has a thing for tall, dark, and bearded guys."

Mallory flushes deep pink with embarrassment, and Mom glances my way with lifted brows.

"Tall, dark, and bearded *hockey players*," Mallory retorts.

I know she doesn't mean anything by it; she doesn't know my history, and she's trying to deflect her embarrassment. However, even though I know it in my head, I'm having a difficult time not feeling it in my heart. Everyone is shooting quick glances at me to see how I'm going to react. I'm not going to react. I don't want to turn a flippant off-the-cuff comment into something that casts a pall over our night.

"Ooh, yeah, let's! Holly and I can look at Dallas's cutie pie center up close." Mom winks at Mallory. "You have good taste. The captain looks like a sexy, growly bear. For a human." Mom giggles at my groan.

I watch them head down to ice level and go to the glass on Dallas' side of the ice. The moms appear to be hollering out, and I'll be damned if the first-line center doesn't skate over. I played against him a couple of times in junior tournaments before my accident. He's a skillful player. He laughs and calls his captain over and skates away. Mr. Growly Bear smiles at Mallory, and I want to punch him. He flips a puck over the glass that Mallory catches with ease, flashing him a smile of thanks, and he skates away with a wink.

"Is that her?" Jake asks.

My attention focused on the ice, I didn't realize they'd arrived. "Who?"

"The woman you're trying to impress."

"I didn't say anything," Logan assures me.

"It's the redhead," Teagan says with certainty.

I glance at Teagan before looking back at the ice. "Is that your witchy superpower at play?"

"No, I recognize her from Vegas."

The foursome is headed back up to our box. Mallory is clutching her puck and has a pink flush to her cheeks. She looks so pretty. Mom and Daphne are chatting with each other, and Aunt Molly must have said something funny because Mallory smiles and nods. Mallory's smile fades when she looks up at the box. Uh-oh.

10

MALLORY

I can't believe the captain of the Dallas Stars gave me a puck. It was so embarrassing when Faith and Holly called over their star center to ask for a puck on my behalf, but it was fun. My mom would never do something like that. I love her, but she's so serious and proper. She'd tell me we had a bunch of pucks at our house already and we don't need one just because it was touched by the stick of an NHL player. It's all the same vulcanized rubber, after all. Then she'd tell me how pucks were made and all about the chemical compounds involved. I passed chemistry in high school just fine, and I don't need a graduate-level lesson from my mother.

While the captain is very handsome, and it's a rush to have him wink at me, I can't help but think Liam is more handsome. Holly is gushing about how cute the Dallas players are. It's funny, they aren't much older than her son. Her husband, Mike, is a handsome man. No reason to look anywhere else. Since I know it's all meant in good fun, I just laugh.

My laughter dies when I glance up at the box and see Liam standing close to and smiling down at Hockey Fan Barbie. I can tell by his expression and how they're standing together that they have a close relationship. It doesn't matter. We're coworkers and maybe sorta starting to be friends. He's good-looking and rich. Of course he's going to have gorgeous women all around him.

"About time!" Faith cries out as she rushes the blonde and gives her a big hug.

"Hey, Momma Morgan," Barbie says, returning the hug and giving her a kiss on the cheek.

Momma? I'm assuming this isn't his sister, since she used her last name. I notice the man with her, who is now hugging Faith and lifting her off the floor. Liam comes to my side and brushes his hand against my back. The light touch starts as a tingle, low and lovely, but grows, gathering warmth and pressure until it's almost possessive, even though his touch remains the same—barely there.

"Mallory, these are my best friends, Teagan"—he gestures to the gorgeous blonde woman—"and Jake."

The man smiles and reaches his hand out to me. "Hey, Mallory, nice to meet you." His handshake is firm, and his brown eyes are warm. He's a few inches shorter than Liam and not as broad, but he's a very handsome man with glossy black hair and olive-toned skin.

"Hi, Mallory. That's so cool you got a puck!" Teagan reaches out a hand to shake as well.

Teagan is a woman. A gorgeous woman. The times I've heard about Teagan and Jake, I thought Liam was talking about two guys. Not a guy and a woman who should walk the runway or grace magazine covers.

I remember myself. "Hi. Nice to meet you both."

Daphne comes up, and the greetings repeat. I guess she hasn't met them before either.

"So great to finally meet you, Teagan. I've heard so much about you!" Daphne gives Teagan a hug. She's such a sweet person. I want to kick her. Which is ridiculous. I love Daphne, and there's no reason to be jealous over Teagan. Yeah, she's gorgeous and Liam's best friend, and she seems friendly. His mom really seems to like her. Now his dad's hugging her. Mike is giving her a fist bump. Yeah, she's part of this group. No reason to be jealous.

Teagan smiles warmly. "I've heard so much about you too! I'm so glad you and Logan finally got together so he can stop being a mopey bird." She elbows Logan in the side, and he grunts.

Mopey bird? That's a weird phrase.

"Logan is a golden eagle shifter," Daphne tells me.

"Really? That's cool. I haven't known any avian shifters. They aren't as easy to tell as wolf or other mammal shifters. No scent," I say.

"Do you shift, Mallory?" Teagan asks.

I suppress my sigh. I miss the days when discussing shifter status was still taboo, and you needed a secret handshake to alert others.

"Nope. But I come from a pack of wolf shifters. I'm the weird one. How about you?" I don't sense anything, but I'm just a human. What do I know?

Teagan and Jake give me appraising looks. What the hell is up with that?

"No, I don't shift," Teagan says.

"I'm an avian shifter too," Jake says.

I turn to him. "Really? An eagle like Logan?"

"Nothing so regal. I'm a shore bird."

That could be anything from a duck to a heron to a piping plover. Living on the coast and near the wildlife refuge, I'm not surprised there are shore bird shifters. I'm curious what kind, but if he wanted me to know, he'd tell me.

"Cool," I reply simply.

I'm saved from trying to think of anything else to say by the request for us to stand for the national anthem. Daphne and I move to seats at the front of the box so we can look down on the ice and watch the start of the game. After the anthem and the puck drop, Logan sits next to Daphne, and Faith sits next to me with Holly on her other side. I can hear Liam with Teagan and Jake behind me. I wasn't expecting Liam to sit with me. We aren't attending the game together. We just arrived in the same vehicle. He should hang out with his friends. Right?

"What the hell, ref! Are you blind? That was tripping! Boo!" Faith screams. I was not expecting that level of passion from her.

Daphne leans in. "I'm not the only crazy fan. It's great." Her laugh borders on the maniacal.

All righty.

Liam leans forward. "You're sitting between the loudest two. Probably should've warned you to wear earplugs. Sorry."

I look over my shoulder. "All good. It's nice to watch with people who care."

Logan stands and asks what we all want to eat and drink from the spread in the suite behind us. I would love to get used to this level of comfort and convenience to watch a hockey game. No being jammed in general seating and getting beer spilled on me. The seats are comfortable, the view of the ice is incredible, and most importantly, we have our own bathroom. I accept my pretzel and Coke with a smile. Daphne has a hot dog and a soda too. Apparently, she gets really spunky watching "her guys," so she's decided it's for the best if she doesn't drink beer tonight. I can't imagine sweet Daphne acting that way, but Logan showed me a video on his phone of her screaming abuse at the refs after what she considered a bad call, so I know it happens.

"Do you go to a lot of games, Mallory?" Faith asks as she rips a piece off her pretzel and dips it in cheese sauce.

"No. I haven't been to a hockey game in years. My younger brother used to play, so I'd go to his tournaments, and we went to a few games here as a family growing up, but now that we're all grown and all over the place, there's no one to go with."

"Oh, that's a shame. I hope you come to more games and watch in the company box with us. You're fun."

"Thank you! That's so kind." I'm touched when Holly leans forward to add her hope I join them in the future too.

Faith sighs and leans in. "Sitting here is way different than sitting in the arena watching a tournament all weekend. We spent many a weekend at tournaments for Liam. I miss watching him play. He should be down there with them playing, not up here watching. He was going to be first-line right wing for his college's team, but then the accident happened."

"Oh." I don't know what else to say. I had no idea Liam played hockey. What accident? Was he truly good enough to be on the first line of a college team, or is that just a proud mom talking? He's a few years older than Trevor, so they wouldn't have been on the same teams growing up or at the same tournaments. Not that Trevor played in college. The university he's attending doesn't have a hockey team, and he joined the cheerleading team instead. Pretty sure it was to be around all those girls.

While society generally accepts shifters, professional sports are one of the last frontiers where shifters and other paranormal folks mostly aren't included. There are some paranormal sports leagues, but no human/shifter mixed professional leagues. It's silly. Shifters and humans play together growing up, but once shifting starts around puberty, shifters drop out of organized sports with full humans because their typically superior speed and strength becomes more apparent, and it would have raised questions in the past. When shifters were still hiding, they couldn't risk calling that kind of attention to themselves.

Now that shifters and other paranormal are living openly, the only remaining reason to not play together professionally and in the Olympics is the human worry that they're at a disadvantage. I guess they don't realize that shifters have been dealing with people like me who come from shifter lineage and possibly have the strength and speed of shifters without shifting ability. I'm sure if we looked at the family trees of some of the greatest athletes, we'd find shifters among the branches, even though the athlete is just a "normal" human.

Faith and Holly get up at the first intermission to mingle. I use the restroom and grab a selection of snacks for the second period and retake my seat. To my surprise, Liam sits next to me instead of sitting with Teagan and Jake again.

"May I?" He gestures to my bag of popcorn.

I tilt it toward him, and he takes a handful.

He munches as we watch the game in companionable silence. Lots of turnovers, but no great plays. Our elbows brush each other on the armrest between us, and goosebumps break out on my arm. It feels too natural, too comfortable, being here with him. The heat radiating off him is like a soothing balm in the chill of the arena, and I want to slather it all over me. Oh, Mallory, this is not good.

"Are you enjoying the game?" he asks.

I sigh dreamily. "Yeah..."

I clear my throat and try again. "I am. Thanks so much for this."

Liam tilts his head as he looks at me, an eyebrow quirked. Is it amusement because he knows how he affects me or confusion? Does it matter?

"Of course. The moms meant it when they said they hope you'll attend more. They don't just say that. They like you."

I can't hide my smile. "I really like them too. They're fun."

"Go!" Daphne screams, jumping to her feet.

Liam and I turn our attention back to the game in time to watch the Flyers' right wing break away with the puck and streak to the goal, dodging Dallas defenders. He shoots...he scores!

"Yes!" Liam yells, jumping up from his seat and raising his fists in the air. I realize he's wearing the jersey of the scoring player. I wonder if it's because he was a right winger when he played.

I stand and cheer too. Liam shocks me by turning my way, hugging me, and lifting me off the floor in his excitement.

Wow. I know he's just being exuberant, but I haven't been in any man's arms since Liam's in Vegas, and it feels wonderful. Comfortable. Right. He smells so good, like my uncle's Christmas tree farm. Oh no, Mallory, stop this. Coworkers. Casual. Friends. Maybe fuck buddies. Nothing more.

Liam sets me back on my feet and turns to high-five Jake behind us. Daphne hugs me while jumping up and down, forcing me to jump up and down with her. You'd think we just won the Stanley Cup, not merely scored a goal. Whatever. It's nice to be with people who are enthusiastic fans. Nothing worse than watching a hockey game with polite, quiet people. If I wanted to be bored, I'd turn on golf.

After the second intermission, Teagan sits next to me. Did the women in Liam's life arrange a schedule ahead of time so they knew who would interrogate me when, or are they leaving it to opportunity?

"You're a friend of Daphne's?" Teagan asks.

Okay, this is the way we're going to go.

"I am. We work together at Morgan Development. You grew up with Liam?" Two can play this game.

"Yes, from grade school through college. Jake too, except for high school. He went to school out of state." She smiles. "We're the three musketeers. They're like the brothers I never had."

"Do you have sisters, Teagan?" I ask.

"No. I'm an only child. How about you?"

"I have an older brother and sister and a younger brother."

"Did you grow up around here?" she asks as we're both watching the action on the ice.

"Yeah, I'm the only one still here. My parents retired to Florida, my sister lives in New York, my eldest brother is in Maryland with his family, and my younger brother is in law school." I cheer as the home team scores again. Fifteen minutes left in the game, and we're ahead by a goal. I hope we can hold on.

We watch the game and sip our sodas. It's a little weird, but not that bad. Oh, what the hell.

"When do you switch spots with Jake?" I ask. "Do you have a signal worked out or a specific time in the third period?"

Teagan's eyes widen, and then she laughs.

"I guess we haven't been subtle, have we?"

"Not really. You know we're just coworkers, right? We aren't dating or anything."

"I know, but he likes you, and I care about him—as a friend—so I want to check you out. You never know. Maybe things will change…"

"Not happening," I insist. "I don't date coworkers, and I definitely won't date a boss." I take a deep breath and lean in. "I care about my career and what people think about me. I don't want anyone to say I got where I am, if I get anywhere, because of who I was dating or who I was friends with. I want to be judged on my merit."

"I get that. I like you, Mallory. I hope we can grow to be friends." A slow grin spreads across Teagan's face, and maybe that's respect shining in her eyes. Then she looks to the back of the box and yells out, "Yo, Jake! Want your turn checking out Mallory?"

I want to climb over the railing in front of my seat and escape the suite. Of course, her bellow comes at the one moment during the entire game the Wells Fargo Center was silent. I swear the players on the ice look up to our suite and judge me. Okay, maybe not really, but I'm pretty sure Gritty is giving me the googly side-eye.

"Hey, how you doin'?" Jake asks as he sits next to me, sounding so much like Joey from *Friends*, I can't control the burst of laughter that comes from me. Jake is the definition of tall, dark, and handsome at a smidge over six feet tall with wavy black hair just touching his collar, rich brown eyes that hint at mischief, and a charming white smile with dimples to drown in lighting his face. He's lean but muscular. To put it simply, he's a hunk.

"I'm good. How are you?" I respond.

"Great, thanks. I really don't have anything to interrogate you on. I think everyone covered it, so wanna just watch the game?"

"Or I could grill you," I suggest.

Jake laughs and takes a sip of his soda. "Shoot."

"You grew up with Liam and Teagan?"

"Yeah, we went to school together. Well, I went to high school out of state, but we reconnected for college. We're the three musketeers."

I nod. I can see that they have a close friendship. Maybe more.

"Are you and Teagan dating?"

It's his turn to let loose a guffaw. "Oh, God, no. She's like one of my sisters!" He shudders. "I love her, but not like that. We've always just been friends." He gives me a shrewd look. "Liam and Teagan feel the same. Just friends."

I watch the game and think about what else I want to know. *Is there more I want to know?* I can't have a relationship with Liam. We work together. It doesn't matter if his best friends like me or not, we're probably never going to see each other again unless we run into each other at a future game or they come to the office holiday party.

"Do you work for Morgan Development?" I can't consider dating Liam because we work together, but Jake is another bowl of ice cream. He's hot, he has good taste in friends, and he's a Flyers fan. Hell, if he was a wolf shifter, I could have his shifter babies. There's no spark though, not like I've had with Liam from the moment I first saw him in that bar in Vegas. Darn.

"Nah, I work in the casino industry with Teagan. Liam is the real estate guy of our group. You're a paralegal for Morgan?"

"Yep."

The Wells Fargo Center erupts in cheers as the Flyers score on a power play. Jake and I cheer along with the rest of our suitemates. The game ends in a victory for the black and orange. My foursome says our goodbyes to everyone and starts the drive home from Philly.

The mood in the car is festive since we won. Liam and I are in the backseat of Logan's Jeep with Logan and Daphne up front.

"Did you have fun?" Liam asks me as we traverse the Walt Whitman Bridge and reenter New Jersey.

"I did! I'm so glad I went. Thank you for letting me know about it and pushing me into going." Normally, being manipulated is the fastest way to piss me off, but for once, it isn't bothering me. I'm not going to think about what that means now.

We chat during the hour it takes to return to Daphne and Logan's, arriving right after 11:00 p.m. It's early enough I could make the drive home, but I don't want to appear ungrateful for the invitation to stay over.

"Liam, do you want to come in?" Daphne asks as we get out of Logan's Jeep.

"No, I need to get ready to hit the road in the morning. Thanks though," he responds.

Logan claps Liam on the shoulder, and Daphne gives him a hug, wishing him a pleasant trip as they go into their house, leaving the door slightly ajar for me.

"Goodnight," I say, smiling at Liam before turning to follow them inside.

"Um, Mallory?" Liam asks hesitantly.

"Yeah?" I stop and look up at him before I go up the porch steps.

Liam walks over to me. "Would it be okay if I texted you while I was gone?" The glow of the multicolor Christmas lights bathes his handsome face and makes the blue of his eyes even more vibrant. He's so handsome.

"Um...okay," I stammer.

I know texting and getting to know each other more is probably a bad idea, but I can't help it. I like him. He's always been respectful, even when he was boinking my brains out behind a plant in Las Vegas. He obviously loves his family, which is hot. Even though my family annoys me sometimes, I love them, and I want someone who is close to their family too. The way he was with that mouse he could have easily killed has stuck with me. How he cradled that frightened little critter gently in his palm and carried it outside says a lot. He was kind and patient with me when I was scared. He didn't know I was me; I was just a strange woman freaking out over a mouse, and he didn't mock me. He's a good man. And he's hot as hell. Why does he have to work for his family's company? It would be so much easier if he was an astrophysicist or a grocery store clerk.

Standing out here feels like coming home from a date in high school and wondering if I'm going to be kissed or not. Of course I'm not getting kissed tonight. I've made it clear I'm not looking for that sort of relationship with him. But I wish things were different.

"Cool." He grabs the back of his neck, looking boyishly awkward and adorable. "I guess I'll head home then. I'm leaving tomorrow to check out the centers in Delaware, Maryland, and Virginia. I'll be back late next week. Maybe we can all hang out when I get home?"

"Maybe. That sounds like fun." Do I wave? Offer my hand to shake? How do I say goodbye?

"Well, have a safe trip. I hope everything goes smoothly." I give a lame-ass wave.

"Thanks. I hope everything goes smoothly for you too." Liam returns my wave and starts backing toward his truck parked at the curb. "Thanks for going to the game tonight."

I smile at him even though he probably can't see me and turn to go inside.

"Mallory."

I look over my shoulder.

He's standing at the tailgate of his old red truck. "Sweet dreams."

"You too, Liam." My throat feels tight. I enter the house and close the door behind me.

"Want anything to drink, Mal?" Daphne calls out from the kitchen.

"A bottle of water, please." I smile at my friend and accept the bottle she offers.

"Are you okay?"

Her perceptive nature is part of what makes her such a good friend, but I wish she'd turn it off.

"Yeah, I'm fine," I fib, unscrewing the cap and taking a sip of water, hoping to dislodge the lump that's formed in my throat. It's silly to miss someone I don't even know. He'll be gone for a week. Big whoop. I only really met him a week ago. You can't count our sexy times in Vegas since we mostly kissed and screwed each other. We were strangers then and intended to remain strangers. You can't miss someone after a week of knowing them. I know that. Then why does his absence feel like a shadow, and why am I already eager for his return?

11

LIAM

Entering my home, I put my keys on the table next to the door and wander into the kitchen to grab a beer. I stuck to soda through the game because I didn't want to be the only one drinking in our group. Mallory only had soda. Daphne gets crazy when she mixes alcohol and hockey, so she's a teetotaler at games, saving her crazy for home, and Logan doesn't drink a drop when he's driving. I take a deep swig and sigh. It was a good game, and everyone liked Mallory. I knew they would.

Walking into my bedroom, I set my bottle on the dresser as I pull my bag from the closet and place it on the bed to pack for the next week. I start with a couple of suits, a selection of dress shirts and ties for the dinners with outlet center managers I'll have to attend. I add my dress shoes to the bottom of the garment bag and zip it up. Next, I start with the business casual clothes I'll need for my tours. I can do this packing in my sleep, so I let my thoughts drift back to Mallory.

I don't think it's my ego talking when I say I don't believe she's not interested. I think she is, but for some reason, she feels she must deny it. She liked me just fine in Vegas. She seemed like she was cool with seeing me socially back here in Jersey until she learned my last name and my position in the company.

I'll be gone for a week. Maybe my absence will make her heart grow fonder? She didn't say no to keeping in touch while I'm gone, so we'll see how that goes. If nothing else, we become friends. I know I'm not entitled to her friendship or anything else, but considering we're close to Logan and Daphne, we'll end up together a lot socially, so getting along with each other is for the best.

Stripping out of my clothes, I climb between the cool sheets, thinking about Mallory staying over with Daphne and Logan. She's sleeping in the same guest bed I stayed in the other night after Logan and I spent the evening watching football and drinking beer. Is that the closest I'm ever getting to sharing a bed with Mallory Carter?

I toured the outlet centers in Rehoboth, Delaware and outside Ocean City, Maryland today and am pleased to see that they're operating smoothly and looking good. They're decorated for the holidays, and the special programs planned to enhance the shopping experience are in place. I had dinner at a local steakhouse with the management teams from the centers. I've been working with most of these people for a couple of years, so dinner is relaxed but productive. Tomorrow, I'll start traveling to our other centers throughout Maryland. Virginia is slated for early next week, and I'll head home next Thursday.

I check the time on my phone. It's just past 9:00 p.m. Is it too late to text Mallory? I decide to send a simple greeting and see if she responds.

Me: Hi

I wait for a response, but one doesn't come. I fire up my laptop and type notes from today's visits. When it's 11:00 p.m. and I still haven't heard from her, I turn off my laptop and go to bed. Maybe she said I could text her just to appease me and get me to leave last night? Tell me what I want to hear to avoid confrontation? I hope not because while I want to be in touch with her, I don't want to be thought of as the type of man you need to coddle and appease to avoid unpleasantness. I'm a grown-up. I can accept rejection.

A chime in the early light of dawn rouses me from my half-dosing, don't-feel-like-moving state to check my phone where it's charging on the nightstand. I can't stop the grin that forms when I see it's a text from Mallory.

> Mallory: Hey, sorry I missed you last night. I had a headache and went to bed early.

> Me: I hope you're feeling better?

> Mallory: Yeah, all good. What's up?

I glance down at my morning wood. I don't think that's what she's asking about.

> Me: Went to the Delaware and coastal Maryland centers yesterday. Going to other Maryland properties today. Nothing too exciting.

> Mallory: You're gone until next week?

She cares how long I'll be gone? Is that progress? Or is she asking so she knows I won't be around to bother her?

> Me: Yeah, I should be home next Thursday. The centers in Maryland and Virginia are bigger, so I can't go through them as quickly. I have dinner with the management teams too.

> Mallory: I hope everything goes smoothly. I need to get ready for work. Have a good day. :smiley emoji:

> Me: Thanks, you too. Talk to you later.

Her message was a welcome surprise. I don't know if she's being polite or if she wants to talk. Do I ask Daphne? I don't want to make anything weird. I guess I'll see if she reaches out to me while I'm gone and go from there. I'm not used to sitting back and waiting. I typically go after what I want. Like I did in Vegas. But this isn't a normal situation. With other women, our only connection has been to hook up. We didn't have friends in common or work for the same company. If things don't work out or turn awkward, the ripple effect will impact many areas of our lives.

After another dinner with managers, I let myself into my hotel room. It's Tuesday night, and I can't wait for this trip to be over. I've been doing this for a few years, and I'm tired of it. I'm tired of traveling, and I'm tired of the talking to people. Obviously, I care that the properties perform well. The livelihoods of many people depend on their success. Of course, my family benefits as well, but at this point, we have enough money for many future generations to live quite well if we stopped everything today. We've always lived way more simply than our bank accounts require. Very few people realize how wealthy my family is. I have my own money, thanks to a trust fund, my salary, and my settlement from the accident. I'll have even more money in the future from inheritances. However, I'd gladly go without that money to keep my loved ones with me. I can't wait to see them when I get home.

I haven't heard from Mallory in days. That's disappointing. I know from conversations with Logan that she and Daphne have been extremely busy working on everything that needs to be done to close the collections department. Daphne's been coming home exhausted each night, and I imagine the same to be true for Mallory, since she handles so much more than Daphne does. No shade on Daphne. It's just that with Mallory's legal background, I know she handles a lot of things that Daphne doesn't. Mallory's also closing out all the files in the system, and that's a lot of physical work—moving the files, doing the computer input, boxing them. If there are any left when I get back home, I'll try to help her. At the very least, I can haul them out of the drawer and to her desk and then box them so she's not up and down all day.

I loosen my tie and remove my jacket, releasing a weary sigh as I sit on the edge of the bed. I take my phone out of my pocket and consider shooting a text to Mallory but resist the impulse. She has my number. If she wanted to talk to me, she could reach out. As much as I want to know her better, I can't be the only one making the effort. If she doesn't want to know me, so be it.

Ding. Wow, not only can I shift, but I apparently can compel Mallory to text me. I swipe to open her message.

> **Mallory:** Hey, what's up?

> **Me:** Nothing much, just got back from dinner. How about you?

> **Mallory:** Watching hockey, Stars and Canucks.

> **Me:** Watching your boyfriend?

I know if she went to whatever bar the Stars hung out at after the game last week, the captain would've chatted her up.

> **Mallory:** Ha. The other games have already finished.

> **Me:** I just turned it on.

> **Mallory:** Wanna watch it together for a while? I'm bored.

> **Me:** How would we do that?

> **Mallory:** FaceTime.

If we're going to FaceTime, I'd rather be doing something more... titillating...than watching hockey, but I'm not going to turn down anything she wants to do now that she's finally reached out to me first.

Me: Sure.

I accept the FaceTime request from Mallory.

"Hey, let me switch over to my laptop. Hold on. Well, I guess you can come with me." I carry my phone to the desk and put it down to open my laptop bag.

"Ooh, give me a tour!" she begs as I grab my MacBook and charger and put them on the bed.

"Do you stay in luxurious suites?"

I can't hold back the bark of laughter. "Definitely not luxury. It's clean and comfortable. Basic Holiday Inn. Here, look."

I hold up my phone and do a slow circle around the room. "It's a bed, couch, and desk. Nothing special."

"Boo," she says with a pout. "I figured you'd stay somewhere swanky since you're an executive and all."

"I drive a partially restored 1990 F-150. Do I seem the swanky type to you?" I roll my eyes at the thought of anyone calling me "swanky."

"I think it's cool you drive a truck. My Uncle Zack has one. I don't know the exact year, but it's of a similar vintage. They run forever if you treat them right."

I settle on the bed with my computer and switch over so I can see Mallory on a larger screen. It looks like she's resting against her headboard too. She's wearing a pink T-shirt. I can't tell if she has a bra on or not. I shouldn't be looking, but I'm a guy. It's instinct to check. She's putting her long red hair in a braid over her shoulder, and it doesn't look like she's wearing any makeup.

"You have freckles!" I cry out with delight. Freckles are adorable.

I hate it when women cover them up with layers of powder and goop.

Mallory's cheeks flush a pretty pink, and she covers her face with her hands.

"You can see them? I hate them. It's the curse of being a redhead."

"Shut up. They're adorable. Freckles have always been my weakness, ever since Amy Looper in fourth grade. Yours are cuter than hers, by the way."

"Seriously? Freckles do it for you?" she asks skeptically.

"Well, I enjoy trying to discover all the spots, other than the face, there may be freckles." I speak with a slow, suggestive drawl and give an eyebrow wiggle for good measure.

"Liam..." A warning.

"What?" I flash a wicked grin.

"No flirting."

"It's kinda my default setting."

"Well, go back to the factory then. No flirting."

I think about that. Can I interact with Mallory without flirting? Yeah, I'm a naturally flirtatious man, but I don't flirt with Teagan. She doesn't inspire those kinds of feelings in me. She'd probably punch me or turn me into a toad if I did. Not that I'm attracted to everyone I flirt with. Sometimes I do it to be funny or to give them a boost. But I want to flirt with Mallory because I am attracted to her. I don't want to make her uncomfortable though. That's an asshole thing to do.

"Okay, no flirting. So just normal friend-type stuff like I'd do with Teagan and Jake?"

"Yeah, or like with Daphne," she suggests.

"Oh, I flirt with Daphne. Always have. It drives Logan crazy. I take credit for them finally getting together." I take a sip of the bottle of water I grabbed from the mini fridge when I entered the room. "I'm going to be the godfather to their baby."

"Baby?" Mallory gasps. "They're having a baby? Oh, my goodness, that's so exciting! Wow!"

"Whoa, cool your jets there, Red," I caution. "No babies yet as far as I know, but when they have them, I called dibs on godfather for the first one."

"Red? Really? That's the best you could do?"

"I can't call you sweetheart or honey, so had to think of something on the fly. I guess I should have gone with Sparky?"

She laughs. "Sparky? Where did that come from?"

I laugh too. "I don't know. It just came to me. You're kind of spunky. Made me think of a spark plug, so...Sparky."

"I like that. I've never had a fun nickname. It's either been Mal or something like Runt or Norm."

"Norm? Like the guy from that old show *Cheers*?"

"Norm, like normal. It wasn't a compliment. Because I can't shift, I'm normal. I hate that one especially."

"I can't believe your family treats you like that. That's horrible." I want to kick some asses on her behalf.

"It's my extended family—cousins and their friends. My immediate family isn't intentionally cruel like that. They're insensitive sometimes, but it's more from cluelessness than cruelty. I imagine it's like if a baby shifter was born into a human family. They love them and care for them the best they can, but they don't understand the shifter side because they haven't experienced it." It's her turn to take a sip from her mug. It's black and says "Perfectly Imperfect" in pink script on it. It suits her. "Their humanness, for lack of a better word, has been filtered through the lens of being a shifter. I think if they weren't all wolves, if it was a mixed family like yours, it wouldn't be as bad. If you were human and not a cougar shifter, it wouldn't be considered something akin to a disability. It's something you got from your mom. Me being human is because something went wrong genetically."

Someone scores, and I'm not even sure which team because we

haven't been watching the game. We've been focused on each other in the waning seconds of the first period.

How to ask this tactfully... "Did they do tests, or is it just assumed that you can't shift because you haven't shifted?"

"Liam, I'm twenty-six years old. If I haven't shifted yet, I'm not going to shift. I didn't decide not to shift. I've tried! I can't do it. There's something wrong with me."

My heart twists, seeing her knuckles whiten as she grips her mug. Her beautiful green eyes go distant. She's hurting, and all I want to do is make it better for her.

"Mallory Carter, there isn't a damn thing wrong with you. You are exactly how you are meant to be. Look at your mug, you aren't perfectly imperfect, you're perfectly perfect."

She looks away from her camera, blinking rapidly and sniffling. Crap, I didn't want to make her cry.

"Shit, I'm sorry, Mallory."

"Don't apologize! Liam, that was the sweetest thing anyone has ever said to me. You're great at not flirting. Thank you."

Huh, that's not something I've heard before.

"Well, there's a first time for everything," I say with a laugh.

"Seriously, thank you, Liam. I need a friend."

Ah, crap, I'm getting friend-zoned. I don't want to be the creepy guy that pretends to be friends with a woman in hopes she'll eventually sleep with him. If I do this, then I'm going to be her friend. That's what I'd want someone to do for Kennie. Mallory is someone's sister, so I need to treat her how I want Kennie treated. Not that it matters what Mallory's relation to someone is. She's a person and worthy of friendship and respect solely based on that. Okay, reset my brain to be friends. Hope my heart follows suit.

"Wow, this got heavy. I'm sorry," Mallory says. "Do you want to keep watching the game, or do you want to go get drunk and cheer up?"

I chuckle. "I'm fine to watch the game if you are. You don't need to entertain me or be fake cheerful. If we're going to be friends, we have to be who we are, right?"

"You're okay being my friend?"

"Mallory, I'm going to be honest with you. I like you. I think you're gorgeous. You're funny, you're smart, and you get along with my friends and family. We know we're compatible sexually. You're the type of woman I'd love to date. But you don't want to date me, and that's your prerogative. You not wanting to date me doesn't negate that you're funny, smart, a good person, and someone I'd want to be friends with, even if you weren't someone I was attracted to. I'm a grown-up. I can handle rejection."

"I'm sorry, Liam," Mallory says. "It's not that I don't like you, it's—"

"You don't have to explain anything, Mallory. It's fine. Let's just leave it as it is and move on. Okay?" I really don't want to hear all the reasons I'm good enough to fuck in Vegas and be a friend with in New Jersey, but not good enough to date. I'm a decent man, but I'm not a saint.

"Okay. So keep watching the game?" There's a tentativeness to her question that I hate. She should never be tentative.

"Yeah, I'd like that. It's intermission. I need to get out of my suit and get comfortable. Do you want me to call you back after I change, or can I point the laptop out the window? You can catch the view of whatever town I'm in now."

"Ooh, let me see you in your suit first!" Mallory requests.

"I already took off my tie, but I'll throw my jacket back on."

I put on my dark gray suit jacket and angle my laptop's camera to show me full length.

"You clean up good, Morgan! Very nice," Mallory says approvingly, a smile gracing her lips.

"Thanks. Mom would be proud. I prefer jeans and flannel, but I'm here to represent the company and need to present the proper image." I pick up my laptop and walk over to the window. I set it on the air- conditioning unit facing a park that has some holiday light displays set up, so there's something to look at.

"Okay, you can enjoy the view while I change. It's some sort of walkthrough holiday light display in a local park."

"Ooh, pretty. Thanks."

I get my clothes out of my bag and unbutton my shirt. It's weird to get changed and not talk, so I continue our conversation.

"How was work? Are you guys all settled upstairs?" There's no response. Did we lose our connection? "Still there, Sparky?"

Mallory coughs to clear her throat. "Um...yeah, we're good. I've been closing out as many files as I can. I normally get an hour or two a day. We have lots to do with regular year-end work. Plus there's the wrapping things up and preparing the open files for whoever the management companies go with for their next counsel."

I drape my suit pants over the desk chair and pull on a T-shirt and a pair of shorts over my boxer briefs. I sleep naked, but I can't get that comfortable while on FaceTime.

"Be right back. Need to brush my teeth," I call out.

"No problem!"

This room's vanity and sink are outside the bathroom proper, so she can probably hear me brush, but big whoop. At least she knows I have good oral hygiene.

"All done." I pick her up from where she was facing out the window. I reach up to close the drapes and notice my reflection in the glass. Could she see me change in the reflection? Judging by the pink flush in her cheeks, I bet she could. I hope she liked what she saw.

12

MALLORY

Wow. I knew Liam was built, but I didn't know he was *that* built until I saw him reflected in the window as he changed clothes. I thank whoever designed boxer briefs—they did a favor to womankind.

"Enjoy the view?" Liam asks with a smirk. That jerk! He must have realized I could see his reflection in the window. I can see my image on the FaceTime screen, so I know my cheeks are bright pink. Damn it.

"I did. The holiday lights are lovely. Is there music too?" Yes, way to deflect, Mallory. Good job, girl!

He quirks his lips. He's not falling for it. "I assume so, but I can't hear it from up here."

"Looks fun. I wonder if there's something like that up here."

"No idea, but I bet Daphne knows."

"Yeah, you're right. She and Logan know all the good places, I'm sure. I think he talked about going to some Christmas markets around here to show that Europe didn't corner the market." I grimace.

He chuckles. "Don't bother saying 'no pun intended.' You totally intended it."

"I didn't! I swear!"

"Yeah, likely story." I can tell by his grin that he's having fun teasing me. He settles on his bed with his back against the head-board, mirroring my pose. The second period is about to start.

"So, who do you think is going to win? Dallas or Vancouver?" Surely hockey is a safe topic to discuss.

"Dallas. Your boyfriend already scored a goal."

"Stop calling him my boyfriend! That's Daphne being obnoxious," I say.

"So, you don't think he's attractive?"

What the hell? Why are we talking about this?

"Yeah, he's good-looking, but there are plenty of good-looking men in the world."

"Is he your type?"

Why is he persisting in this?

"I don't know him, so I don't know if he's my type or not. What's your type?"

Why are we talking about our types? This isn't friendly talk. I'm curious what his type is, though. Probably supermodel beautiful like Teagan.

He lets out an annoyed huff. "What's your type physically? I'm not asking for any deep personality analysis."

I shrug. "I guess he's tall, with dark hair and a beard. I think that's attractive. But I think many things are attractive. I don't have just one type."

"Same. Well, not tall, dark, and bearded. I like women, preferably without beards. But I like all types."

I bet he does.

"Are we watching the game or what, Liam?" I know I sound testy, but I don't want to talk about the type of man I find attractive. My ideal man doesn't work for the same company I do! If we didn't work together, I'd definitely be interested in Liam. I'd want to be repeating

Vegas on every surface we could find. But for the long term, I need to be with a wolf shifter, not any other kind of shifter. I don't want to be a total disappointment to my family.

Liam raises his eyebrows. "Sure."

We settle on our respective beds and watch as the ref drops the puck to start the second period.

He doesn't deserve my bitchiness. It's not his fault I'm screwed up. "I'm sorry. I don't always take being teased well. I get defensive."

"No worries. I'm sorry too. I'll try to do better in the future."

Why does he have to be such a good guy? It would be easier if he was a jerk. I snort. If he was a jerk, then he'd be like every other guy I've dated.

"What's so funny?" he asks.

"What?"

Did I say something and not realize it?

"You snorted like you thought of something funny. I was wondering what it was."

"Oh, um..."

"You don't have to tell me. I can just sit here and make things up in my head, but it may involve you in a tutu on a unicycle."

I can't hold back my laughter. "You're so weird, Liam. I was thinking—emphasis on the was—that you're a good guy. If you were a jerk, then you'd be like every other guy I've dated."

He gazes at me, and I wonder what he's thinking.

"Is that why you're not interested? I'm a good guy? Do you like jerks?"

I sigh. I brought it up. It's only fair I'm straight with him.

"It's not that I'm not interested. I am. But we work for the same company, and you're an executive in that company. My career is important to me, and I want to advance at Morgan. I don't want people thinking I achieved things because of who I'm sleeping with. As if that's not enough, you're the son of the CEO, so you'll probably end up being my boss one day."

"What? No, I won't," he interjects.

"You're going to be CEO one day."

"Nope. No interest in that. It's most likely going to be my cousin Andy." He leans back and tucks an arm behind his head. I try not to drool as his bicep bulges. Focus, Mallory— no getting distracted by the bulging muscles or anything else you may have noticed bulging. I know what all those bulges can do, the pleasure they can bring to my body, how secure and desired they can make me feel.

"He graduates from college this year and will come on board in Operations. He'll be working in all the departments to get a big-picture view." He grins, and it's adorable and boyish. "He loves business and has been interested in the company his whole life."

"Really?" I had no idea about this. I always assumed Liam would follow in Will's footsteps.

"Yeah, really. Logan and my sister are welcome to join the company too. It's just as much theirs as it is mine or Andy's, but they haven't shown an interest."

He sighs like the weight of the world is on his shoulders. "So that's it? Because we both work at Morgan, you won't go out with me? I can resign. No problem."

I laugh again. Like he'd really leave his executive position at a company his family owns just to go out with me.

"Yeah, okay." I can't help rolling my eyes at the absurdity of it. "Well, that's only one reason."

"You have more?" he asks with a furrowed brow.

Oh, boy. Am I just going to be honest and sound like a bitch? Is it fair to ask him to be my friend but then keep things from him? I don't want to string him along. Maybe I should just lay it all out there so he knows there's no chance for us and he can stop whatever this is between us. I take a deep breath and tell him the truth.

"I need to be with a wolf shifter. I know that's stupid, and I should probably be in therapy, but I want my family's approval for once. I've already disappointed them by not being a shifter. I can't help that. It's biology. Being a paralegal is my dream career, but it's not aspirational enough for my mom. I don't want to stop doing that and go to law school. Law is interesting, but not enough to incur tons of debt and have no life. This lets me have a balance. I already had one boss work himself to death. I'm not following him. So the least I can do is to be with a wolf shifter. Then there's a chance my kids won't be like me."

Holy word vomit. I can't believe I just unloaded all that. I feel so much shame, having said that out loud. What the hell is wrong with me? Am I going to pass up a chance with a great guy that seems to like me because I don't want to face my mother's disapproval? Before I can open my mouth to mitigate the damage I just did, Liam nods.

"Yeah, that's a big reason. I can't do anything about not being a wolf shifter. This is a first. Normally I'm sought after for my position, my name, and my money. That's what matters to most women. Whether I can shift or not doesn't factor into it, certainly not what animal I shift into. It's something that would be tolerated to get the other three. This is the first time all the other things are disregarded, and the fact I'm a cougar shifter is the deal-breaker. I knew you were one of a kind from the start, Mallory." The laugh following that statement holds no humor.

"I'm sorry—"

"No, it's okay. I asked, and you told me the truth. I appreciate that. It would have been easier to lie, but you were honest with me. You truly are one of a kind. I mean that in the best way."

I try to swallow past the lump in my throat. The goal horn sounds, and I glance at the TV. I forgot we were supposed to be watching the game. Dallas scored again. Looks like the captain is two-thirds of the way to a hat trick. Woo-fricking-hoo.

For the second time in this conversation, I'm blinking back tears. I'm usually a pro at holding my emotions in check, but something about Liam brings them to the surface.

"I should probably go, Mallory. I need to type up some notes from today and get ready for my visits tomorrow. It's been a long day. We'll catch up after I come home, okay?"

I nod and croak out an "okay" and a "goodnight" accompanied

by a wave. I close my laptop and put it on the nightstand. Settling under the covers, I turn off my light as the tears stream from my eyes and run into my hair. I've left the hockey game on to mask the sound of my sobs—not that there's anyone here to hear them. I'm alone, like always. I had a chance, and I blew it. That goodnight felt like goodbye.

13
LIAM

Well, that sucked.

14

MALLORY

THERE IS NOT ENOUGH UNDER-EYE CONCEALER IN THE WORLD TO COVER THE bags I'm carrying. I slept like crap, and I'm all stuffed up from crying. I wish I'd just called out from work, but that would require more explanation than I want to attempt.

"Good mo— What's wrong?" Daphne's concerned expression as she enters our office is so sincere. And unwelcome. I don't want to discuss what isn't happening with me and Liam, and I don't want to lie to my friend, but between those two options, I'm going with the lie.

"Nothing's wrong. I stayed up late watching the game. This is how I look when I don't get enough sleep."

With raised eyebrows, Daphne deadpans, "Not a good look, friend. Make sleep your priority. The DVR is your friend."

"Yep. Good advice. Thanks. I'm getting some tea. Want anything?" Picking up my red plaid mug, I rise and head to the kitchen.

"I'll come with you." Daphne grabs her coordinating blue plaid mug and follows me out of our office.

I love Daphne, but I was hoping to get away from her. I just can't deal today. Maybe I can hide downstairs and close files for most of the day.

"Your uncle has a Christmas tree farm, right?" Daphne asks as she hands me a tea bag and stands next to me at the counter, unwrapping her tea bag and dunking it in her mug.

"Yeah. Full Moon Farm. They have a whole holiday experience happening—Santa's workshop, a hot cocoa stand, carriage rides, an ice rink, reindeer farm. It's neat." I pass her the Splenda she uses in her tea. "Are you guys going for a tree this weekend?"

"We are!" She bounces on her toes in excitement. "I haven't had a tree the past few years. It wasn't worth all the trouble just for me." Her sigh is tinged with sadness. "I've missed it." A beautiful smile spreads across her face. "It's my first Christmas with Logan, and I'm looking forward to making memories with him."

"Well, check them out. They have nice trees. That's where we get ours."

"Oh, are you getting yours this weekend too? We can go together!"

"No." I remove the tea bag from my mug and throw it in the trash. Daphne follows suit. "We tagged our tree, and my uncle will cut and deliver it right before Christmas. Our tradition is to decorate it on Christmas Eve."

"Well, do you want to come with us? Faith and Holly are coming along to pick out their trees as well." She looks so hopeful. I don't want to disappoint her, but I'm going to.

"Thanks, no. I just want to hibernate at home. I want to catch up on the latest books by Delancey Stewart and Marika Ray."

"You read romance? How did I not know this? We could have spent the past year talking about books!" Poor Daphne looks crestfallen at all the missed opportunities.

We walk back to our office and sit at our desks. I look out the window. Most of the trees are bare of leaves in the early December sun. I love having a window. I can't wait for spring so I can see the trees regain their leaves. It will be nice to open my window and hear the birds. I'm so grateful they gave us this office.

"I can't believe you never told me," Daphne grouses.

"Well, you never told me you read romances either. I figured you were all about cozy mysteries since you worship Jessica Fletcher," I retort.

"It's not so much worshipping as idolizing," Daphne corrects.

She's such a goof.

"I do like cozies, but sometimes you need a happily ever after more than a whodunnit, you know?"

I nod. "I love cozies too. My favorite sugar cookie recipe is from a bakery mystery series, but I *need* romance."

"You do need romance, Mallory," Daphne says earnestly. "If only I knew a single, good-looking guy who isn't a jerk."

"No."

"Good job, nice family, fun..."

"Daphne, seriously. No. Not going to happen. We're friends, and that's all we can be. Don't make it awkward, or else we can't all hang out together."

My friend stares at me. I don't know what she sees other than the bags under my eyes and my hair pulled back in a simple ponytail. I made no effort today. If I could have come in yoga pants and one of Trevor's old jerseys, I would have.

"Okay," she agrees. "When you're ready to talk, I'm here."

I take a sip of my tea and look at our task list for the day. There isn't anything crazy since we aren't taking on new files. I should be able to knock out a lot this morning so I can spend the afternoon downstairs closing files. I grab the files I need for the first few tasks and start preparing what we need to get them off my to-do list and back on the shelf.

We work in silence for a while, but not quite the companionable silence we normally enjoy. The click-clacking of our keyboards creates a soothing rhythm, which helps diffuse some of my tension.

"Did you want to hit Francisco's for lunch?" Daphne asks after a while.

"I don't want to talk about it, Daphne. There's nothing to talk about." Welcome back, tension.

"Okay," she replies easily, "but you still eat, right?"

Dang. Who knew Daphne could be snarky?

"Lunch sounds good. I always love Francisco's."

Now our silence is more companionable. Good. Daphne has become a close friend, and I don't want what is or isn't happening with Liam to affect that.

"You're going to the office holiday party, right?" Daphne asks a little while later.

"Yeah. You are too, right?"

"Of course. It's nice to have brunch at the country club. I never go anywhere that fancy."

Isn't that the truth.

"How dressy is it?"

"Nice dress or dressy sweater and skirt. Nothing crazy." Daphne chuckles. "Well, you can wear an ugly Christmas sweater. Those are fun."

"What are you wearing?" Safety in numbers. If I dress like Daphne, I should blend in.

"I don't know. I need to go shopping. Want to go together on Sunday?"

"Sure. What are you looking for? Nice dress or crazy sweater?" I ask.

"Not sure. Maybe both? My wardrobe is kinda boring. I want to revamp it a bit. Get some date clothes?" Daphne shrugs.

"Ooh, yes! Mall or outlets?"

"I guess we will see what the weather's like. If it's not raining or unbearably cold, do the outlet and support our company. If it's icky, we do the mall."

"Sounds like a plan."

We go back to our respective tasks, and when my stomach lets out a loud growl, I look at the time on my monitor. It's past noon. My...breakup? No. It's not a breakup since we were never together. My whatever with Liam last night had me so upset that I couldn't stand the thought of finding breakfast. My tummy is protesting that now.

"I heard that all the way over here. Ready for lunch?" Daphne raises her gaze from the figures she's computing.

"Yeah, I am. Finish what you're doing though. I'm good."

"Nah, I'm done." She lays down her pencil. "Let's go."

We walk into Francisco's and hear Wham!'s "Last Christmas" playing. I groan because I'd successfully avoided it so far.

"Ugh, I just got Whammed," I complain.

Daphne chuckles. "I lost Whammageddon in the car on December first. How did you make it so long?"

I shrug. "Dumb luck. This is the furthest I've made it."

I order the baked ziti special, and Daphne gets a cheeseburger to eat here and two of the ziti specials to take home for dinner.

"Logan is trying to get shots of the snowy owl that's been seen at the refuge. When he's trying to get nature shots, he'll be completely still in awkward positions for however long it takes, so I'm betting he won't feel like cooking." She takes a bite of her fry and continues after swallowing. "I know I don't feel like cooking, so ziti specials it is!"

I ignore the pang of envy I feel knowing Daphne is going home to someone while I'm going to an empty house.

But I don't want a relationship. At most, I want a friend with benefits, and I'm not even sure about that. The only *friend* I want is Liam, and I don't know how to have the benefits without risking my heart.

15

LIAM

"Hey, man. All good?" Logan asks as he enters my pool house.

I look up from my laptop where I'm typing up notes from the last outlets I visited in Virginia.

"Why? What have you heard?"

Did Mallory tell Daphne about us—about the us that can never be?

Logan's eyes widen.

Crap.

"I haven't heard anything," he says. "What's going on?"

Crappity crap crap.

"Nothing," I assure him. "Just typing up my notes from the last centers I visited. Everything was in good shape."

"Great." He walks over to my fridge to grab a bottle of water. How nice that he feels he can make himself at home. "So, what's going on? Don't bother saying nothing. I can ask Daphne—"

"What would asking Daphne do?"

"She could tell us if Mallory said anything that would shed light on why you're in a mood."

"No."

"No, Mallory wouldn't have anything to say? No, she wouldn't say anything if she had something to say? No, Daphne wouldn't tell me?" Logan chuckles. "It's not the last one. Daph would tell me."

"Why are you here?" I ask tiredly, pinching the bridge of my nose. I am not in the mood for this today. I got home a few hours ago, and I just want to finish these notes, open a beer, and sit on the couch, watching some hockey while moping. I could shift and go for a run, but I'm not in the mood for that either.

Settling next to me on the couch, Logan rests his ankle on his knee and takes a sip of water. "Daph and I are going Christmas tree shopping on Saturday. Mallory's family has a Christmas tree farm. Did you want to go with us?"

"Is Mallory going?" I feel like a desperate teenager asking, but I want to know.

"Does it matter?"

I haven't punched my cousin with any kind of force since we were teenagers, and then it was mostly a joke. I'm not in a joking mood now.

"Okay." He sighs. "I'll stop teasing you. She's not going. Daphne invited her. She said she wants to stay home and hibernate. Daph says she looks miserable and tired, but she won't talk about it. Flat out refuses to discuss it."

Now it's my turn to sigh. I don't know if her mood is because of our conversation a couple nights ago or something else, but I don't want her tired and upset. If it's over our conversation, that doesn't make sense. It was her decision that our relationship wasn't going to develop into anything.

"Nah, I don't want to go. You two will be all huggy kissy and take forever to pick out a tree." I am not in the mood for that. "You can borrow my truck if you want, so you can haul it home."

Logan claps me on the shoulder. "Thanks. That was going to be my next question."

"No problem. Did you just want to take it tonight? I'm not doing anything with it tomorrow. I can use the Bronco for wherever I go."

"I think the moms are going with us. If so, your mom can drive it to our house Saturday morning when we meet up."

"Okay. Whatever works. I don't care."

Logan swallows a sip of water. "Are you going to the company Christmas party?"

It's been a couple of years since I've gone. I should make an appearance. The food is good. I don't see too many people in the company since I travel so much, and when I'm home, I work from here and not from the office.

"Yeah. I should show my face. It's been a few years."

"Uh-huh. Daphne and Mallory are going shopping on Sunday for stuff to wear."

I put my laptop on the coffee table and go to the fridge to grab a beer. My mind isn't on my notes. I raise the bottle to Logan to see if he wants one. He shakes his head.

Opening the bottle, I take a swig of my beer as I pace my living room.

"I just don't get it. She likes me too, but she says no to dating me or having a relationship."

I will probably regret telling Logan anything because he'll run his mouth to Daphne, who may then talk to Mallory. That'll be awkward. But fuck it, it's already awkward. We're going to be together at work stuff, and with Logan and Daphne, and we'll have to ignore that at least one of us is attracted to the other.

"We're talking about Mallory, right?"

I glare.

Logan holds up his hands defensively. "Hey, just making sure we're on the same page. Okay, so you asked Mallory out, and she turned you down?"

"I didn't ask her out." I sigh. Again. "I didn't get the chance to. She told me why we're a no-go before I had the opportunity."

"Ouch," Logan says sympathetically. "So, why not? You had that night in Vegas, and she still," he emphasizes *still* because he's an asshole sometimes, "seems to like you, and it looks like you're compatible."

"That's just it. I think she does like me." I roll my eyes. "You know, we sound like teenage girls using the word like in this context."

"OMG, I know!" Logan squeals like my sister used to when she was with her cheerleader friends, and I chuckle. How can I not laugh at a six-foot-four muscled dude sounding like some little girl from that dancing show Kennie would make me watch?

"Anyway, she won't date me or anything because we work together, and I'm an executive. She says it would be awkward because I'll be her boss someday."

"No, you won't. Didn't you tell her about Andy?"

"I told her about Andy," I inform him. "I even offered to resign. But that's not the big reason we can't be together."

"What's bigger than working together? She likes guys, right?"

"Yeah. She had sex with me," I remind him.

"Oh, yeah, right. And she still likes guys after that?"

I raise a fist and Logan holds up his hands in a protective manner.

"Kidding! Jeez. So, what's the issue?"

"I'm a cougar shifter." I rejoin my cousin on the couch. I'm tired of pacing.

"She comes from a wolf pack, right? Surely, she's not anti-shifter?"

"Shifting isn't the problem." I lean my head against the back of the couch and look up at the ceiling. "I'm not a wolf. She needs to please her family, and she's convinced she needs to 'make up' for not being a wolf shifter by marrying one." I can't believe I did the air quote fingers. Now I'm the teenage girl.

"Who's talking marriage? Go out to dinner, fool around. Keep it out of the office."

I turn my head on the cushion to look at him. I don't know how to explain this without sounding crazy.

"Just say it, Liam." Logan prods me. "I can hear you thinking."

"I know I've only really known her two weeks, and this is crazy, but..."

"You think she's the one."

"Yeah. That's crazy, right?" I sit up and rest my forearms on my thighs, clasping my hands loosely together.

"No. Sometimes you just know," he assures me. "Look at our parents. They all knew from the start they were meant to be together. They didn't always act on it if the stories are to be believed, but they knew." He slaps me on the shoulder. "You guys saw each other across a dance floor and then hooked up. You were both feeling something. I know you're not a monk, but I know you aren't a random hookup guy. You usually at least learn something more about them than their first name before you have sex. I don't know Mallory well, but I don't think what happened in Vegas is normal behavior for her either. Sometimes our animals know what our human brains don't."

"It took you and Daphne years."

"Well, I'm a dumbass," Logan says easily. "My heart knew from the moment she knocked me in the head with her backpack in class she was the one for me. My head was stubborn and insisted it wanted to be free and go on adventures."

He takes a sip of his water and starts peeling the label. "Daphne has abandonment and loss issues, so the blame doesn't solely rest with me. She was afraid to risk being hurt by losing someone again. We needed the time it took for us both to grow up, admit what we wanted, and recognize what we had." He shrugs. "Sometimes we meet the right person at the wrong time."

"So, what do I do? Do I just accept it? Be friends and ignore the fact I want more? Not be friends?" This is the first time we've had a serious talk about adult relationships. We'd talk about flings when we were kids, but we're men now. This isn't kid stuff.

"Can you be friends with her? If she says no for whatever reason, you obviously need to respect that."

"Obviously. How were you able to be friends with Daphne all those years?"

"Why do you think I traveled all the time?"

I laugh. Then I look at his face and the laughter dies.

"Seriously? That's why you became a travel photographer?" In the five years since he's graduated college, he's maybe been home two or three months a year, but not at one time. It would be a week or two here and there throughout the year.

"That's why I stayed away so much. I love to travel and have a talent for photography, but I took all those assignments and didn't come home often because it was impossible to be around Daphne so much and just be her friend. I wanted to make her mine for years, but I had to wait for her to be ready." He gazes at me. "It was hell. Especially when I had to worry about assholes like you swooping in while I was gone."

"Dude, I was never serious about flirting with Daphne. It was just fun. I always knew she was hung up on you. She knew I wasn't serious."

"You're not the only guy who flirted with her. She doesn't realize the effect she has on people. She thinks she's invisible, but she has a way about her that attracts everyone. We went out to dinner, and our waiter flirted with her like I wasn't even there!"

I choke on my beer because I'm laughing so hard.

"It's not funny! She called him on it, and he told her in case she dumped me, he wanted to get in line."

"That's not a bad strategy. It probably works."

Logan nods. "It has. We went back last weekend and saw it in action. It's impressive when it's not my girlfriend he's trying to pick up."

He puts his water bottle on the coffee table and turns to look at me. "So, what's your plan with Mallory? Just be friends?"

I shrug. "I don't see what else I can do. She has her reasons, and I must respect them."

"Are you going to be all Zen spouting 'what is meant to be, will be' bullshit?" Logan's smirk shows the unlikeliness of me being able to pull that off.

"Maybe all of this is just envy from seeing you and Daphne happy. Maybe I'd be into any girl that came along right around now.

Logan scoffs. "Do you really believe that?"

"No. I think it's Mallory."

"Well, it's the holidays. Find yourself some mistletoe and see what happens," he suggests.

"Great idea, genius. Let's throw a sexual harassment complaint into the mix." I shake my head. "HR would love that. And our dads would rightly kick my ass."

"So, hanging out in the friend zone for the time being? Sorry, man."

"Whatever. This is how my parents started out. Mom didn't want to date Dad because she was Grammy's student teacher. She didn't even know he was a shifter since we were still secret back then. They overcame that obstacle, so there's hope." I turn my head to look at my cousin. "Right?"

Logan claps me on the shoulder and stands. "There's always hope. I think you guys have a spark. If that's enough to overcome her hangups, I guess we'll have to see." He drains his water bottle, gets up, and puts it in the recycle bin under my kitchen sink.

"You know what you should do?" he asks.

"I'm afraid to ask."

"Text Trevor and see if his sister will let you use the rink. I think skating again and burning off some aggression shooting pucks during the weeks you're home will be good for you."

I consider the suggestion. It's a good one.

I nod. "Yeah, maybe I'll do that. They should be home for break soon so we could skate together. It was fun. I missed skating. I felt it the next day though."

"Me too. Rugby doesn't use the same muscles."

Standing, I put my almost empty beer bottle on the breakfast bar and walk Logan to the door.

"Thanks for coming by, man. I appreciate you listening to me." I hold out my hand to shake. Logan takes it and pulls me into a hug, slapping me on the back.

"Anytime, Liam. Other than Daph, you're my best friend. I want you to be happy. I love you."

I try to clear my throat of the lump that's just formed. We're fortunate we were raised by men that are comfortable showing affection, but it's not something Logan and I typically express to each other. We have each other's backs, no doubt, and we love each other, but we don't tell each other. Tonight, we do. It's nice.

"Love you too, man."

I watch him walk to his Jeep and get in, then wave as he drives away before closing my door.

Picking up my phone, I shoot a text to Trevor. Since Thanksgiving, Logan, Trevor, and I have had a group chat talking about sports. I've watched some videos posted of the stunts he and Randi do for cheerleading—they're amazing. Dude is crazy strong, and she's fearless. I know from the years Kendall cheered how dangerous it is, and the fact that Randi is taller than the average cheerleader makes it even more difficult and impressive. Trevor can bench press more than either me or Logan.

> Me: Hey, Trev, what's up?

> Trevor: Nothing much, studying for finals. What's up with you?

> Me: Shit, I'm sorry. Don't want to interrupt.

> Trevor: You're good. Tbh I've been checking out the hottie shelving books. Totally sexy librarian vibe.

I laugh, remembering my own "productive" library study sessions. Especially that study room on the third floor of the main library...

Me: I was wondering if it would be okay to use your rink for some skating time and shooting drills?

Trevor: Sure. Just let me text Lory so she knows.

Me: Thanks. I'll work around her schedule. I don't want to bother her.

Trevor: She won't care, but that way, she knows why there's a car parked there. She uses the gym too. Usually before or after work, you probably won't see each other.

Me: Cool.

Trevor: I'll shoot her a text and get back to you, and I'll be home next week. Hopefully we can skate while I'm on break.

Me: Hope so. Thanks.

Trevor: No problem. Let you know. Bye.

Me: Bye.

Skating and shooting pucks aren't how I want to expend my tension, but it looks like that's my option for the foreseeable future. I wonder if Trevor's sister is single.

16

MALLORY

My phone flashes with a text notification from Trevor. He better not be saying he's not coming home for Christmas. It was hard enough to be without backup for Thanksgiving. I don't want to do Christmas on my own too. Okay, that's not fair. Thanksgiving was better than usual, all things considered, but I miss him.

> Trevor: Hey, Lory. Everything good?

What has he heard? Who told him?

> Me: Hey, Trev, yeah, everything's fine. Why?

> Trevor: Just asking. Would it be okay if my friend uses the rink for skating and shooting drills?

> Me: Sure. Have they been there before? Do they have the code?

> Trevor: He's been there, and I'll give him the code.

> Me: As long as he locks up, cleans up after himself, and doesn't need me for anything, I don't care.

> Trevor: Thanks, you're the best.

> Me: You'll be home for Christmas, right?

> Trevor: Of course! I'll be home on Wednesday.

> Me: Good. Go back to studying.

> Trevor: Yes, ma'am.

Looking out the window, I see the touch of frost on the window-pane. It's one of those sunny days that doesn't look cold, but it is. My favorite kind of day. I don't have anything planned for today. Daphne's going Christmas tree shopping with Logan. I could go over to my uncle's Christmas tree farm to join them or just to help. They can always use extra hands, but I can't deal with the crowd I know the farm attracts. Things are always crazy in the two weeks leading up to Christmas. Even if a family already has their tree, they'll return to the farm for the other events or to pet the reindeer.

I wonder if Trev's friend is coming by today or not. I could text him back and ask, but it doesn't really matter. I should've asked who it is, but that doesn't really matter either. I should go for a run. Yeah. Maybe some fresh air and physical activity will get me out of this funk. It's been forever since I've run outside. I normally just use the treadmill in the rink's gym. Okay, I know what physical activity would really get me out of this funk, but no chance for that now because I told Liam there was no chance for us.

The rink lights are on, and an old SUV is parked alongside it as I approach the barn rink after my run. Trevor's friend must be here—I should peek in and make sure everything is okay. I let myself in the door that enters directly into the gym portion of the building so I can grab a bottle of water from the fridge. I take a sip as I walk to the doorway to look out over the rink and...promptly start choking.

What the hell is Liam doing here? Is he the friend Trevor told me about? Since when are they friends? This makes no sense. He glides over the surface beautifully, his feline grace clear with each long, smooth stroke and the flexing of his powerful thighs. I remember other long smooth strokes and flexing of thighs, and my core tightens with longing.

He moves the puck with ease as he does a drill, guiding it through cones effortlessly. I've tried this same drill before while playing around with my brothers, and it's not as easy as he makes it seem. I understand why his mom misses seeing him on the ice. If he can move like this after not playing for years, I can only imagine the force he was on the ice in his prime.

"Mallory? What are you doing here?" Liam asks.

Did I unknowingly sigh and alert him to my presence? Or was it my choking half to death on my water? Or did he sense me in the doorway?

"This is my rink," I say, approaching the boards. "I should ask what you're doing here. Since when are you friends with Trevor?"

"You're Lory?" He looks at me quizzically. His eyes widen as realization hits. I could drown in their clear blue depths. "Oh, short for Mallory."

"Yep. How do you know Trevor? Did you play hockey together? He's a few years younger than you. I wouldn't think you were on the same teams."

"We met at Thanksgiving. He's friends with my sister Kendall." He skates over to the boards where I'm standing. "We got to talking hockey, and he helped me and Logan put up the lights at their house. We came here to skate while we were waiting until the girls finished shopping."

"Wow, small world."

"Yeah." Liam leans on the board in front of me. In his skates, he's at least a full foot taller than I am. I feel tiny, not a feeling I get to enjoy that often. That's why I feel that thrill. It's not that Liam is close to me, flushed with exertion and smelling deliciously manly. I've smelled way more sweaty hockey gear than any woman should have to in her lifetime, but for once, I'm not gagging.

He flicks the end of my ponytail playfully. "You realize even if we hadn't met in Vegas, we would have met each other eventually with all the connections we have? It's fate."

His grin is a mixture of boyish exuberance and sexy man. It's not fair I have to resist the tug I feel when I'm near him. Is it fate that we found each other that night six months ago? Twenty-five plus years here in South Jersey without our paths crossing. It's crazy, considering how many of our orbits intersect. It's amazing we haven't been tripping over each other our entire lives.

"Yeah." I look up into his gorgeous eyes. "I'm glad we met then and had that night without knowing how complicated things are."

"They don't have to be complicated. We like each other, we do our own thing and live our lives."

That could work, and it's exactly what I've been looking for. "Friends with benefits? We'd have to keep it just between us. No telling Daphne or Logan. Trevor can never know. Nothing at work."

Liam nods. "Friends with benefits."

Now that we have that settled, I can't wait to reap some benefits.

17
LIAM

She wants to be friends with benefits. No dating, no relationship, just hooking up.

I don't believe that's what she really wants. I'm pretty sure she wants me, and I think she wants more than hookups, but she won't admit it. Why agree to lunch with me twice? Why FaceTime with me when she knows I'm not what her parents want? When she looks at me, it's not just like she's checking out my ass. She sees me, and she likes me. That has to mean something. I want more than hooking up, but for now I'll go along with her idea and work on changing her mind.

I'm too sweaty and gross to reap the rewards of our new benefits arrangement, but I can at least get a kiss out of this. She's flushed, and I don't think it's just from her workout.

"Did you go for a run?" I ask.

When she nods, I continue, "How far?"

Shrugging, she responds, "About six miles. There are trails through the woods. I set my watch for an hour and run until it goes off."

She checks her watch. "6.2 miles. I normally do four or five miles a few times a week on the treadmill, but it's nice out, and I wanted to be in nature. I spend too much time cooped up inside."

Trevor had said his sister appreciated nature more than anyone else in their family. I can't believe I didn't put the pieces together sooner. They each spoke about living out in the woods and having siblings. I assume Logan doesn't know, or maybe he does and suggesting I come out here is his attempt to play matchmaker.

I raise my hand and place it against her soft cheek, running my thumb along her rosy skin. I lean down and press my lips to hers, tasting and savoring in a way we didn't before. In Vegas, our kisses were hungry and passionate, a product of desire and desperation. Now, we can take our time and enjoy learning the feel of each other's lips, give each other teasing, nibbling kisses, deep kisses, playful kisses. I want all the kisses with Mallory.

Her sigh as our lips meet and the way she rises on her toes to press her lips to mine show she's as eager to kiss me as I am her. Her hand rests against my chest where my heart's pounding, not just from the exertion of my skating but from the thrill of being near Mallory again. From kissing her again. I never thought I'd have this opportunity and would have to make do with the scant memories I collected from our too-brief time together in Vegas. Her nails scrape lightly against my chest as if her hand can't rest, as if it needs to claw me, mark me as hers. Her other hand grasps my bicep to pull me closer.

I wish we didn't have the boards of the rink separating us, but maybe that's for the best. If I could pull her body against mine and feel all her luscious curves, I don't think I could stop at just kissing. The sound of multiple car doors closing pulls me from the bubble our kisses have cocooned us in.

"Are you expecting anyone?" I ask, lifting my head.

"No, were you?"

The voices I hear cause me to close my eyes and groan.

"It's my cousin. He suggested I ask Trevor. He must have seen my Bronco as he drove back from the tree lot."

"Hello! You here, Liam?" Logan calls out as he slips through the barn doors to the rink. Daphne follows. With our mothers. Fuuccckk.

Mallory's eyes widen when I push away from the boards, and she gets a clear view of our quartet of visitors.

"Oh, wow," Mom says as she looks around the space. "Liam would have loved something like this when he was younger." She hasn't seen me yet.

"Hey," I call out, skating over to where they're approaching the boards, hoping to draw their attention before they notice Mallory. By his smirk, I can tell Logan's eagle eyes have caught sight of her, but he's not saying anything.

"Oh!" Mom cries out, seeing me on skates for the first time since my accident. Tears flood her eyes, and her chin wobbles. "Oh, Liam, I didn't think I'd ever see you skating again. Is everything okay?"

I reach to open the gate so I can hug my mother without the boards between us. I don't know why I'm surprised by her emotional response. She knew how much I missed skating and playing. Skating again for the first time with Trevor and Logan after Thanksgiving had me choked up.

"Yeah, all good," I answer. "I was doing some puck handling drills."

Mallory approaches us and nods.

I tilt my head her way. "And then Mallory came in from a run."

"Mallory! What are you doing here?" Daphne asks in surprise.

"Hi, everyone. It's my family's rink. Trevor's my younger brother. Small world, huh?" She smiles. "Trev texted asking if his friend could use the rink, and of course I agreed. I was finishing up my run and saw the Bronco, so I peeked in to see who his friend was. Turns out it was Liam, so we were just laughing about all the connections."

"Turns out there's another connection, Mallory," my Aunt Holly says. "Mike and I went to law school with your father. I knew your uncle Zack back then too, so it was a mini reunion seeing him at the farm."

"Wow, that's crazy." Mallory looks over at me. Is she thinking about how our meeting was inevitable or fate or whatever like I am?

Mom looks at the skating surface and then at Mallory. "So that isn't ice? Your mother invented it?"

"Yeah. It's a synthetic surface. My mom is a chemical engineer, and she developed this special polymer that's more durable with less friction to better emulate an ice surface. We were her guinea pigs testing it out."

"Wow. Your father is an attorney, and your mother is an engineer—"

"And here's me, just a paralegal," Mallory finishes.

"What's this 'just a paralegal' bullshit?" Aunt Holly asks bluntly. "All I've ever heard is how good you are and how eager Mike is to get you in leasing. I practice family law and without my paralegals, I'd be lost."

Mallory blinks at my aunt.

Mom chimes in. "What I was going to say was that it's no wonder you're so brilliant. Will raves about you. He has since you started. You stepped up after Martha and George retired and kept the collections department going. You and Daphne."

Daphne laughs. "Oh no. It's all Mallory. I'm just her wing woman."

A pretty blush climbs Mallory's neck and spreads across her cheeks. I don't think she hears how smart she is and how much she's appreciated often enough. Her family has done a number on her, and I don't like it.

Swallowing and then coughing to clear her throat, Mallory appears to be trying to control her emotions. I wish I could reach out and rub her back or hold her hand.

"You're all too kind," Mallory says. "I love working at Morgan and am excited to work on leasing. I enjoy contracts and leases much more than litigation. Anyway, did you get your trees? Did you get some of Aunt Carol's hot cocoa?"

"Yes!" Mom's practically dancing with enthusiasm. "It was so much fun! Such nice quality trees, and the activities there really make it a fun experience beyond tree hunting."

"It is fun. I worked there when I was younger. I worked at all the farms. Another uncle has blueberries, and one has a corn maze. I haven't been to the tree farm yet this year. I'll have to go sometime."

I hope I'm picking up on what she's putting down when I suggest, "The four of us should go sometime. Are they open only on the weekends or weeknights too?"

"Oh, yes! We need to go together!" Daphne is so excited at this idea she's practically doing a Tigger bounce.

"Starting this weekend, they're open every night through Christmas Eve, until 9:00 p.m. on Sundays and weeknights, 11:00 p.m. Friday and Saturday." Mallory looks at me, and I nod. I'm not sure why.

"I'm good any night," I say. "My schedule is wide open."

Her smile must be why I nodded. I enjoy making her happy. I want more of those smiles aimed my way.

"We're going shopping tomorrow," Daphne says. "We could meet for dinner and then go over."

Mallory nods. "That works if it's okay with the guys." She looks to me like I'm not going to agree with anything she suggests that enables us to spend time together.

"Yeah, sounds good," I say.

"Oh, why don't you guys come over tonight and help decorate the tree!" Daphne suggests, doing a clappy-clappy-excited-bounce thing.

"It's your first Christmas tree," I remind her. "Don't you want to be all romantic and junk with just the two of you?" I figure this is one of those romance milestones couples celebrate. I look to Logan for confirmation, and he just shrugs.

The moms have just been listening. Very unlike them. I almost forgot they were there. Aunt Holly nudges Mom and says, "Remember how we used to decorate each other's trees before we had kids?"

Mom laughs. "Yes! You could tell when the liquor kicked in. I oversaw the tinsel and at first, I'd be very deliberate and place it strand by strand. As the eggnog kicked in, I'd start being less meticulous. By the fourth cup of Grammy Morgan's eggnog, I'd be throwing it on the tree in big globs."

I laugh. "You still do that!"

"I fix it once I sober up," Mom protests with a giggle.

"Anyway," Aunt Holly says, "decorating with couple friends is fun."

"Oh, we're not a couple," Mallory rushes to say.

"Okay, dear," Aunt Holly says with a whatever-you-say tone to her voice and a smirk.

Mallory shoots me a glance, and I just shrug. I know Aunt Holly can smell the pheromones we're putting off since she's a cougar shifter like I am. Mom and Daphne are human, so they don't have that clue. Logan, as a golden eagle shifter, doesn't have a super keen sense of smell, but nothing escapes his notice.

"Thank you," Mallory says, "but I really just want to stay home tonight." She softens her rejection with a smile. "It's been a long week, and we'll be going shopping tomorrow and to the farm tomorrow night, so I need tonight to recharge."

"I'm not being a third wheel, so I'm out," I say.

"Maybe we can see it tomorrow before we go to the farm?" Mallory suggests. She's good at being tactful. I tend to be too blunt.

"That's a good idea, I guess," Daphne concedes. "Speaking of letting you recharge...we should probably head out. Sorry to have just dropped in randomly. We didn't realize this was your rink. I can't get over how small of a world it is!"

We all chuckle. For once, I'm grateful that this world is small and there are all these connections and ties between me and Mallory.

"I know Mike still talks with your dad, Mallory," Aunt Holly says. "I'm surprised they never made the connection."

Mallory giggles. "I'm not surprised. With the way Dad laser

focuses on things, random connections like that wouldn't occur to him."

Aunt Holly winks. "Sounds like Robert hasn't changed then. His hyper-focus was legendary in law school. We used to try to break his concentration when he was reading case law, and it was impossible. The only thing that would do it was your mother walking into the library. It was like radar. She'd walk in, and suddenly she was the focus of his attention."

"Really? That's so sweet. I never think about them back in college or dating. They're just Mom and Dad." I love the soft expression Mallory's face has, and I hope to inspire that look one day.

"Well, we should go," Aunt Holly says. She's my favorite aunt. "Great seeing you, Mallory. You'll be at the company party on Friday?"

"I will. Looking forward to it. Are ugly sweaters really okay?"

"More than okay. We encourage them!" Mom bounces on her toes. What is it with everyone being all bouncy today? First Daphne and now Mom. Maybe it's a human thing? "Are you going to wear one? We have a contest."

"Maybe. Still thinking about it." Mallory grins. She has a mischievous twinkle in her eye that I can't wait to get to the bottom of. Can't wait to get to her bottom.

Okay, Liam, stop that train of thought before your thoughts become evident to everyone. I feel Liam Jr. stirring, and without the cold of an ice rink to help keep things tame or a cup to keep things contained down there, we're going to have a situation. I fidget and glide away to snag a puck, hoping being in motion will disguise things. Skating with the start of a hard-on isn't that comfortable, but neither is having an erection in front of your mother. Lesser of two evils and all that.

I feel Logan's gaze follow me as I skate and, when I glance his way, his smirk tells me he knows exactly why I started skating. Jerk.

"Liam, I'll leave your keys under the front seat?" Mom asks. "I borrowed his truck to carry the trees," she tells Mallory.

"Yeah, that's fine." I weave my way through cones with the puck on my stick. The concentration it takes is helping resolve my issue south of the equator.

From the corner of my eye, I see Mom wrap Mallory in a hug. Mallory is several inches taller, so she bends a bit to accept it and hugs her back. I'm glad my mother likes Mallory. She couldn't stand Tiffany, the last real girlfriend I had back when I was in college. She was polite to her, but she wasn't warm. Nothing like how she's been with Mallory since the moment they met.

She never said anything, but I think she blames Tiffany for my accident. If she hadn't insisted I come home to take her to that party, we wouldn't have been on the road—but that's not fair to her. The accident wasn't her fault. It was my choice to come home to appease her. But we *can* blame her for dumping me when it was obvious I'd no longer be a hockey star. With maturity and experience, I know now I never loved her, but back then, it was just another loss I suffered, and it hurt like hell.

Thank goodness she dumped me. I shudder to think what life would be like being shackled to her. The thought of missing out on Mallory is so distressing, I rub a hand over the ache in my heart.

I wave goodbye as they leave, and Mallory graciously walks them out. I continue to skate my drill under her appreciative gaze. After shooting the puck into the net, I reenact my old goal celly of gliding on one knee and pumping my fist to make her giggle. It's a sweet sound, and I skate over to where she's standing, hoping to resume what we were doing before my family popped in.

"He shoots, he scores!" she says with a grin.

I wink. "That's what I'm hoping for."

"I may be able to help make that happen," she purrs. "Do you have a change of clothes?"

"Yeah. In my car."

"Good. I need a shower after my run. Care to join me?"

All the skating drills in the world couldn't distract Liam Jr. from that invitation.

"Hell yes," I growl. "Let me get these skates off."

18

MALLORY

IF I DIDN'T SEE HIM TAKE OFF HIS SKATES WITH MY OWN TWO EYES, I'D assume his skates evaporated off his feet, considering how fast Liam had his sneakers on and was holding my hand as we rushed through the band of trees separating the rink from my house.

"Wow, Mallory, this is nice," he says as we enter my kitchen through the back door.

"Thanks, I'll give you the tour." I spin to press a quick kiss to his lips, pulling away before he can deepen it and derail my train of thought. "Later. First, I want to show you upstairs." I tug his hand to lead him up the back staircase. "Especially my shower."

Chuckling, Liam follows me upstairs and down the hallway into my bedroom. Its blue-and-yellow color scheme always makes me feel like I'm outside on a sunny spring day with soft sunlight warming my skin. It makes me happy. I carried the theme over to my bathroom with the daisy shower curtain and yellow towels. It's a very feminine space, but Liam doesn't look silly here. He belongs. I turn on the shower, and we kiss hungrily, removing each other's clothes. I reach into the vanity drawer for some condoms, and Liam's ardent gaze follows my actions.

"I like the idea, but the next time I fuck you, it's going to be in a bed. We deserve it," he murmurs against my neck as he gives a gentle nip and then presses a soothing kiss to the spot.

I am so wet, and it has nothing to do with the steam coming from the shower. I peel my shirt off over my head and admire the broad chest Liam exposes when his shirt follows mine to the floor. Our first encounter in Vegas was all about our sexy bits fitting together. We didn't have the opportunity, or the lighting, to see each other's bodies and admire them. I'm sorry I missed that. The reflection in the hotel room window during our call didn't do justice to what I have here in front of me today.

He is glorious, with his broad shoulders and firm pecs covered by a light dusting of brown hair. I'm so glad he doesn't shave his chest bare. I appreciate thoughtful manscaping as much as the next girl. No one wants to be boinking Chewbacca, but I want some hair to show that I'm with a grown man. Maybe it's the dormant shifter genes in me, but I appreciate a bit of manly fur in certain spots. No back hair, but a bit of chest hair to run my fingers through is nice.

I refocus to follow the light trail of hair down his tight abs to where it's hidden by the waistband of his athletic pants. They need to come off. Now. He's kicking off his sneakers while reaching to remove my pants too. Eventually we're down to our underwear— black zip-front sports bra and cotton panties for me, navy-blue boxer briefs for him.

"You're gorgeous," he says reverently, resting his hands on my cotton-clad hips and pulling me toward him. His boxers contain his heavy erection, but it still presses against my belly as he moves his hands from my hips to the cheeks of my ass. I'm wearing the least sexy undies I own, but I feel like a goddess nonetheless.

"May I?" he asks, reaching for the zipper of my sports bra. I nod, grateful I chose this one, so there were no awkward contortions trying to get out of a pullover sports bra. I'm a full-figured woman— my sports bras serve a purpose and are feats of engineering. They aren't decorative. The rasp of the zipper lowering joins the sound of the water flowing in the shower. The look of lust and awe that comes over Liam's face when he sees my naked breasts for the first time is something I'll remember forever. Glancing in the mirror, I can see the seam lines from the bra pressed in my skin, but in this moment I don't care. The flush crawling up my chest is from desire, not embarrassment.

I shimmy out of my panties as Liam shucks his boxer briefs. Wow. I've had the man inside me. I'm well aware he's been blessed with length and girth. I just wasn't expecting his cock to be so... pretty. That's such a ridiculous thing to say. Penises are big, jutting, curved to the left, whatever. They aren't pretty. But his is. It's straight and proud, bobbing a bit toward his belly button like an excited racehorse ready to enter the starting gate. The vein that runs along the shaft to the broad head of his erection—oh lord, I can't believe I used a phrase right out of a romance novel—is prominent and just so manly.

"Come on." I grab his hand and open the door to the shower. The steam billows out around us. "Time to get cleaned up so we can get dirty."

The warm water rains down on us, and I revel in it. Liam's body is glorious, with the water cascading over his muscles. I can see the feline grace of his body now and, man, I want him. Shower first, then sexy times.

Strong hands flex on my hips, pulling me closer to his body.

"You are so sexy," Liam rasps, placing passionate kisses along my shoulder and up my neck.

Even though we're under the warm spray of the shower, goosebumps break out on my skin from his kisses.

"You're pretty hot yourself, cowboy." I tilt my head so he can better access my neck for his kisses.

"Cowboy? What kind of weird fantasy do you have?" Liam asks with a chuckle.

"Shut up and kiss me," I demand. No way am I sharing my love of cowboy romances and my current Netflix binge about a Canadian horse ranch and the drama that goes along with it.

I love it when a man listens to me, and the kiss Liam plants on my lips doesn't disappoint. Why have I been denying myself this for weeks? His lips are firm and mobile against mine, and the strokes his tongue makes against mine remind me of what it felt like to have other parts of him stroking inside me all those months ago. As fun as this is, the sooner we shower, the sooner we can fall into my bed and continue this encounter to a mutually satisfying conclusion.

With reluctance, I pull back from our kiss and grab the washcloth I snagged from the linens shelf and my body wash. I know it's crazy. I'll have sex with this man but won't share my loofah. Loofahs are so personal. I squirt some body wash on the cloth and rub it to get it to lather.

I push on Liam's shoulder to get him to turn around and run the washcloth along his broad shoulders and down his back. I look at the marvel that is his ass. He may not have been skating for years, but he still has the butt and muscular thighs of a top-tier hockey player. I can't wait to see him in a suit in person. I got a glimpse when we FaceTimed a few days ago, but I want to appreciate it fully. He must get them tailored so they accommodate his trim waist, apple-shaped ass, and thick thighs. I stop washing at his waist and start on his arms. I run the cloth from his shoulder to his wrist on the right and go to repeat the motion on his left arm. The long, thin scar running down the back of his upper arm stops me. Liam looks over his shoulder and finds me looking at it.

"I forget it's there. Got it in the accident. Compound fracture. They had to put a titanium plate in to put the bone back together. They told me I was lucky it didn't affect my shoulder or elbow." He gives a mirthless laugh. I assume he didn't consider it lucky. "You can't hurt it. You can wash it."

I run the cloth over it and then press my lips to it. I rest my forehead against his shoulder and close my eyes. How bad must the accident have been that it caused that kind of damage?

As if he can read my mind, Liam reassures me. "I'm okay, Mallory. That wasn't the worst injury. It just left the most dramatic scar. Well, that and the burns."

"Burns?" I jerk my head from his shoulder and shake my wet hair from my face.

"Just on my leg. All healed." He turns and extends his left leg. Now that I know where to look, I can see faint scars on his upper calf and lower thigh. "Engine fire. I'm good. Let's refocus."

How can he be so nonchalant about what he's been through? Or feign nonchalance so well? If these injuries weren't the worst, what else has this poor man been through? A few scars have no effect on my attraction to him, but I can't help to think about the pain he must have suffered, not only physically but also emotionally from losing the ability to play the sport he loves. I know shifters heal more quickly from injury, but to have these scars despite his shifter constitution, they had to be severe.

He tilts my chin and claims my lips again. This kiss isn't as hungry, but it does the trick to stop me thinking about anything other than us naked in my shower.

Pulling back this time, he suggests, "How about we each wash ourselves to get the job done efficiently and then spend as much time as we want exploring each other horizontally?"

"Good idea," I agree. There are over six feet of muscled glory I want to spend hours exploring. And a good nine inches I want to pay special attention to. Wow!

I grab my loofah, squirt some body wash on it, and add a squirt to Liam's washcloth to refresh it. He washes himself quickly and is generously washing my back for me when I hear a sound from my darkest nightmare.

"Mallory? We came home early for Christmas. Dad's getting the bags from the car, but I'm going to suggest we go to the tree farm to say hi. I can buy you and your...friend half an hour, maybe an hour to, um, finish up."

Any sexy thoughts I was entertaining desert me. Turning around and glancing down at Liam's cock, I see Mom's appearance had a similar effect on him.

"Hey, Mom," I croak out. "Welcome home. See you in a bit."

Liam's wide eyes meet mine in disbelief.

"Your parents are here? Were you expecting them?" he whisper-shouts. Not that it matters. Mom has superior wolf shifter hearing. We're not keeping anything from her.

"Of course not! They weren't supposed to get here until Tuesday. If I knew they were going to be here, you wouldn't be!"

The flash of hurt that crosses over his face squeezes my heart. Damn.

I reach out and rest my hand on his chest. "Hey, I didn't mean it like that. It's just awkward to be in the shower with a man and have your mother knock on the door."

Nodding, he covers my hand with his and gives a light squeeze.

"Sounds like we have thirty minutes at most to get out of here. Can I use your shampoo, please?"

"Yeah." I hand him the bottle and hold out my hand for a dollop as he gets his. We switch places so he can rinse the lather from his locks as I shampoo mine.

Since he's finished first, Liam exits the shower, pressing a soft kiss on my bare shoulder as he passes by and dries off. I rinse my hair and don't bother with conditioner. I know I'll regret this decision, just one of many, but I don't have time for all that. I'll braid it later, and that will be good enough.

Turning off the water, I open the shower door and step into the towel Liam holds open for me. Wrapping it around me and grabbing another towel for my hair, Liam laughs.

"Someday, I swear we're going to have uninterrupted time together. In a bed."

I laugh too. "Hashtag goals."

We dry off, and Liam pulls on clean boxer briefs he had in his bag as I enter my bedroom to grab clean clothes.

"Do you want me to stay?" he asks.

I sigh. "Will you be offended if I say no? It's nothing personal. It's just...this is awkward, and I don't know what Mom's going to say or what Dad knows."

"I get it. This isn't the first impression I wanted to make on your parents, anyway." He sits on the corner of my bed to pull on his socks and shoes. He bounces slightly and grins. "The mattress feels good. Hope to test it in the future."

My cheeks flush, the curse of being a redhead. There's no hiding my embarrassment.

"If you don't get out of here before my parents return, you may not be alive to try it out." I say while stepping into black yoga pants. I grab a hoodie that says, "Addicted to Love Stories" and pull it on, taking a moment before popping my head through in hopes the flush to my cheeks subsides.

Liam is fully dressed and running his fingers through his hair to give it some order.

"Your hair curls! I love it!" Reaching up, I finger one of the curls forming along his neck. This time it's his turn to blush.

"Yeah, when it gets too long, it does that. I need to get it cut."

"No!" I cry. "It's adorable." I imagine a little boy with copper-tinged brown curls and bright blue eyes and—I gasp. No, no, no, no. I can't think about precious little boys with curls and mischievous glints in their eyes. Not going to happen. Can't happen.

"You okay, Mallory?" Liam asks, concern clear in his voice.

I cough to clear the frog that has leaped into my throat. "I'm fine." I don't think my smile is convincing, but Liam lets it go.

"Okay, I'm going to head out. Text or call me later?" Grabbing my hand and leaning forward, he brushes a quick kiss across my lips.

It's too quick. I wish we could linger. My parents have the worst timing. I guess it's better they came home when we were only in the shower and not in the middle of making the most of my mattress.

"I'll walk you out." I lead the way down the back stairs, stopping at the bottom to look around and make sure we're alone.

"They aren't here," Liam says behind me. "I'd smell them. If I wasn't distracted earlier, I would have noticed your mom as soon as she entered the house. I'm sure she scented me right away."

Great. She has to know he's a cougar. Not bad enough to have a man in my shower, but for him to be a cougar shifter will bring some questions, I'm sure.

"Right." I pull open the back door and turn to Liam. "You can get to the rink okay? It's right through the trees there. You have your keys and stuff?"

He steps closer to me and wraps the arm not carrying his bag around me. "Give me a kiss, and I'll have all I need."

I stand on tiptoe to press a kiss to his jaw. He tightens his grip and adjusts the angle of his head to kiss my lips, lingering. With a sigh, I reach up and run my fingers through his damp curls. I open my lips and run my tongue along his bottom lip. I hear a rumble, almost like a purr, and it makes me smile. Instead of accepting my invitation to deepen the embrace, he breaks it and steps past me to the deck outside the kitchen door. In his eyes, I can see his reluctance to leave warring with his determination

"I'll see you tomorrow night. Call me. Please." He gives a sheepish grin. He's learning commands don't work on me.

"Yeah, see you tomorrow. Drive home safely."

He lopes off toward the rink, stopping at the tree line to look back at me and wave. I raise my hand to return the gesture and watch him slip into the trees. Just a minute or two later, I hear the powerful engine of his Bronco come to life and watch the headlights as they drive through the early twilight December brings to southern New Jersey. I close the door and sigh. My parents will be home soon, and I am not looking forward to that conversation.

19

LIAM

WELL, THAT DIDN'T GO HOW I EXPECTED. NOT THAT I WAS EXPECTING TO see Mallory or have sex when I went to the rink. I didn't know she'd be there. But after we came to our "friends with benefits" agreement and got rid of my family, I was expecting something more than some soapy shower time fun and an interruption from her parents.

I start my Bronco and drive through the woods in the winter twilight. It's nice out here. I grew up in a well-to-do suburban neighborhood, so I've never lived somewhere this rural. It's incredible how much of a difference a few miles make, even in the same town. Shifting Pines goes from marshes and coastland to deep forest in the Pine Barrens, farms to housing developments, houses older than the United States to mansions. It's so incredibly varied. I wonder what it was like to grow up with space like this. Did they have free rein to run all through the woods? Kendall and I could shift and run around on our property, but that was just a couple acres, nothing like having a forest at your disposal. Logan's lucky. He has the entire sky to fly in. We land shifters are limited to the land available.

I bet they had snowmobiles and ATVs growing up so they could zoom around the woods. Mallory probably kicked ass racing, and it would be something they could include her in without shifting. I'll have to ask her about it.

Maybe that's something we could do together.

She doesn't want to date and be out in public. We can't spend all our time in bed. Or in the shower. Well, we could, but regardless of what Mallory thinks, there's more to us than a physical relationship. I'll be patient, but my plan is to convert this no-strings friends-with-benefits thing to a genuine relationship with a future.

My mind wanders to the property in Atlantic City I've been checking out. Things have progressed a lot more quickly than we expected it to, but I'm thrilled. This is the challenge I've been searching for.

As I pull in next to the pool house, I see Mom returned my truck. I glance in the bed and it's empty, so Dad must have hauled the tree inside already. Flicking on the lights in my living room, I walk to the kitchen to see what I have for dinner. I haven't been shopping, so it'll probably be whatever I can forage from my freezer. I fish my ringing cell phone out of my pocket. It's Mom, and disappointment washes over me, followed closely by guilt. I was hoping it was Mallory. Mom must have been watching for me to get home.

Sighing, I answer. "Hi, Mom."

"Hi, honey. We're having tacos for dinner. Want to come over? We have plenty."

I know that "we have plenty" is code for "bring Mallory with you if she's there." I run my hand through my hair. It's pretty much dry.

"Thanks. I'll be over in a few."

I change into jeans and walk over to the main house, letting myself in through the French doors off the patio.

"Just me," I call out, pulling the door shut behind me.

"Hi, Liam. Can you give me a hand?" Dad calls from the living room. He's trying to stand up the tree in front of the big front window.

"Sure." Looking at the evergreen, I admire how full and symmetrical it is. Mom always finds the prettiest trees. "Do you want me to hold it so you can adjust the stand?"

"Just let me know if it looks straight. Your mom got one of those fancy stands where it adjusts by stepping on a pedal. No climbing under and turning the screws."

"Cool." I step back and assess it, leaning to view from a variety of angles. "I think it just needs to move a smidge that way." I gesture to my left.

He makes the adjustment and stands next to me. "Looks good to me. Want a beer?"

"Yeah." Walking into the kitchen, I press a kiss to Mom's cheek because it makes her smile. "Smells good. Thanks for the invitation."

"You know you don't need an invitation! This is your home. You can bring friends too. There's always plenty."

"Thanks. I know."

Grabbing the platter of tortillas and the carrier that has taco sauce, sour cream, and salsa, I ask, "Table or island?"

"Breakfast nook," Mom suggests.

We grab the taco stuff and carry it to the table. Before I can even take a bite out of my taco—your basic variety with meat, cheese, and onions—my dad hits me with the probing questions.

"So you were skating today?" Dad asks.

I nod, chewing my first bite.

"Oh, Will, it was wonderful! I wish I had thought to record it, but I was so surprised, it didn't occur to me," Mom gushes, tears in her eyes. I didn't realize it meant that much to her to see me skate again.

"Yeah, felt good. I skated with Logan and Trevor after Thanksgiving and figured I'd do it some more. Get used to being on skates on again."

"So, Kendall's friend is Mallory's brother?" Dad asks. "Small world. I didn't know Trevor played hockey. Wonder if we were at the same tournaments?"

"He's a few years younger, so even if we were, we wouldn't have had much overlap in ice time."

I pick up my second taco. Skating and showering worked up an appetite in me. But thinking about Mallory is going to cause reactions that aren't appropriate while sitting at my parents' table. Gotta move the conversation on to topics that are not Mallory.

"They converted a barn to a rink. Their mother is a chemical engineer and invented a synthetic ice surface, so they use that. No cooling needed, no Zamboni. It's a suitable surface to skate on. Not as fast as actual ice, but fine for recreation or practice. I'm surprised they don't use it at some of the outdoor games. It would be ideal for warmer weather. We could have a game at the beach. There's an anti-glare coating." I'm sounding like a salesman, so I shut up and start in on taco number two.

"So, Mallory," Mom starts.

"No," I say firmly.

"No what?" Dad looks up from his taco.

"Mom's trying to play matchmaker."

"I don't think you need me to do anything, Liam," Mom teases.

Crap.

"You and Mallory? Dating?" Dad looks at me with a furrowed brow.

"No, we're not dating." Technically, I'm telling the truth.

"Good. There's nothing against it in the company handbook, but you're an executive, so there are appearances to be considered. And Mallory's an outstanding employee. We don't want to lose her if things don't work out."

"What do you mean, if things don't work out? Why wouldn't they?"

Mom and Dad share a glance.

Dad smirks. "If you're not dating, what does it matter?"

My jaw clenches. "It doesn't," I mutter into my taco.

"Oh, Mike and Holly went to law school with Mallory's dad," Mom says. "Robert?"

"Yeah! I remember him. Very serious." Dad shakes his head. "Crazy how connected we all are."

"Hmm," I say around a bite of my third taco. My best strategy will be to keep my mouth full of food so I can't say anything.

My parents chat about Mallory's uncle's tree farm and how Dad will put the lights on their tree tomorrow, but we won't decorate it until Kennie comes home on Wednesday.

Finishing my fourth taco, I rise from the table and grab my plate. "Dinner was delicious, Mom. Thank you. I need to do laundry and handle some email, so going back to my place." I rinse my plate and put my beer bottle in the recycling bin. "Have a great night," I call to my parents as I let myself out the patio door.

Laughter reaches me as I pull the door closed. I know my parents know I'm trying to avoid discussing Mallory. They aren't stupid, but there's nothing to discuss yet.

Entering my home, I consider what Dad said. I know Dad likes Mallory a lot. Any reservations about us being together aren't personal. If my father and uncle are her bosses, and they like her and appreciate her work, then I don't see how us being together would impact her career. It shouldn't matter. We don't really work together. I have nothing to do with her job. Hopefully, spending time together will show her it doesn't matter and there's no reason to hide things.

I can't wait for us to hang out with Logan and Daphne tomorrow night. I think the more we hang out with an established couple, the more Mallory will see we can have the same thing and relent on just being friends with benefits. If we ever get to the benefits. I'm okay being patient, but it's like the universe is conspiring against us.

20

MALLORY

WHY DO THINGS KEEP GOING WRONG FOR US? JUST ONCE, OKAY, AT LEAST once, I'd like to have sex with Liam and be able to bask in the afterglow. Or at least not have someone a few feet away, waiting for a break in the action to talk to me. I thought it was embarrassing with Ashley in Vegas. It's a billion times worse with my mother in my house. Ashley never changed my diaper, and we won't wear matching pajamas on Christmas morning.

I'm making a cup of full-strength black tea. May as well add some caffeine to the situation. My phone dings to indicate a text, and I pick it up, hoping it's Liam. It's not.

> Mom: Leaving the tree farm now.

> Me: Okay. Want me to start anything for dinner?

> Mom: Raided the concession stand.
> Supposed to rain tomorrow.

It is? That will kill the plan to hang out there tomorrow night. I hope Mom's wrong. I'm excited about tomorrow now, looking forward to wandering the farm with Liam in the moonlight.

I wonder if he has plans for New Year's. He's probably going to a club or a casino. Hanging out in the woods around a fire, getting drunk among the unsold Christmas trees couldn't compete.

> Me: Sounds good.

> Mom: I snagged enough for your…friend.

Groaning, I tilt my head back and gaze up at the ceiling. She's not going to ignore this. I didn't really expect her to, but it is the season for miracles and everything.

> Me: Hope you're hungry because it's just me.

> Mom: Oh. See you soon.

A few minutes later, the headlights of my parents' SUV bounce down the driveway. I wish they would've let me know they were coming earlier so I could have made sure everything was just right. It's only me living here full-time, and I'm neat, but Mom can be so particular about things. She likes the glasses lined up just so in the cabinet and the condiments in a certain order in the refrigerator door. I guess it's the engineer part of her brain that likes perfect order. I'm not an engineer.

"There's my Mallomar!" Dad calls out as he and Mom enter the house carrying bags of treats. I can smell the greasy goodness of chicken fingers, mozzarella sticks, and French fries. I pull out the ingredients for a basic salad in hopes of counteracting all the cholesterol we're about to ingest.

Dad sniffs the air as he enters the kitchen. "Why does it smell like a wet cat in here?"

My parents laugh when they see my expression. I don't know exactly how I look, but I'm assuming it's a combination of wide eyes, slack jaw and either pale from blood draining or bright red from blushing. I may be cycling between the two for all I know.

"Just kidding. Your mother told me. Where is he?"

"He left. We are not in a 'meet the parents' kind of relationship. It's just casual." I hate having to say that to my parents. Not that I have any reason to be ashamed of being a sexually active grown woman. But just like I don't want to know about their sex life, I don't want them knowing about mine.

I dump the salad mix in a bowl with a sliced onion, cherry tomatoes, and jalapeño slices. It's basic, but it's not fried, so that's a win. While Mom unpacks all the food, Dad grabs dishes, glasses, and silverware. I dish up salad for each of us and grab the bottle of Italian dressing out of the fridge. We sit in companionable silence, eating for a few minutes. I enjoy it while it lasts because I know the interrogation is coming.

Three...two...one.

"So, Mallory, tell us about your friend," Mom says.

"No," I answer.

Mom sighs the sigh mothers are gifted after going through the pain of labor. I guess it's like compensation.

I can feel myself weakening. Be strong, Mallory. There's no reason for them to know about any of this. There's no relationship, and there's no future.

"There's nothing to tell. It's casual." I finish my chicken finger and get up to rinse my plate and put it in the dishwasher. I grab my glass of Diet Pepsi from dinner and nod to my parents. "Welcome home. I'm going upstairs to read. See you tomorrow." I turn before they can say anything else. Or before I cry. It's no longer as easy to say there's nothing between me and Liam, that it's only casual. It's starting to feel like a lie.

21

LIAM

I FIRE UP MY LAPTOP WHEN I GET BACK TO MY PLACE. YEAH, MY PLAN WAS TO spend my Saturday night working, but for a moment, I had a much better offer with Mallory that beat any plans I had. Fucking hell. Clicking through my email, I see one that commands my attention. I'm dialing my dad as I finish reading it.

"Dad, can you come out here? I have news on the pier deal."

"On my way." I hear him call out to Mom as he hangs up.

A minute later, the door opens, and Dad comes in, carrying his coffee mug. "What's up?"

He sits on the stool next to mine at the breakfast bar, and I slide my laptop in front of him so he can read the email I received.

"Wow," he says. "I thought it would be about six months before they were ready."

"Yeah, I know. I guess they decided they were done. What do you think?"

The deal we are considering is buying a pier on the Atlantic City Boardwalk. Currently it's a mostly vacant shopping mall in need of updating. It's a great location, right across from Devil's Den, the casino Teagan owns.

Sipping his coffee, Dad looks at the email. "Are Teagan and Jake ready?"

Picking up my phone and dial. "Yeah, but let me get them on the line."

"Call your uncle too," Dad advises.

"Hey, you're conferenced in and on speaker. My Dad is here," I tell them when they each answer their phone.

"Hi, Liam, what's up?" Jake must've been on the casino floor because I hear the *ding-ding-ding* of slot machines fading as he probably enters a hallway behind the scenes.

"Got an email from the real estate agent. They're ready to sell Sand Dollar Pier now and are offering to us first. Price is right where we want, and buying now stops another six months of neglect. You guys still in?"

"Hell yeah!" Teagan yells.

"Absolutely," Jake affirms.

I look at Dad.

"Mike, what do you think?" Dad asks.

"You're the businessman, Will, but I think you'd be stupid to pass up this opportunity." Uncle Mike clears his throat. "Of course, all of this depends on inspections and our due diligence going as expected, but based on what we've done already, I don't foresee any issues."

"You've covered your ass well, Mike. Your lawyerly duty is done," Dad says, his blue eyes twinkling with his laughter. "We're buying a pier!" he calls out, raising his arms like he just scored the winning goal.

We all cheer and discuss the next steps. Morgan Development is purchasing the pier, but it'll become a joint venture with Devil's Den and Penhall Enterprises. I email the agent with our intent to purchase, and the information needed to start the process of contracts and inspections.

Wow! I've just taken the first step of my future. I hope it'll lead me right to where I want to be—working for myself, coaching, and if

I can ever woo her in the right direction, in a relationship with Mallory Carter.

Dad stands to leave. "Well, I'm going back up to the house. Congratulations, guys. I'm excited to be working with you."

"This speeds up our timeline," Teagan says. "Do we want to submit our franchise application now?"

This is it. We're finally doing it. This pier will provide the home arena for a team in the very first Paranormal Hockey League. I pump my fist in the air. Finally, shifter players like me and Trevor will have opportunities to play after college. I can't believe I'm finally getting my dream.

"Absolutely," Jake states firmly. "Get in as an inaugural team and have a say in how the league is run. We can't pass up on an opportunity like that."

"Listen to you, making managerial decisions already," I tease Jake.

"Okay." Teagan types on her laptop. "This is really happening. Our franchise application has been ready to go. We just needed word on the pier. We have Boardwalk Hall as a backup plan if the pier falls through, but I trust all will go well."

We spend another hour discussing our plans and what we need to do to implement them. My brain is buzzing with everything on the horizon. I always knew a career playing professionally wasn't an option for me since I was a shifter, but I was hoping to work for an NHL team behind the scenes as a coach or in the front office. After the accident derailed my college playing career, I sidelined those dreams.

Now I have a chance to achieve not only my dream but to help others achieve their dreams of playing professional hockey. It's heady stuff.

I want to call Mallory and tell her about all of this, but until we're under contract for the pier and our franchise application is approved, there's nothing to tell. Anyway, according to her, we're just friends with benefits. Our plans for the future, our dreams, don't factor into it.

According to her. According to me, she's part of my plans for the future, part of my dreams. She just doesn't know it yet.

22

MALLORY

Sunday morning arrives with a deluge of rain outside my window. The tree farm will be closed, so there goes our plans to hang out there tonight. I was hoping Uncle Zack's instinct was off when he sent home food with my parents, but, as always, he's spot-on with the weather. That's a handy trait for a farmer, I suppose.

Daphne and I are supposed to go shopping today, but I'm not feeling it. The mall is going to be packed with holiday shoppers, and it's too rainy to do the outlet center. According to my closet, I don't need to go shopping. I don't want to bail on her though. My phone dings, and I pick it up from the nightstand. It's Daphne.

> Daphne: How much would you hate me if I said I didn't feel like shopping today?

> Me: I wouldn't hate you at all. My closet is telling me I've shopped enough. LOL.

> Daphne: It's icky, and the mall will be so full of people.

> Me: Did you want to do something else?

Daphne: The guys are going to be watching football, so the moms were going to have a craft day making ornaments and drinking wine. That sounds fun...

It does sound like fun, and I know Daphne misses having her mom to do things with and having a family for the holidays, so she needs to do this. But I can't ditch my mom to go hang out with them, and I don't want to bring her along. Yeah, I can imagine the introductions. "Mom, you know that guy I was in the shower with yesterday? This is his mom."

That wouldn't be awkward at all.

I know reading minds isn't a wolf shifter trait, but I swear Mom has it anyway when she taps on my door.

"Mallory, are you awake?"

I shoot Daphne a quick "brb" so she knows I'm not ignoring her.

"Yeah, Mom, come in."

My door opens, and Mom enters wearing capri leggings and a T-shirt, her straight brown hair in a ponytail. She looks healthy and cute. Mom rarely dresses this casually. When she works out, she showers immediately and gets dressed in her clothes for the day. She somehow looks formal in jeans and a sweater. I like this look on her.

"Good morning. Did you want waffles for breakfast?"

"Yeah, that would be great! Thanks. I'll be right down."

"Okay. Oh, Mike Morris texted your father and invited him over to watch football with him and his family." Feeling my eyes widen at this information, I nod.

"Your father went to school with Mike and his wife Holly. I guess Holly ran into your Uncle Zack yesterday when she was getting her tree. I didn't realize you worked with him."

I want to tell her that's because she never asked for details about my job. Instead, I keep my mouth shut and nod again.

Mom mirrors my nod. "Holly's having a 'crafternoon' making Christmas ornaments and invited me. And you, of course. We won't go if it makes you uncomfortable." She schools her face to appear nonchalant, but her bright eyes betray her desire to go. She was so cute making air quotes around *crafternoon*. Mom is not an air quote type of woman.

Mom is typically introverted and doesn't spend a lot of time with women her age, as far as I know. Unless it's my aunts. Maybe she has friends in Florida. I hope she does, but I think spending time with Holly and Faith would be a treat for her.

"Yeah, that sounds fun."

"Are you sure?" she asks. "I don't want to make things awkward for you."

"It's fine. I like Holly and Faith, and my friend Daphne will be there too."

Swinging my legs out of bed, I scoop up my phone and text Daphne back.

> Me: Mike & Holly invited my PARENTS over for football and crafting.

> Daphne: Your parents are here? Since when?

> Me: Since yesterday evening.

> Daphne: So…we're crafting?

> Me: I'll pack my glue gun. :winky face emoji:

Daphne fills me in on the details of when and where everything is happening. I don't know how this thing with Liam has gone from no-strings-keep-it-to-ourselves to our parents meeting and everyone hanging out. Everything feels out of control, and I don't like it.

———

I take my car because I'm afraid this afternoon isn't going to go well, and I don't want to be trapped in a car with my parents or subject to their schedule. I really want to be confident that everything is going to be great and my parents won't embarrass me, but experience has taught me that their filters don't always fully engage, especially if I'm the topic of conversation.

When I was younger, I created a bingo card on some random website and would mark off the obnoxious things my parents said or did. Each bingo earned me a little treat, like new nail polish from Target. I had so many nail polishes I could have opened a nail salon. No boring French manicures for this girl. That drove Mom crazy. We'd go for mother/daughter manicures, and she and Valerie would get demure French manicures, and I'd get bright colors and fun nail art. Just another way I'd confuse and disappoint her.

I pull up in front of Mike's house. It feels weird to be socializing with my boss, but no way am I letting my parents loose unchaperoned. Grabbing the tray of chocolate-covered pretzels I picked up, I survey the cars to figure out who's there already. I see Logan's Jeep and Liam's truck. That's good. My parents pull up at the curb behind me. We'll walk in together. Damn. I was hoping to be able to talk to Liam alone before my parents arrived to make sure we have our story straight. I guess we're going to wing it and hope for the best. Dad's carrying a bottle of wine—they must've stopped at the liquor store on the way. I try to get a glimpse of the label to determine if it's something I like. Not that it matters. I bet I'm drinking whatever they're serving.

Mike opens the front door as we approach the porch. The house is a stately brick colonial, with candles in each window and lighted garlands wrapped around the pillars of the front porch. Normally I'm a fan of multicolored Christmas lights, but the white lights they're using complement the house perfectly.

"Welcome!" Mike says. "Come on in. You lucked out arriving between rain showers."

He leads us into the kitchen where Holly and Faith greet us.

Holly smiles warmly at Dad. "Robert! Great to see you again! I heard you had moved to Florida. How are you liking it down there?"

She hugs Mom as Dad tells her they love living among the theme parks they enjoy so much.

Faith hugs me as my parents become reacquainted with Mike and Holly.

"Daphne's gone with the guys to pick up pizzas. They should be right back," she tells me.

No sooner has she made that pronouncement when the door opens and Will, Liam, Logan, and Daphne come in bearing pizzas and subs. It did not take all four of them to make that run, especially since the pizza place they went to delivers.

The kitchen is suddenly Grand Central Station with the food being put on counters and my parents meeting first Will and Faith and then Logan and Daphne. The moment I've been dreading is now upon us.

"And this is our son, Liam," Will says. "He works with me at Morgan Development as Vice President of Operations."

Liam holds out his hand. "Nice to meet you, Mr. Carter, Mrs. Carter."

Dad shakes his hand first. "Have we met before? You seem familiar."

Kill me now.

Mom shakes his hand next. "Robert, hush. Nice to meet you, Liam. Please, call us Robert and Beth."

Liam smiles, nods, and turns to me. "Hey, Mallory."

"Hey, Liam," I respond.

We stand there awkwardly, looking at each other, unsure what to do next. What's the proper protocol for seeing each other after being caught in the shower by one set of parents and now spending the afternoon with All. The. Parents? Heck, we have parents who aren't even ours here to share in the awkwardness. Yay.

Daphne, bless her heart, comes to our rescue. "It's almost kickoff! You better get your food and settle in so you don't miss any of the game. Gotta watch the Eagles kick some ass." There's a bloodthirsty gleam in her eye.

I laugh. "You're like this about football too? I thought you were only a freak for hockey. You're so sweet until game time."

"Hockey is Daphne at her worst. Her football reactions are mild in comparison," Logan says, wrapping an arm around Daphne's shoulder and pressing a kiss to her temple. I sigh at the tenderness of the gesture. I wish I had something like that in my life. But I don't. And I'm not going to. My arrangement with Liam is for mutually satisfying hookups to keep my lady bits from getting cobwebs. It's not for temple kisses.

"What about baseball?" Mom asks. That's her favorite sport.

"I don't care about it that much unless Andy is playing," Daphne answers.

Mike and Holly explain that their son Andy is the star pitcher for his university's baseball team. He'll be graduating this spring and then joining Morgan Development as well.

The guys take their food and drinks and settle in the family room just as the coin flip is taking place. Daphne and I join the moms at the table in the breakfast area.

"Wine?" Holly offers.

Hell yes. I may end up sleeping it off in Holly's guest room, but I think wine is going to be how I survive this afternoon.

23
LIAM

WE SPREAD OUT AROUND THE FAMILY ROOM WATCHING THE GAME. LOGAN and I have claimed the loveseat, and Uncle Mike has his recliner, leaving Dad and Mr. Carter, um...Robert, on the couch. I chose the loveseat because it gives me a clear view of Mallory in the breakfast area between the family room and the kitchen. Her discomfort is clear in the tense set of her shoulders. I don't know if it's being here with my family or if it's because of her parents or something else. All I know is I want to make it better. I wish I could go over and massage the stiffness in her shoulders, press kisses against her neck, nibble her earlobe until she giggles. I'm willing to do anything to make her comfortable. Having her parents hanging out with my family is probably awkward as hell for her. I don't love it either. I don't know if they know for sure it was me naked in the shower with their daughter yesterday afternoon, but I'm assuming they do, based on the comment from Robert about me being familiar.

"So, Logan, what do you do?" Robert asks my cousin.

Logan lifts a finger to show he'll answer when he finishes chewing his bite of pizza. When he swallows, he says, "I'm a travel photographer."

Robert furrows his brow. "You just travel around and take pictures? You can make a living at that?"

Mike and Will exchange glances, but Logan only smiles. "Yep. I travel around and take pictures. I make a decent enough living at it. I've been published in several magazines and sell the images on different media. I'm also going to do photo tours, taking people to locations and helping them learn how to take quality images."

"Oh," Robert says, turning to Dad. "At least your son works in the family business."

Logan shakes with silent laughter next to me. Uncle Mike looks ready to shift into his golden eagle and peck out some Lycan eyeballs, but when he sees how unconcerned Logan is with Robert's ignorant comments, he relaxes.

Dad's wearing his CEO smile. The one that looks polite but really means he's going to eviscerate you. "I enjoy working with Liam. He's an asset to the company."

Robert nods. "My youngest is in law school. It's nice that at least one of my children is following me into the legal field."

What the hell?

"Mallory's in the legal field," I say.

"She's not an attorney. She's just a secretary."

Just a secretary? There's not a damn thing wrong with being a secretary, but Mallory isn't one, and it's ridiculous her father can so casually dismiss her. Dad stares at me, silently commanding me to hold my temper. Aunt Holly would be pissed if we got blood on her furniture.

I glance toward the kitchen to see if the ladies have noticed our conversation. Mallory's cheeks are flushed, and by the quick glance she shoots our way, she's either heard the conversation or experienced this kind of bullshit often enough to know what's going on.

Uncle Mike, the diplomat of our group, diffuses the situation. "Mallory is an excellent paralegal. She's a key component of our legal team. You must be very proud of her."

Robert must realize he can't say anything more on the subject without making it obvious he's not proud of Mallory and her career, so he shuts up. Good. What an asshole. He keeps his mouth shut for the rest of the first half except for discussing football. At halftime, we go back into the kitchen to grab more food and refresh our drinks.

The ladies are chatting and working on their ornaments. Logan whispers something in Daphne's ear that makes her blush. Mallory's seemingly focused on spreading glue on a piece of felt. More focus than the task entails. I tune into the conversation in time to hear her mother take her turn being an asshole.

"My eldest has two little boys. They should start shifting in a few years, thank goodness." She makes the sign of the cross either in gratitude to a higher power or to ward off the curse of being a non-shifter. Maybe both.

"Both of your kids shift, Holly?" Beth asks.

"Yeah. Logan is a golden eagle shifter like Mike, and Andy is a cougar shifter like me," Aunt Molly answers.

"And Liam and Kendall are both cougar shifters, Faith?"

What's with all the shifter talk?

"Yeah, they take after Will," Mom answers.

"You don't shift?" Beth asks.

"Nope," Mom says, popping the P. She's getting annoyed.

"Neither does Mallory, the only one of our kids not to. She's not prey-driven like them. That's probably why she isn't that ambitious." Beth takes another sip of wine. She must be drunk. Please let her be drunk and not like this all the time.

I look around the room. Everyone's gobsmacked. Robert's filling his plate, oblivious to the bullshit his wife is spouting. They're perfect for each other.

"She's always been the runt of the litter," Beth says with a giggle. "If she ever gets married and has kids, if they shift, she won't understand. How did you handle it, Faith?"

How the hell did Mallory and Trevor end up so normal? This is crazy. Mom is just staring at her. Aunt Holly looks like she's ready to shift and cut a bitch. Daphne is near tears.

Mallory laughs and holds out her wineglass for Mom to refill. She's obviously heard this countless times. She's trying to act like this isn't affecting her, but it's like Mallory's getting smaller and smaller right before my eyes with each comment out of her mother's mouth. The words are chiseling off little chunks of her. She's sitting tall and proud like this doesn't mean anything, but her shoulders are even tighter than before. Her hand is trembling ever so slightly as she raises her glass to take a sip of the wine she has a hard time swallowing.

I want to defend her and pull her into a hug to tell her how wonderful she is, but she raises her eyes to meet mine and gives the slightest shake of her head, telling me to stand down. I'll do it. This time. Because she's asked me to. But this isn't okay. People don't get to treat Mallory like this and get away with it.

"Hey, Daph," Logan cuts in, "didn't you want to show Mallory that thing upstairs?"

Daphne nods slowly. "Yeah, I did."

She reaches out to take Mallory's hand. The one not holding the wine glass.

Mallory drains her glass in two gulps, puts it back on the table, and stands up to go with Daphne to see the thing.

"Coming with us, Liam?" Logan asks.

There must've been some silent communication happening among our parents, and we're supposed to skedaddle. I'm good with that.

"Sure am," I say, taking up the rear of our group going up the back stairs.

I assume we're headed to Logan's old room. Maybe we're being slick and going down the front stairs and leaving out the front door? I'm all for getting the hell out of here.

Logan's room it is. Daphne leads Mallory over to sit on the navy-blue comforter on Logan's old bed. Logan leans against his closed door with his arms crossed over his chest. I take the chair at the desk and move it over to the bed. I need to be near Mallory.

"Are you okay?" Daph asks softly, still holding Mallory's hand.

"I'm fine," she assures us. "I'm used to this. Well, doing this in front of my employer is a new twist, but this is what I've heard all my life. It is what it is."

"What it is, is bullshit," I say. "What the fuck is wrong with them?"

"Liam."

"Why do you care about their opinions so much? They don't care about you."

Mallory's suddenly too-wide eyes and Daphne's sharp intake of breath clue me in that I probably shouldn't have said that. Too bad. It's true. You don't treat your own child, or anyone you care about and respect, the way they are treating her.

"Liam! They're my parents. Of course they care about me." Mallory's shoulders slump as she lets out a weary sigh. "I know they aren't like your parents, but they're who I have."

Mallory looks to Daphne for support, like it's better to have those asshats as parents than to be an orphan like Daphne is.

"I don't know what to say, Mallory. I miss my parents every day, but our relationship wasn't like yours."

"They are who they are. They're old-school shifters. I just ignore them and move on."

I reach out and take her other hand, giving it a gentle squeeze. "You weren't ignoring them, though. I could see you shrinking with the blow of every word she let loose. I hated seeing you like that. You're wonderful, and you deserve to be treated like the treasure you are." I press a kiss to the crown of her head as she sucks in a shuddering breath. My heart constricts at the sound. I want to protect her from anything that hurts her or makes her sad. I'm falling for her. I wish she was falling for me.

Daphne watches us with wide eyes. I think we just confirmed what she was hoping for. She's going to be so disappointed when she finds out we aren't dating. We're just sleeping together. Well, trying to sleep together.

Mallory squeezes my hand and looks up at me. Her normally bright green eyes are more like a pine forest in fog now. It kills me to see her like this and feel powerless to make it better. Taking a deep breath, like she's centering herself, she musters a smile and turns to Logan.

"What are we going to say you showed me up here?" Mallory asks. "Mom is probably going to be curious, and I want to have an answer handy."

"Oh, yeah," Logan looks around his room. He hasn't really lived here for a couple years, although he crashed here when he was in the country between assignments. Once he and Daphne became a couple, he moved in with her full-time.

Mallory looks at the framed photos on the wall above the desk. "What's that one?" She asks, pointing to a castle.

"It's Inverness Castle in Scotland," Logan says.

"Let's go with that. I'm Scottish on Mom's side of the family."

"That explains where the red hair comes from," I say teasingly.

Mallory sticks her tongue out at me. If she can tease me back, then she's doing all right. Some of the tension leaves my body. We can go back downstairs, and I can make it through the rest of the game without going ballistic. If Mallory is okay, I'm okay.

Logan and I go downstairs first, Daphne and Mallory trailing behind, talking. I assume Daphne asks what's going on between us because I hear Mallory answer that we're just friends.

My cougar stirs restlessly at that. He apparently has decided Mallory Carter is his mate and his to protect. Down, cat. We need to be patient. He growls in protest, and there's a rumble in my chest. Logan looks at me with raised eyebrows. I shake my head. Now is not the time to share that Mallory Carter is my mate. I can see our future so clearly, including more afternoons like this with my family. Thank goodness her parents live in Florida. We should only have to put up with them infrequently. Date nights with Logan and Daphne. Nights at her home, making use of that bed. In time, we could get married and start having kids. I don't care if they shift or not—I would love them because they come from me and Mallory.

I can see it all so clearly. If only Mallory would consider it and see it too. Maybe since she doesn't shift, she doesn't feel the mating call the same way I do, but how can she not feel the connection we have as a man and a woman? We've had it from the moment our eyes met across the club in Vegas. Hell, considering all the connections we have and how many of our orbits overlap, it truly is fate. We would've met eventually if we hadn't met in Vegas.

I'm grateful now we met in Vegas first and could connect without all the baggage Mallory insists on carrying. Maybe I can't convince her we're fated mates in the shifter sense, but she'd have to be purposely blind to not see the hand fate has played in our being together now and how right it is.

The second half of the game passes amazingly well. Mallory's parents stop with the snarky comments and are polite guests. I'm assuming something was said while we were upstairs. Hopefully we'll get the scoop later. Robert and Beth leave in a flurry of hugs, handshakes, and "we should do this again" proclamations.

Yeah. No.

As soon as her parents pull away from the curb, Mom and Aunt Holly hug Mallory and reassure her she's smart and beautiful and her parents love her. I want in on it, but Daphne is the lucky one chosen to be included.

"Did you read them the riot act?" Logan asks his dad.

"Gently," Uncle Mike says.

The group hug has broken up, and the ladies are fixing themselves mugs of tea.

"Your mother hasn't changed since I first met her in law school when she was dating your father, Mallory," Aunt Holly says.

"Believe it or not, she's mellowed a bit," Mallory says.

That's her mom mellow? Wow!

"I know they love me in their way. But they don't understand me. I'm nothing like my sister Valerie."

"Wait, you're a twin?" Daphne asks.

"No, why? Oh, the matching names!" Mallory shakes her head and laughs. "Mom just picked Mallory at random. I don't think she ever said it out loud to realize it rhymes with Valerie."

She lifts her teacup and blows on it to cool down the tea. The steam rises, framing her face in its curly tendrils.

"Funny story time," she says. "My brother Ethan is eighteen months older than Valerie, so my parents had two kids under two. Mom didn't bounce back as quickly after Valerie's birth as she did after Ethan's, but figured that was normal because two kids are four times as much work. Plus, she was working and all that stuff."

Mom and Aunt Holly nod. They must remember what it was like when we were little.

"After four months, Dad convinced Mom to see the doctor because he's worried about her. She's exhausted, irritable, not losing the baby weight like she did with Ethan, and it's bothering her. So, Mom goes to the doctor and surprise! She's three months pregnant with me."

The moms gasp, and the dads are doing their best to not hear anything. If they could put their fingers in their ears and go "la la la," I think they would. Not that it would help. They have excellent shifter hearing.

"Mom is insisting that can't be true because she and Dad haven't done anything. She's been too tired. To be honest, I think that was Dad's biggest concern." Mallory laughs. "Turns out they were both so exhausted they didn't remember the one time they slept together after Valerie was born."

The room is silent. No one knows what to say to that.

"She was three months pregnant and didn't know?" Daphne asks. "Aren't shifters supposed to be especially in tune to all that stuff?"

Everyone turns to look at Aunt Holly since she's the only one here who would know.

"Don't look at me! I spaced my kids out, so I was awake for all of it!"

Logan groans.

Mallory shrugs. "I'm not a shifter, and I've never been pregnant, but I guess they were so tired and overwhelmed they just didn't notice?"

"So, your sister is less than a year older than you? Were you in the same grade?" Daphne asks.

"No, Valerie was a year ahead of me in school because of how our birthdays fell. However, since our names rhymed and we were so close in age, many people assumed we were twins, and I was the dumb one held back a year. I've always been smaller and not as fast or as strong as Valerie, so it was like I was the lesser twin and not the younger sister." Her lips twist in a wry smile. "You know how clueless people can be."

Mom puts down her mug of tea with a clunk. "Okay, I'm just saying what everyone is thinking. What the ever-loving hell? Are your parents stupid?"

We all laugh. Mom is a tiny blonde and the sweetest woman I've ever known, but she's from South Philly, and sometimes it shows.

"Not generally, but I guess parenthood sucked out their brain cells?" Mallory says. "It's amazing I have any self-esteem at all with that origin story."

I want to tell her she's amazing, but this isn't the place for it. I will tell her one day. She deserves to hear it, and I want to be the one to tell her. One day. Every day. Forever.

24

MALLORY

Since the football game on Sunday, I haven't seen Liam all week. He hasn't been in the office, and in the few texts we've shared, he's only said he's been busy with something for work, but he'd see me at the party. Not that I care. He can do what he wants. It doesn't matter to me. I only wondered because we need to figure out a time to hook up. My parents are here through the new year, so my house is out. Liam lives in his parents' pool house, so I'm not crazy about that either. I guess we could wait until after my parents leave, but that's almost two weeks, and since I didn't have any satisfaction after our shower, I'm brimming with unfulfilled lust. That's what it is—lust. Not feelings or longing or loneliness. It's pure horniness.

The office Christmas party is brunch held at a local country club. It's the Friday before Christmas, and after giving the valet my keys, I approach the door of the club. Nervously, I tug on the hem of my sweater. I've seen other folks wearing their ugly sweaters, but I worry my sweater is exceptionally ugly. Oh well, I love it.

"I'll take your coat, miss," the coat check clerk offers. Smiling at her, I remove my green wool peacoat and hand it to her.

"Wow! I love your sweater!" Her eyes have gone as wide as her smile.

"Thanks," I say, taking the claim ticket. "I hope I don't ruin anyone's appetite."

I'm wearing a black knee-length pencil skirt and a white blouse under my sweater, so if I've really missed the mark, I can take off the sweater and still look presentable. Taking a deep breath, I approach the dining room. Will, Mike, and their spouses are near the threshold, along with other members of the senior staff. I don't see Liam—not that I was looking for him.

Faith spots me first and gives a squeal of excitement.

"Oh my goodness, Mallory, look at you! Where did you get your sweater?"

Her exclamation has caused others to turn my way. I rock uncomfortably on my black heels.

"My Nana knit it for me. She made sweaters for all the grandkids to wear for Christmas, and this is mine."

"Holly, check this out! Holly knits, but I don't think she's ever done anything like this," Faith says.

Holly runs over, mimosa in hand. "Wow, that's incredible! Turn around, Mallory."

I do a slow turn, feeling self-conscious.

"The detail is incredible! May I?" Molly reaches out a hand as if to pet my sweater.

I nod.

She gently strokes my arm. "I love how there's Fun Fur and actual googly eyes sewn on. She's captured Gritty perfectly!"

Yes, I'm wearing a handmade Gritty ugly Christmas sweater for my company's holiday brunch. Nana found just the right shade of Flyers' orange yarn at her favorite shop and knit me a Gritty-themed sweater, complete with orange Fun Fur for his face and the bottom of the sleeves. She even added plastic googly eyes that shake and wobble with every move I make. The saving grace is that the eyes aren't where my nipples are. That would be a bridge too far, even for me. It's hideous, but I love it, and my Nana is the best Nana in the whole wide world.

More people have wandered over to check out my sweater. It has its admirers, and, for some, the ridiculousness is the attraction. I feel awkward being the center of attention like this. I knew Gritty would get a reaction, but nothing like this.

"You and Liam will have to pose together, and we'll tag Gritty and the Flyers when we post it on the company's social media," Daphne says, handing me a much-needed mimosa of my own and giving me a hug.

"What? Why?" I ask. This is a work function, not the senior prom. Liam and I do not need to pose for pictures together.

"Logan, check out Mallory's sweater!" Daphne calls, looking over my shoulder and waving someone over.

"Hey, Mallory." Logan leans in to kiss my cheek.

"Wow! That's incredible. Puts my light-up cactus sweater to shame," he says with a laugh.

Liam joins us. Oh no. He's wearing a Flyers sweater too. His sweater straddles the line between gaudy and classic, unlike mine that never saw the classic line as it zoomed straight to gaudyville. It's orange and black, the Flyers team colors, just like mine, but where I'm Fun Fur and googly eyes, he's intricate stitching marrying a classic Nordic snowflake design with the stylized "P" of the Flyers' logo. It spans his broad shoulders, and the hem falls at his narrow waist, accentuating his athletic build. He's rolled the cuffs of his black button-down dress shirt over the pulled-up sleeves of his sweater, like he's a freaking male model. I wonder how absorbent the yarn Nana used is because I'm fairly certain I'm drooling.

"Great sweater! I can't believe we coordinate. That's crazy." Liam gives me a one-armed hug in greeting. His hand lingers at my waist and gives a slight squeeze. The heat in his eyes as he gazes down at me makes my breath catch. That is not a "nice sweater, coworker" look; it's a "I want to strip you naked and do sexy, naughty things with you" look. I glance around to see if anyone noticed, but every-one's hugging each other, so it's unremarkable.

"Too crazy," I agree. I think his sweater was knit from magical unicorn fur full of pheromones because all I want to do is drag this man to the coat closet, rip his sweater off him, and have my way with him.

"Our table is over here," Daphne says, grabbing my arm and leading me to a table close to the bank of windows overlooking the golf course. I'm seated between Daphne and Liam. Logan's on Daphne's other side. Miller joins us, as does our coworker Ben, intro-ducing me to his lovely wife, Heather.

"Another hockey fan!" Ben says, checking out my sweater. "I knew I liked you."

Laughing, I reply, "What's not to love?"

"Do you play or just watch?" Ben asks. I'm surprised. No one ever asks if I play.

"I played some when I was younger, but just with my siblings, not on a team. My younger brother did travel hockey when he was a kid. How about you?"

Ben inclines his head toward Liam. "I played with this guy when we were younger. Now I help coach our twins' pee-wee team. Here. Check 'em out." Ben takes out his phone and shows me his lock screen. Pictured are two little blond-haired cherubs decked out in hockey gear. The little boy is smiling hugely, cheesing it up for the camera. The little girl is looking fiercely at the camera with her braids falling over her shoulders.

"That's Asher and Emma. They're in kindergarten. Emma plays defense, and Asher is the leading scorer." Ben's voice swells with pride.

I feel the sappy smile spread across my face, looking at them. "Aww...they're adorable! Emma looks fierce!"

Heather laughs. "She is! She's a bruiser. She'd be checking everyone into the boards if contact was allowed. She's fearless."

"I didn't know there was a rink around here," Daphne says.

"There isn't," Heather replies. "We drive to Voorhees for practice and games. It's a shame. If they could get more ice time, it would help with their skills a lot. The kids that live closer have an advantage."

"I have a synthetic rink at my house that almost no one uses. Maybe over Christmas break, you could bring them over and let them skate and shoot. It's in a converted barn. My parents set it up when we were younger so Trevor could practice."

"It's a great surface," Liam says. "Not as fast as ice, but great for drills or rec skating."

"You're skating again? Man, that's great!" Ben says with a huge smile. "Maybe you and I can pass the puck sometime."

"That would be great," I say. "My younger brother is home from law school. I bet he'd love to skate some drills with you guys. And my nephews will be here for Christmas. They're six and eight. They could skate with Asher and Emma."

I exchange numbers with Heather so we can figure out a plan to get everyone together.

"Thanks so much, Mallory. I tried to convince them to play basketball like I did so they only needed a ball and some sneakers, but no, they want to play hockey like their daddy."

I laugh. "My eldest brother played baseball, my sister swam and played lacrosse, and Trevor played hockey. It absolutely thrilled my parents that I ran cross-country, so they only needed to keep me in sneakers and send me outside. I love to run through the woods near my house."

Miller looks at me. "I didn't realize you were a runner. I did cross-country too. Do you do any races?"

"I haven't raced since college. I just run for stress relief now. I usually set my watch for an hour and just run. Normally four or five miles a few times a week." I take a sip of water. "I run outside when I can. Otherwise, I'm on the treadmill."

Servers approach the tables to take our brunch orders. I get cinnamon swirl pancakes with a side of ham. Liam gets steak and eggs. They leave carafes of mimosas, orange juice, and water on the table. As the servers retreat, Will stands at the front of the room with Mike and Holly. I forget Will and Holly are siblings and that she's most likely a partner in Morgan Development, even though she's not involved in the day-to-day operations.

"Thank you, everyone, for joining us today. It's been an exciting year with some things ending, but there are other, more exciting things coming in the new year." Will looks out over the room fondly. "Liam, please come up here and join us."

"Excuse me," Liam murmurs, pushing back his chair and rising. He joins his father, aunt, and uncle.

Servers swarm the dining room with trays of champagne flutes. The four at the front each take a flute, as does everyone at the tables.

"One of the exciting things coming in the new year is the development of a new property. Morgan Development has gone under contract to purchase the Sand Dollar Pier in Atlantic City, and we will redevelop it as a combination retail and entertainment property. Liam will spearhead the project. We're excited to continue to change and improve the landscape of Atlantic City."

Will raises his flute, and we all follow suit. "To Morgan Development, and to all of you. May this coming year be the best yet."

The sound of glasses clinking tinkles across the room. I take a sip of the champagne and try to collect my thoughts. Wow. A new project, and Liam is in charge. Does that mean he won't be traveling as much? Is his role in the company changing? We haven't spoken much this week because he's been busy. I guess he was busy with this deal.

Daphne leans in. "Did you know about this?"

"I had no idea. Did you?"

"Nope. Neither did Logan."

Liam rejoins us.

Ben holds out his flute in a toasting gesture, and they clink glasses. "Congratulations, man. Sounds like a cool project."

"Thanks. It's exciting. I'm glad I don't have to keep it a secret anymore." He glances at me quickly. "We need to finish our inspections, but if everything goes as we expect it to, it'll be a game changer for the region."

I wonder if it's going to be a game-changer for us too. I want to invite Liam over and find out more, cash in on some of those benefits, but the rest of my family is arriving this weekend, and the house will be packed—I barely hold back my snort-laugh at my pun—until after New Year's. I won't get any alone time with Liam that way, and definitely won't get to find out more about his new project. If the game's changing, it's becoming a marathon instead of a sprint.

25
LIAM

THE INSPECTIONS ON THE PIER HAVE BEEN GOING SMOOTHLY, BUT BETWEEN them and the holidays, I haven't been in the office and haven't seen Mallory since the party last week. We've been texting, but it's not enough. I want to see her, hold her, kiss her. Just be near her.

I'm in the office today, the Friday after Christmas, but Mallory isn't here. Daphne's here, and she's roped Logan into helping her pack up the files that Mallory's closed so we can take them to storage. We have file clerks that can help with that, but this way, Daphne and Logan can be together. They'll probably be able to make out in the file room like I long to do with Mallory.

I have my choice of desks to work from since we aren't fully staffed over the holidays, so I choose Mallory's desk. If I can't be with her, at least I can be in her space. Wow, creepy much, Liam? I scoop up my phone when it vibrates on the desk, hoping it's Mallory. It's a Carter, but not the one I was hoping for. I open the text thread with Logan and Trevor.

Trevor: Hey, hope Christmas was good. Did you want to come skate? Lory mentioned a friend of yours had kids who could skate with my nephews. I'm good either Saturday or Sunday, whatever works for everyone.

Me: Yeah, Christmas was good. I'd love to skate, no plans. Want me to check with Ben?

Trevor: Yeah.

Logan: Hey Trev, I'm up to skate. Let me know when.

I pop out of Mallory's office and walk over to Ben's desk. Smiling, I take in the pictures of his family and children's drawings that decorate his space. I want that. A crayon drawing with "I love you, Daddy" in childish printing is more precious than the Monet my parents have in their home.

We arrange to skate tomorrow afternoon, and I return to Mallory's desk. Hopefully, she'll be there too. Maybe skate with us. I spend the rest of the day trying to concentrate but eventually give up. All I smell is Mallory, and it causes my mind to wander and my dick to harden. Neither is conducive to a productive afternoon at the office, so I pack up and go home.

Back at my place the next day, after skating with Mallory's family and Ben's kids, I plop on my couch with a groan. Yeah, it was nice meeting her older brother and skating, but I really went there hoping for some time with Mallory. I was kind of hoping she'd skate with us. I'd love to see her stick handling. Not gonna lie, I was hoping she'd handle *my* stick.

Sighing, I start a FaceTime call with Jake and Teagan. From the looks of it, Teagan is in her penthouse apartment at Devil's Den.

From the background noise and activity behind him, Jake is at his parents' house.

"Hi. Is this a bad time?" I ask.

"I'm good," Teagan says. "I'll be going down to the security booth to watch things for a while, but I have time now."

"Let me find someplace to hide from the mob," Jake says. "We're doing Feast of the Seven Fishes tonight since we couldn't get everyone together on Christmas Eve. It's a madhouse here."

In the background, I hear his sisters and mother shouting at each other. They aren't fighting; they're just loud. Very loud. I've always felt bad for his dad. He's human. At least Jake could shift and fly away. I never understood how quiet Mr. Whitman could handle the loud and wacky Mrs. Whitman, but their six kids show they're compatible in at least some ways.

"Okay, what's up?" Jake says, clicking on a light and pulling a door shut.

"Jake, are you in a closet?" Teagan asks.

"Only place I can be alone, but they'll find me eventually, so make it quick."

"Right," I say. "I want to keep the rink open year-round. Have it open for pee-wee and junior hockey leagues, host tournaments, sponsor kids' teams, available for rec leagues. Maybe get ice hockey in the high schools. We can have figure skaters too. We can do open skates and have private parties, as well. I think we can support a rink full-time."

"I'm good with that," Jake says.

"Me too," Teagan adds. "And we can bring in touring ice shows or maybe have an ice show in residence like they do in Vegas. They're good family entertainment, or we can cater to an adult crowd, maybe have two shows. That's what you called about? Could've been an email."

Ouch.

"You're both invited to spend New Year's Eve at Full Moon Farm. Mallory's uncle owns it, and they end the season with a New Year's

Eve party. They have fire pits and igloos to hang out in if you want to be outside, and they have the barn at the Carters'."

"Um...I have a whole casino to party in. Why would I want to be out in the woods in the cold and dark?" Tegan asks.

"What she said. Is this just to get you laid? I didn't realize you still needed me to be your wingman," Jake says.

"Fuck you both. You're invited. Attend or not. I don't care. You can party at the casino any time. But whatever."

"Chill out, Liam. I'm just teasing you," Tegan says. "Is it a party or a hangout? Who do I RSVP to?"

"It's a hangout. It's Mallory's siblings, Logan, Daphne, maybe some of the Carter cousins. Low-key. If you're going, tell me, and I'll tell them."

"Give me Mallory's cell, and I'll let her know, see if I can bring anything."

"You don't need to bring anything, Teagan, and you don't need her number," I say.

"What are you afraid of, Liam?" Jake asks. Asshole.

"I'm not afraid of anything. I don't want to be rude and give out her number without her permission."

"Oh, never mind. I have it from the Flyers' game," Teagan says.

Shit.

"Teag, please don't make it awkward."

Jake snorts. "Pretty sure that ship has sailed, dude."

"Well, I'm going for sure. Liam has a crush. No way am I missing this," Teagan teases.

Groaning, I close my eyes. Why do I bother? Why can't I have normal best friends?

"I'm going too," Jake says. "Text us the address."

Pounding and muffled yelling carries across the call.

"Tell Ma I'll be right there!" Jake yells back. "I gotta go. Send the address."

It's only me and Teagan left on the line.

"Are you okay, Liam?" she asks.

"Yeah, I'm fine."

"You know you can talk to me, right? I may tease you, but I'll always listen."

I know that. It's why we've been best friends all these years.

I sigh, then say, "I know. Thank you. Nothing really to talk about now."

"Okay. But when there is, I'm here for you."

"Yeah. Same."

"Thanks, but I'm good the way I am. No attachments. My casino and our team are all that I need," she says.

I know she thinks that's the case, but I hope one day she finds a man to make her consider being in a relationship again.

"I'm going down to see what's happening on the casino floor. Was there anything else you wanted to talk about?" she asks.

"Nah, I'm good. I'll send you guys the address and details for New Year's Eve. Thanks for coming."

"You got it. Bye."

"Bye." I disconnect the call.

Drumming my fingers on the arm of my couch, I wonder if I should give in and make another call. I don't want to be clingy, but it's been over a week since I saw Mallory. It would be one thing if one of us was traveling, but we're in the same freaking place. Kinda hard to be friends with benefits if we never see each other. Not that I only want the benefits. Of course, I'm dying to sleep with Mallory again, but it's more than that. I like her. I want to talk to her. I want to hang out with her. And then sleep with her. I guess she doesn't feel the same way about me.

The phone rings in my hand, and I jolt. A Cheshire Cat grin spreads across my face when I see it's a FaceTime call from Mallory. I take a deep breath and accept.

"Howdy, stranger." I can't believe I just answered my phone like that. Can I be any more of a dork?

Laughing, Mallory replies, "Hey, you. Have you always been so weird?"

I grin. "Yeah, but normally I'm able to hide it better."

"Don't hide it. It's cute."

She thinks I'm cute. If I was a twelve-year-old girl, I'd blush and giggle. Since I'm a manly man at twenty-seven, I hold back the giggle, but I'm betting there's a touch of red underneath my beard.

"I met Ethan," I say. "He seems nice. Your nephews are cute."

"Yeah, they're adorable. Ethan liked you."

"I was hoping to see you this afternoon," I admit.

Mallory sighs. "Me too, but Valerie needed some sister mani/pedi time. She's going through some stuff."

"Is she okay?" Valerie is the only Carter sibling I have yet to meet. From what I can tell, she's kind of intense.

"She will be. Anyway, I did a thing," she says flirtatiously.

"Oh, you did, did you? What kind of thing did you do?"

"Well...you know how we haven't seen each other in over a week and we're friends with benefits who haven't had any benefits yet?"

"Yeah? " I say with a mix of curiosity, eagerness, and caution.

"My house is full, yours is too close to your parents, and it's too cold for your truck, so I got us a room at Devil's Den." She bites her lip nervously, like she's afraid I won't think that's a brilliant idea.

"Really? That's awesome! I'll pick you up. I can be there within the hour." I sound like an overeager beagle, but I don't care.

"I'm already here, just waiting for you. If you want to come." Her sexy smirk and double entendre have my cock suddenly hard. I think the loss of blood to my brain has made me lightheaded. Thank goodness I'm already sitting down.

"Hell yes, I want to come. What did you want to do for dinner? I can get us a reservation," I say.

Mallory gives me a devilish grin. "How about room service?"

"Perfect. What's the room number? I'll be there within the hour." I'm already up off the couch and heading to my bedroom to throw a change of clothes and a box of condoms in a bag.

She gives me the information I need and asks, "Should I order now? Or later?"

"Order sandwiches so we can snack. Later." I'm starving, but not for food.

Mallory giggles. "Okay. Get here soon. Drive safely."

Like anything is going to keep me from finally being with my girl again.

26

MALLORY

I can't believe I'm doing this. I'm not a sexually shy woman, but this is the first time I've rented a room and invited a man over for a booty call. I didn't know how else to get alone time with Liam without having a quickie somewhere. Been there, done that, and thoroughly enjoyed it, but I want a bed this time and the opportunity to take our time and enjoy each other without interruption.

I don't know who's going to arrive first, room service with the tray of sandwiches and chocolate cake I ordered, or Liam, so I'm staying dressed.

The room is elegant, like the rest of the casino. The bed is a king-size four-poster made from a dark wood. Maybe cherry? The decor is warm and understated, and there's an air of elegance about it. I feel more like I'm at a grand home in the English countryside than a casino in Atlantic City.

There's a knock on the door, and the butterflies in my stomach take flight. I check the peephole and am disappointed. Room service.

"Good evening, miss. I'm Frederick, and I'll be serving you tonight. May I wheel in your meal?" The room service attendant's deep brown eyes are friendly in his weathered face.

I step back and gesture for him to enter. "Thank you, Frederick. How are you today?"

Wheeling the cart over to the small table, Frederick smiles over his black-suit-jacket-clad shoulder. "No complaints, miss. Would you like me to serve your meal?"

"No thanks, Frederick. I'm waiting for a friend to arrive. We'll take care of it." I sign the bill and add a tip above the gratuity already included. 'Tis the season, after all.

Frederick unloads his tray on the table and rolls his cart to the door. "Please don't hesitate to let us know if you need anything to make your stay with us more enjoyable."

"Thank you. I hope you have a happy New Year, Frederick."

"You too, miss." He opens the door.

Liam is standing there, ready to knock.

"Good evening, sir," Frederick says.

"Perfect timing," I say with a smile. "He's my guest, Frederick. Thank you."

"Hello," Liam says to Frederick as they switch places. Liam closes the door, drops his bag, and engages the locks before turning to me.

A slow grin spreads across my face as he stalks toward me, his feline grace never more evident. But I don't feel like prey, I feel like treasure. His treasure.

"Are you hungry?" I ask, not at all innocently.

"Starving."

"I ordered sandwiches."

"Don't care." Liam's growly voice makes my core tighten and my lady bits tingle.

He reaches for me, grasping my hips and pulling me toward him. His kiss is hungry, and I open my mouth, eager for my tongue to tangle with his. Kissing Liam is wonderful, but I want so much more. My greedy hands slip under his blue sweater. The skin on his back is warm, and his muscles ripple and bunch as he mirrors my movements and pulls my sweater up my body. The green cashmere is soft, whispering against my skin. We break our kiss for a moment so that we can remove our sweaters.

Calloused fingers replace the softness of the cashmere, and the difference makes me shiver.

"Are you cold?" Liam asks as he kisses down my neck to where it meets my shoulder. Goosebumps break out, but not from any chill.

"No, not cold. Hot. Very hot." I'm surprised I could string that many words together. My brain is scrambling with desire. I don't want to talk. I want to feel.

"So hot," Liam says. His blue eyes burn as they take in my breasts. I'm glad I'm wearing my best black lace bra. I know it shows them off spectacularly. My nipples pebble under his heated gaze. As much as I am enjoying his eyes on me, I want his hands and his mouth on me even more. Liam must read my mind because his large hands reach up to cup my breasts, thumbs brushing my nipples. His hands need to be on my skin. I don't want any barriers, even black lacy ones, between us. I reach behind to unclasp the bra.

Liam lets out a low chuckle. "Eager, huh?"

"Yes, I am." I stretch to reach his lips again as my seeking hands drop to his belt buckle. In a flurry of kisses, caresses, and murmurs, we're both undressed and gazing hungrily at each other.

"You are so beautiful," Liam says huskily.

"So are you." I run my hands over his powerful chest with the light covering of hair. I trail my fingers down his abdominals, past his belly button, following his happy trail to his erect cock, jutting proud and strong from his body. A drop of precum glistens on the tip, and I drop to my knees so I can lick it off.

Liam's groan as I take his cock into my mouth is music to my ears. I cup his balls and run my tongue along the underside of his heavy shaft. I love having his pleasure within my control. I continue licking and sucking, reveling in the grunts and groans my attentions draw from him.

"Ahh...Mallory, love, you gotta...stop. I'm going to come, and I want to be inside you."

I run my hand up and down his shaft as I glance up at him with a smirk. "You are inside me."

He bends to put his hands under my arms and lifts me effortlessly. I gasp at the brief feeling of weightlessness as I rise through the air, but then wrap my legs around his hips, nestling his cock between us. We each recognize that the slightest shift would put him at my entrance, and a thrust would have him inside me. Bare. I'm not ready for that, and Liam must see that in my eyes and agree because he carries me to the bed. After slowly lowering me to the comforter, he reaches out for the strip of condoms I have on the nightstand.

I expect him to sheath himself hurriedly and push into me, but instead, he places them on the bed next to my hip and leans down to kiss me. His weight on top of me is warm and heavy, but not confining. His lips move to my jaw and travel to a sensitive spot under my ear that makes me sigh. I tilt my head to offer access to my neck, and Liam takes the hint, kissing his way down my throat, giving a light nip where my neck and shoulder meet.

I know what that means.

I may not shift myself, but I understand. Biting is how shifters claim their mates. That nip wasn't a claiming, but only because Liam is holding back. Because I've been adamant that this is nothing.

Claiming is so much more than nothing. It's everything.

I want everything. With Liam.

I gasp, my entire world tilting with the revelation.

He chuckles, misinterpreting the sound of shock as a response to pleasure. He continues kissing downward to my breasts. While his lips have been on the move, so have his hands. Calloused fingertips have been running up and down my sides and along my thighs. Now one hand caresses my breast as the other slips between my legs.

"Oh, Liam," I sigh as he parts my folds to rub my clit.

His lips are busy too, drawing a taut nipple into his mouth. His tongue flicks over the tight bud, mimicking what his finger is doing to my clit. Both feel so good, I don't know where to focus. I move restlessly underneath him, enjoying his attentions, but needing more.

"Liam, please. I want you," I beg.

"You have me, Mallory," he murmurs as he turns to my other breast.

"Inside me." I can hear the whining tone of my voice, but I don't care. Foreplay is nice, and Liam is very good at it, but I want him in me. Now.

"As you wish," he says.

Jinkies, a *The Princess Bride* reference. I can't help but giggle. He knows that's one of my favorite movies, and I'm touched he remembered, especially at this particular moment.

He reaches for the strip of condoms, rips one off, and sheaths himself quickly. I open my legs wider so he can nestle against me. I can't wait to have him inside me. He rubs his cock against me, coating himself in my wetness. I wrap a leg around his hip as he presses himself in me with a slow, firm thrust. He feels so good, long and hard inside me. I squeeze my walls around him, and he starts to thrust, slowly at first, but I need more. I pull his head down into a kiss and use my tongue to show the rhythm I want our lower halves to match. He takes the hint, and his thrusts become harder and faster. I love it. I roam my hands over his back, my nails lightly running along his spine. I grasp his firm ass, and the muscles flex as he pumps into me.

"Oh, Mallory, you're so tight. So good," Liam pants as he thrusts into me.

"So good," I echo. "I'm close. Please, Liam."

I don't know what I'm asking for, but Liam does. He gets a hand between our bodies and presses his thumb to my clit. Apparently, that was all I needed because I'm suddenly tightening everywhere and crying out as my orgasm overtakes me. A few more deep thrusts, and Liam is voicing his own pleasure as he comes.

In the afterglow, I enjoy Liam's weight on top of me. I could lie like this forever with him. I wish it was possible. Maybe it could be. If our lives were completely different and we weren't who we we re. I sigh as I run my hands up and down his back, my fingers tracing each bump of his spine. Liam's breathing is slow and even. I wonder if he's fallen asleep when I feel the rumble coming from him. Wait...

"Liam, are you...are you *purring*?"

"Mmm."

He presses a kiss where my shoulder meets my neck, and I shiver.

"Maybe. I'm happy. All of me is happy. My cougar is happy, and when he is, he purrs."

I smile. If I had the ability to purr, I'd be doing the same.

"Wow," I say after a few minutes of holding each other.

Liam's moved slightly, so his weight isn't fully on top of me. Chuckling, he tightens his arms around me. "Wow because of what we did, or wow that we weren't interrupted?"

I laugh. "Both?"

Liam gets up to take care of the condom, and I admire the view of his firm ass. Stretching, I enjoy the slight ache in places that haven't been touched in so long. I shiver as Liam reenters the bedroom.

"Let's get you under the covers," he says. "We don't want you catching a chill." He pulls back the covers and settles me under them.

"Ready for dinner?" he asks.

"Yeah. We worked up an appetite."

Liam hums tunelessly as he examines the sandwich selection I ordered and makes a plate for us to share.

"Wine?" he asks, handing me the plate and some napkins.

"Nah, I'm good with water."

He nods and grabs two bottles from the mini fridge. I watch his beautiful body with its graceful movements and think briefly of the accident he was in years ago and the miracle it was he recovered from his injuries. I say a quick prayer of gratitude as he slides under the covers to join me.

We eat our sandwiches, and it's both normal and weird to be naked in bed, enjoying a turkey club with Liam.

"How offended would you be if we turn on the Flyers' game?" I ask.

"Oh, Mallory, I think you're my ideal woman." Liam laughs and hands me the remote.

We settle in with our sandwiches and entertainment, and I think about how I've missed this. I've missed him. This is so good, but so bad. This is a booty call, friends with benefits. I can't be catching deeper feelings.

I'm afraid it's too late.

27
LIAM

THIS IS MY FIRST TIME WAKING UP NEXT TO MALLORY, AND I HOPE IT WON'T be the only time. I'm propped on my elbow, head resting on my palm, watching her sleep. She's curled on her side, facing me, her hands tucked under her cheek. I can count the freckles scattered over her nose—twenty-three. I'd love to wake her by kissing each and every freckle, especially the one on the tip of her nose. It's adorable. Maybe she sensed my thoughts because her long lashes flutter and her sleepy green eyes look into mine.

"Good morning," she murmurs, a slow, sexy smile forming on her lips.

"Good morning," I respond, a matching smile spreading on my face. "Do you want room service for breakfast, or would you prefer to get something after we shower?"

"What time is it? Checkout is at eleven."

"We're good," I assure her. We are. I already arranged for the charge for the room and food to be put on my account, and checkout is whenever we want to leave. Being best friends with the owner has its perks.

"Where would we go? I take breakfast seriously."

I enjoy learning that about her.

"Go Fork Yourself?" I suggest a mom-and-pop place near my house that's legendary for their omelets and pancakes. And rude service. That's what happens when badger shifters are the proprietors.

"Oh, yeah. I haven't been there in forever." Mallory stretches and winces slightly. We were busy last night. After our sandwiches, we went another round that included some creative use of the frosting on the chocolate cake she'd ordered for dessert. Then we had to shower and finally had time to do everything we'd wanted to do when her mother interrupted us. The shower was fun, but I loved being in a bed and having all night to savor her body.

"You okay?" I ask. We were very energetic. I hope I didn't accidentally hurt her.

She gives me a wink and a grin. "Yeah, I'm good. Very good. My muscles aren't used to that kind of workout."

I lean down and kiss her. I can't help it. I could kiss her all day long, but her stomach growls, signaling that it's time to find my girl some food.

"I'm happy to help you with this new fitness regime. Consider me your personal trainer. But first, I guess I'm your nutritionist." I throw back the covers and get up from the bed. I don't miss the way her eyes sweep over my naked figure.

"Nice flex there, stud. Subtle." Mallory rolls her eyes as she teases me. She grabs a T-shirt off a nearby chair and pulls it over her head before she gets out of bed. I don't know why she's being shy now. I've seen, touched, kissed just about every inch of her body in the past fifteen hours.

"What's your plan for today?" I ask.

"Nothing too exciting. Laundry, play with my nephews, avoid awkward questions about where I was last night, read. The usual. What about you?"

My gaze follows her as she goes into the bathroom and closes the door behind her.

"Have breakfast with you," I say, pulling on my clothes. "I need to go over some reports and figures for the pier project."

She opens the door and motions toward me with her toothbrush. "The pier is going well? No nasty surprises from the inspections?"

She brushes her teeth, and I lean against the doorframe, watching her.

"No surprises. We did a ton of inspections beforehand because we knew this was going to be an extensive project. We usually build our outlet centers from the ground up. They aren't rehabs like this."

She nods, showing she's listening.

"Plus, it's a pier, so the ocean and all that must be considered. It's going to be a mammoth undertaking, but it's exciting. We've been working on it behind-the-scenes for a while, so a lot of planning and designing has already been done. Our plan was to move quickly once the property came up for sale. We have crews lined up to start the structural work it needs."

"I can't wait to see how it all comes together. It's an eighteen-month timeline? There's a lot to do in that time."

She doesn't know the half of it. When it's done, it's going to be so much more than another shopping center. It's going to be a destination for fun and the home of my dreams for the future.

We finish dressing and gather our overnight bags. I took care of the express checkout, so we don't need to go to the desk. Mallory still thinks she's paid for our night. I'll explain it if she ever asks about it.

I open the door to our room and allow Mallory to step out first when I hear, "Mallory!" called out from down the hall. The voice is familiar, but I can't quite put my finger on it. I go to peek when Mallory grabs the door handle and pulls it shut behind her, leaving me in the room and damn near taking my nose off.

"Janet, imagine seeing you here!" Mallory's voice in the hallway is muffled by the thick door. "How was your holiday?" Her voice is softer now, more difficult to hear. She must have walked away from the door.

Janet is the biggest gossip at Morgan Development. She works in

the leasing department, and she's...adequate at her job. I can understand why Mallory wouldn't want her to see us together, leaving a
hotel room. We hadn't made plans other than breakfast. We were
going to get our cars from the valet and drive to breakfast separately.
I take out my phone and shoot her a text.

> Me: Waiting a couple minutes to leave the
> room. I'll meet you at the Fork. Drive safely.

Mallory sends me back the thumbs-up emoji.

I hate having to sneak around and hide our relationship or
friends with benefits or whatever this is. Okay, I know Mallory calls
it friends with benefits, but to me, it's so much more. Shifters know
when they've found their mate. Last night confirmed she was mine.
My cougar longed to sink its teeth into her, to mark her, claim her as
ours. I appeased us both with a small nip. Even though Mallory
doesn't shift, she knows about claiming. I heard her gasp, and I know
it wasn't only from the pleasure I was giving her. She's mine, and I'm
hers. Now to get her to see it too.

I peek to make sure the coast is clear when I leave the room a few
minutes later. I'm waiting for the valet to bring the Bronco around
when I get a text from Logan.

> Logan: Apparently we're meeting Mallory for
> breakfast at Go Fork Yourself, and I'm
> supposed to invite you. So...want to join us?

> Me: Yeah, see you in thirty.

I get in my truck and tell my phone to call Mallory.

"Hello?"

"Hi. Logan and Daphne are joining us for breakfast?" I ask.

"Hey. I thought you were calling to cancel." She sighs. "Yeah, I
invited them. I figured if they were there, it wouldn't look odd that
we were out together. Logan's your cousin, and Daphne's my friend,
so it makes sense we do stuff together."

She's quiet, and I can picture her chewing on her bottom lip. I love kissing that lip.

"Is that okay?" she asks.

"Yeah, it's fine. Just making sure you still wanted to do breakfast," I say. Do breakfast, be with me, be my mate...but we'll start with breakfast.

"I'm starving. I'm having breakfast. Whether you're there or not is up to you."

Ouch. I get on the highway out of Atlantic City and head toward the mainland.

"Mallory, are you okay?"

"Ugh. I'm sorry, Liam. I'm just freaking out because of Janet. You know she's such a gossip, and I'm not sure she even cares about the truth. She'll be telling people about me being there, and who knows who she'll say I was there with."

"Does she know you were there with someone?" I don't care personally if she says I was there with Mallory, but I know she doesn't want it out there, so for that reason alone, I care.

"I told her I was there to get away from the full house with my family visiting, but I don't think she believed me. But even if that was the truth, she'd twist it to make it seem like I was there with a lover."

"Well, try not to worry about it. If she spreads shit at the office, HR can step in."

"No! Then it just lends credence to her tales."

"Okay," I say slowly, drawing out the word. "So, you're just going to stress over this?"

"Pretty much. And stress eat."

I laugh. "As long as you have a plan."

Mallory laughs too, so that's a win. "I'm pulling in at the Fork. I'll go in and get us a table. Did you want me to order anything for you?"

"Coffee and OJ, please."

"Okay. See you soon."

She hangs up.

If we just didn't worry about keeping whatever this is we have a secret, then Janet or anyone else wouldn't have anything to talk about. But that's a topic to tackle another day. Now that we've finally gotten started, I'm not going to risk Mallory changing her mind. I'll do what it takes to convince her to be more than my friend with benefits. I'm going to convince her to be mine.

28

MALLORY

I SNAG A TABLE FOR FOUR AT GO FORK YOURSELF AND IGNORE THE DIRTY looks I garner for having prime real estate. Thankfully, Daphne and Logan arrive right after I sit down so it no longer looks like I'm taking up a four top all by myself. Logan goes to look at the pastry case and Daphne turns curious eyes on me.

"Shut up," I tell her before she can get a word out.

"I didn't even say anything!" she protests.

"I don't want to talk about it."

"He's meeting us," Daphne says.

"Who is?" I know she's talking about Liam, so I don't know why I'm even questioning it. Blargh. This is such a mess.

"Miller. I think he has a crush on you, and since nothing is going on with Liam, you should give him a chance. He's a nice guy."

"*What?*" Oh no, no, no. Miller is a nice guy, but he's not the guy for me. That will be even more awkward. I don't want to hurt Miller. I like him. But not the way I like Liam. If I'm being honest, I've never liked anyone the way I like Liam.

Daphne smirks. She's been teasing me. Bitch.

Speaking of Liam, he walks in the door and joins Logan at the pastry case. After a moment, they walk to our table and sit down. Logan sits next to Daphne, who's laughing at my panic at the thought of being matched with Miller, which leaves the chair next to me open for Liam to drop into.

"Hi, Daphne, what's up?" Liam asks.

"Hey, Liam. It's okay. We know," Daphne says.

A beautiful smile appears on Liam's face as he turns to face me, and my tummy flips in a way that has nothing to do with being hungry.

"You told her?" he asks, pleased surprise clear in his voice.

I give Daphne a death glare. "No, I didn't."

She smiles back serenely.

"Oh." Liam's smile fades. He picks up the coffee I ordered for him and takes a sip as he looks over the menu.

Damn it. Why does this have to be so complicated?

Our server arrives to take our order. I'm hungry, but I've lost my appetite for the decadent gourmet specialty pancakes they offer. I end up ordering a stack of regular plain pancakes, scrambled eggs with cheese, and a side of ham. Everyone else gets omelets with toast and home fries.

"So, what do you have planned for today?" Logan asks.

"I think I'm going to go for a run," Liam answers.

That could be fun. We haven't run together yet.

"I'll see if Dad feels like it. We haven't shifted and run together in ages. Shame Andy isn't here. Did you want to fly along?"

Oh. He wants to shift and run. I can't keep up with that. I shouldn't have hurt feelings over it, but I do. Is he excluding me because I don't want to be public with our relationship?

Our meals arrive, and we dig in. The food is delicious, but I can't enjoy it with the lump in my stomach.

"Trevor and Ethan are usually always in the mood to run if you're okay with wolves," I offer.

"Yeah, good idea. I'd love to explore the woods out your way."

"You're welcome anytime. Same as with the rink." And my bed.

"You're sure?" Liam asks.

I don't know if he's asking if I'm sure about Trevor and Ethan wanting to run or something else.

"I'll text them and see." I grab my phone and get to work, then relay the response after I get it. "My parents took the boys to the movies, and Ethan is dying for a run. Haven't heard from Trevor."

"Okay, thanks."

"No problem."

Daphne nudges Logan. "You should go fly with them. Mallory and I can hang out." She turns to me. "We can catch up."

She isn't fooling me. She wants the scoop on me and Liam. There is no scoop.

"Sure." I hold back my sigh.

We decide we'll all head to my house after breakfast. I hope they puke from running after eating.

I look around the café to keep my gaze from straying to Liam. I love the country cottage charm of the place. The blue gingham plastic tablecloths and pale-yellow walls set off the white chairs and tables. The blue vases filled with daisies on every table remind me of my bedroom and bathroom. The red lighthouse accents all around add a nautical touch. It's a cheerful space.

The bell above the door dings to signal a new arrival, and my gaze drifts there.

"Shit," I say.

Liam looks up and groans.

Daphne and Logan have their backs to the door and turn around at the same time.

"No! Don't turn around!" I whisper hiss.

"We have to stop meeting like this, Mallory!" Janet says with a fake-ass laugh.

"We do, Janet!" My tone is similarly fake, but I mean every word.

Janet leans in conspiratorially. "I ran into Mallory as she was leaving her room at Devil's Den. I was so surprised!"

"I bet," Daphne says. "What were you doing there? I must have just missed you. Mallory and I had a girls' night since Logan and his cousins were watching college football all day long."

I love Daphne.

"Oh! Have you met my boyfriend, Logan? Honey, this is Janet. She works with me and Mallory. Janet, this is Logan Morris, my boyfriend."

"Morris? Are you related to Mike Morris?" Janet asks. She knows damn well he is.

"Yes, he's my father. Will is my uncle, and Liam's my cousin."

Liam coughs to hide his snort-laugh. I'm pretty sure if we had crayons at our table, Logan would have offered to draw Janet a family tree.

"Well, it was so nice to meet you, Logan. Great to see you, Liam. Daphne, Mallory, I'll see you in the office." With another fake smile, Janet walks away to peruse the pastry case.

"Not if I see you first," I mutter.

Janet gets her Danish and coffee and leaves, giving our table a lingering glance as she walks out the door. Good riddance.

We decide Daphne's going to ride with me. Liam is going to drop his Bronco off at his house, and he'll ride with Logan to my house to go run with Ethan. I'd rather get the interrogation over with on the ride so we aren't overheard by Valerie if she's around.

No sooner have I pulled out of the parking lot when Daphne turns in her seat to look at me directly and asks the dreaded question.

"So, you were at Devil's Den with Liam last night?"

I take a deep breath and release it slowly. "Yes."

She bounces up and down in her seat and squeals. "I knew it! How was it? How long have you guys been dating?"

May as well get this over with.

"We're not dating. It's just a friends-with-benefits thing. We met and hooked up in Vegas when I went for that bachelorette party. It was a one-night stand."

"What? I thought you just met at Thanksgiving!"

"We didn't know each other when we hooked up in Vegas." I'm embarrassed to admit this. Daphne is such an innocent. "We only exchanged first names, and it was a quickie in a dark corner of the club. We weren't going to ever see each other again. Scratch an itch and all that."

"So, you hooked up there and then randomly find each other here and have all these connections in common?"

I glance over to see Daphne sitting there with a dreamy look on her face and her hand pressed to her heart. Uh-oh.

"That's so romantic! It's fate that brought you back together!" She sighs. I bet she's picturing her bridesmaid dress...or maybe a double wedding. Not happening.

"Vermin brought us together. It's not fate, and it's not romantic. It's nothing. We both like sex, and it's convenient. I don't want people knowing our business because I don't want anyone thinking I get anything at work because I'm sleeping with the boss's son."

"I understand that, but everyone knows how good you are at your job. You don't need to sleep with anyone to get ahead."

"Thanks. But you know how Janet and her crew of mean girls are. I don't want to deal with it."

"Yeah," Daphne agrees.

I remember something. "Oh! You'll probably meet my sister, Valerie. Do not say *anything* about Liam in front of her. She made me swear to never date a coworker, and even though what Liam and I are doing isn't dating, she'll freak out. She just got out of a bad arrangement with a coworker, and it's messed her up."

"Oh no! Is she okay?" Daphne is so sweet.

"I hope so. She's normally so strong, but this has really shaken her." I grimace. "One more thing. I told my family I was hanging out with you last night. They think we were watching chick flicks and drinking wine because you had an argument with Logan." I glance over apologetically. "Sorry."

"Whatever. All good."

I park in the driveway and chuckle as Daphne stares up at my house with her mouth hanging open.

"This is your house? You grew up here?" she asks in awe.

"You didn't see it when you came to the rink?"

"No, we came from the tree farm, so we didn't pass it, and I was focused on the barn. I didn't look around."

"Yep. It's been in the family for generations."

"Wow..."

It's a beautiful house. It's big and white with green shutters, which always makes me think of *Anne of Green Gables*. It's mainly colonial in style, but my ancestors have added on through the centuries, so while it's an architectural mishmash, it works somehow.

Walking through the butler's pantry into the kitchen, I see Valerie sitting at the counter with a bottle of wine in front of her. Normally she's perfectly groomed, but today, she's still in her pajama pants, and there's a glob of dried yogurt on her T-shirt. Uh-oh. This does not bode well.

"Hey, Valerie. This is my friend Daphne. Daphne, my sister Valerie."

"Hi, Valerie. Nice to meet you."

"Hello," Valerie responds. But she's not paying attention to Daphne. Her attention is focused on me. "I kinda sorta accidentally-on- purpose gave my notice this morning. Via text." With that pronouncement, she drains her wine glass and promptly refills it.

"Wow. I bet that was unexpected," Daphne says.

"I don't see how it was. My cheating ex is a sleazoid. No way was I going to work for him. Especially since he took my promotion." She takes another deep sip of her wine. "Never get involved with a coworker. It's a clusterfuck waiting to happen."

Oh boy. This isn't good.

"Do you have something else lined up?" I ask. Please let her have something else lined up.

"Nope." Valerie pops the *P*.

Okay. This isn't her second glass of wine. Possibly not her first bottle.

"What are you going to do?" I think I know the answer, but I'm praying I'm wrong.

"Well, roomie, I arranged to sublet my apartment for the last two months of my lease, and then they'll sign their own lease. I have a severance package, so I don't blow things sky high for those assholes while I figure out what I'm doing next."

For the first time, I see insecurity in my big sister.

"Is that okay, Mallory? I know this is your place now, but it's a big house. I'll stay out of your way..."

I pull Valerie into a hug, and she lets me, even though she's usually not a hugger.

"Valerie, this will always be your home. Of course it's okay. You do what you need to move forward. I've got you."

Oh shit, oh shit, oh shit. I meant it when I said this was her home, but her being here means collecting benefits from Liam has gotten even more complicated. I can't afford Devil's Den every week.

My phone dings with a text.

> Liam: Almost there. Are we meeting at the barn?

Good question.

I go to the foot of the back stairs. "Ethan, Trevor! You in here?"

Daphne's eyes widen. She's an only child. She's not used to the bellow.

My brothers thunder down the stairs, sounding more like a herd of elephants rather than a pair of wolf shifters. They shoot wary glances at Valerie as they enter the kitchen. I'm betting they were afraid of Valerie and waiting for me to get here to be a buffer. For a couple of wolves, they're big chickens.

"You rang?" Trevor asks slightly snarkily.

"Should Liam and Logan come to the house, or were you meeting them at the barn?"

"Who are Liam and Logan?" Valerie asks.

"Logan is Daphne's boyfriend, and Liam is his cousin." I shoot eye daggers at my brothers to keep them from saying anything more. They have powerful senses of self-preservation and keep their mouths shut except to say they should come to the house.

> Me: Come on up to the house. You can meet my sister. She's going through stuff—please don't mention we work together. Just be Logan's cousin.

> Liam: Okay...

> Me: You'll see.

> Liam: Pulling up now.

"They're here," I say to my brothers and walk to the front door to see Liam and Logan emerging from Logan's Jeep.

"Hi," I say to them, "come on in."

"Wow, this is some house," Logan says, looking around. "Daphne asked to move in yet?"

Liam follows him, but he doesn't glance around the entry or anything else. I'm the focus of his attention. I hope Valerie is too deep into her wineglass to notice.

"You know Trevor and Ethan, obviously. This is our sister, Valerie. Valerie, this is Logan and Liam." Logan moves next to Daphne and slips his hand around her waist, and Liam just stands there awkwardly. In gray sweatpants. Damn it! The man is wearing gray sweatpants, and I'm not supposed to want to jump his bones? Promises to my sister and the need for secrecy be damned.

"Nice to meet you," Valerie slurs, waving her wine glass.

How much has she had to drink that she's this drunk? Wolf shifters metabolize alcohol quickly. It takes something like Nana's special eggnog to knock us on our asses. It's essentially jet fuel with a touch of nutmeg. A glance in the sink shows a glass with the dregs of eggnog. So the wine is the chaser to the eggnog? This isn't good.

Trevor follows my gaze and must realize the same thing.

"Ready to go?" he asks the rest of the guys.

Logan nods.

Liam reaches into his pocket and pulls out his wallet and phone. "I forgot to leave these in the car. Okay to leave them here?" He holds them out to me.

"Sure." I take them from him and put them on the counter.

Daphne and I follow the guys out the French doors in the breakfast room and across the patio. I've seen my brothers shift countless times, but I'm dying to see Liam in his cougar form. I'll never understand the magic that makes shifting with your clothes on possible, but I'm grateful for it. Well, usually. No one wants to see their entire family naked, but I quite enjoy Liam in the buff.

The guys walk across the back lawn and, with a slight cosmic vibration that never fails to cause the hair on my arms to stand on end, shift.

Logan is regal as his golden eagle form takes flight, his massive wingspan casting shadows as he circles above. I shift my gaze to Liam.

"Oh." I can't help the sigh that escapes as I take in the tawny form of Liam as a cougar. He's all sleek feline grace with his muscles rippling as he stalks away on his massive paws. My brothers are big men, and their wolves are huge, but Liam eclipses them both. Wowzers.

Before they enter the tree line, Liam looks back at me. His eyes are the same blue as always but even more vibrant with the black fur rimming them. He gives a wink and a happy kitty chuff, then follows my brothers into the woods. I look up and see Logan flying high above the treetops, soaring in lazy circles. Occasionally, he gives his massive wings a flap, and I swear I hear the leaves rustle from the draft they create.

With the guys off on their adventure, Daphne and I reenter the kitchen. Valerie is still sitting there, but gone is my morose wine-guzzling sister of a few minutes ago. In her place is a furious woman, appearing stone-cold sober, glaring at me. Daphne steps behind me.

"You lied to me," Valerie spits out.

"What?" I ask.

"You're sleeping with him."

"Who?"

"Liam."

"Okay. I never said I wasn't." I keep my voice calm and modulated in hopes it calms Valerie down as well.

"You work together!" she screeches, flinging something at me as I approach the counter.

It's Liam's business card. I look around and see Liam's wallet in front of Valerie. I scoop it up.

"You went through his wallet? What the fuck is wrong with you?" I slam my palm on the counter as my scream tears through the kitchen. Valerie should be grateful for the counter between us because if I could reach her, I'd be yanking out fistfuls of hair.

She snarls. "It's obvious you're screwing each other. I could smell him all over you. I was making sure he didn't have a picture of his wife and kids in there. Can't have us both make the same mistake, can we? And you promised, you *swore*, you wouldn't sleep with a coworker. You lied to me just like everyone else does."

"I know he's not married! And it's none of your business what I do!"

"You're my little sister. It makes it my business, Mallory. Sleeping with your boss? Really? Going to sleep your way to the top? I'm not surprised. You always were a failure. I guess fucking your way up the corporate ladder is a valid strategy for those without brains or ambition, but I stupidly expected better from you."

I rear back like she struck a physical blow. This. This is why I don't want people knowing about me and Liam. No matter what the truth is, it will always boil down to me sleeping around to get ahead. My intelligence and skills won't factor into it. Well, maybe my blow job skills, but not my legal skills.

Daphne steps in front of me to confront my sister.

"Valerie, you know nothing about Mallory and Liam's relation-ship. I'm sorry you're having a crisis, but that doesn't give you the right to say things like that to your sister. Liam isn't Mallory's boss, he's not married, and he's a good man."

Valerie turns her heated gaze to Daphne, and I'll be damned if Daphne doesn't just glare back at her. I don't know where this bravery and loyalty is coming from, but my sister angry is a scary sight. She makes my brothers turn tail and run. However, Daphne's standing up to her. In my defense. That's never happened before.

And Daphne isn't finished.

"I don't know what is wrong with all of you, but Mallory is a great paralegal, and the success she has, and will have, is all because of her hard work, dedication, and brilliance. She's not an attorney because she doesn't want to be, not because she can't be. Attorneys are a dime a dozen. Paralegals really get the job done, and your sister is stellar at that. So take your head out of your ass, sober up, and then apologize for being a bitch to Mallory."

I stare in awe at Daphne. No one has stood up for me like that before. Hell, *I've* never stood up for myself like that before. I don't think anyone has ever confronted Valerie like that. My sister is physi-cally intimidating. She's almost six feet tall and leanly muscled. Even if you didn't know she's a wolf shifter, it's obvious she's strong. Add in her keen intelligence, confident attitude, and general air of "I take no shit," and she's a force to be reckoned with. And Daphne reckoned with her. For me. Tears spring to my eyes.

Valerie continues to glare at Daphne, but now I swear I see a glint of respect in her hazel gaze. With a huff, Valerie grabs what remains of her current bottle of wine and storms out of the room. She tromps up the stairs and slams her bedroom door. I hope she takes Daphne's advice and sobers up. I don't expect an apology. That's not how we do things. We just ignore the issue and move on.

I wrap Daphne in a hug, and I'm surprised to feel her trembling.

"Holy shit. I was afraid she was going to turn into a wolf and eat me!" Daphne says, giving a shaky laugh and lowering herself to a stool at the counter when I release her.

"What? No! Really? You were afraid? And you stood up for me anyway?"

"Have you met your sister? She's scary! I thought I was going to pee myself." She looks around. "Do you have anything to drink? I know she took the wine, but is there anything else?"

With a teary laugh, I turn to rummage through the fridge. My search is successful, and I emerge with a carton of orange juice and half a bottle of champagne.

"Let's grab some blankets, turn on the patio heater, and have mimosas while we wait for the guys to get back."

That's how we spend the afternoon. If it wasn't for the shadow Valerie cast with her outburst, it would have been perfect. Logically, I know I should just shrug off her words, but I can't. I've been chasing her approval my whole life. I want her to like and respect me. We're sisters. We're supposed to be best friends, but she doesn't want me. Yet again, I'm not good enough for this family. Will I ever be?

29
LIAM

WE RUN FOR ABOUT AN HOUR. THE WOODS AROUND THE CARTER FAMILY home are great. I assume these are the trails that Mallory runs on. Hopefully we can run them together sometime. When we reach a clearing with some old wooden Adirondack chairs and a cooler, the Carter brothers shift back to human form. I follow suit, and a moment or two later, Logan lands and shifts as well. Trevor opens the cooler and holds up a bottle of water, silently asking if we want one. When we all nod, he tosses them around our group, and we settle into the chairs.

Chuckling, I look around. "Cozy setup you have. How'd you get it out here?"

Trevor takes a pull of his water and nods. "Yeah. We're civilized. There are ATV trails throughout the woods. We hauled them in that way. Later this week, one of us will come restock the cooler and take any empties. I'm sure our Lycan ancestors are rolling their eyes at us for not drinking out of the river as God intended, but...ew."

"Your property goes to the river?" Logan asks.

"Yeah. It was a great place to grow up. I hope the boys like growing up here," Ethan says.

"Don't you live in Maryland?" I ask.

Ethan nods. "My wife and I are divorcing, and I'll have primary physical custody of the boys. We decided it would be best if they were raised away from DC. They'll finish out the school year there, and then we'll move up here in the summer."

"Does Mallory know this?" Trevor asks.

"I don't know. We haven't discussed it."

He's moving here-here, like...in with Mallory? Is he really that clueless?

Trevor shakes his head. "Don't you think you should, Ethan? It's our home, but it's hers now. We can't just keep treating it like a Holiday Inn. She's never going to turn any of us away, but we should do her the courtesy of asking her and not just assuming we can crash here whenever we want."

The tips of Ethan's ears turn red, standing out against the black of his slightly shaggy hair. I guess he really is that clueless.

"Crap. You're right. I didn't think about it. It's amazing she puts up with us." Ethan tips his bottle toward me. "Don't think that just because we're inconsiderate clods that you can get away with treating Mal that way."

I hold up my hands in a "not me" gesture.

"How long have you two been dating?" Trevor asks.

"We're not dating," I say reflexively.

"Bullshit," Logan says with a cough to cover it.

I shoot my cousin a glare.

Trevor quirks a brow. "Lory will insist you aren't dating because Valerie is constantly hounding her to promise she'll never date a coworker, and Lory wants Val's approval, but I have eyes, and you two are together. I think you're a good match."

Ethan nods. "I love our sisters, but they're a handful. Mal is the mellower of the two though."

I do a spit take. Mallory. The mellow one? I use the sleeve of my T-shirt to wipe the water I dribbled off my chin.

"It's true. Lory is stubborn, but Valerie's so moody. She just broke up with a guy she worked with who turned out to be married with kids, so she's gone off the deep end." Trevor looks at Ethan. "Did you get the guy's name? I'd like to pay him a visit."

"Nah," Ethan says. "She's not talking. She'll just drink her wine and lick her wounds in private." Ethan turns to me. "Mallory must really like you a lot if she's involved with you even though you work together. She's never gone against what Valerie says before."

I shrug. "I'm not her boss or in her chain of command. Yeah, we work for the same company, but I have nothing to do with her job. What's the big deal?"

"The big deal is that our mother has gone on since the girls were old enough to understand that they had to be strong and succeed on their own merits," Ethan says.

"What's wrong with that?" Logan asks.

"Nothing. But Mom felt she lost out on promotions to men or that other women got ahead because they slept their way to the top. Maybe they did. I don't know. So, she drummed it into their heads that there could be no appearance of favoritism or whatever. Then Valerie hooks up with whatever schmuck and loses out on a promotion to him. It's like it flipped a switch and she's doubling down." Ethan finishes his water, crushes the bottle, and puts it in a bag in the cooler next to him.

Trevor picks up the thread of conversation. "Mom and Val have always kinda double-teamed Mallory. They have very forceful personalities and Lory is mellow, like we said, so she goes along with it. Have you met our parents?"

"Oh, yeah," mutters Logan.

I nod.

"They don't realize it, but they've treated Mallory differently than the rest of us. I think because she doesn't shift, they don't know what to do with her. Mom doesn't understand her because they're so different. Mallory keeps trying to earn their approval. She especially wants Valerie's, and I don't think it's possible," Ethan says.

"She needs to say fuck it and just do what she wants to do," Trevor says.

I agree wholeheartedly. But if she won't, and us working together is the impediment to us being together, then I'll remove that obstacle as soon as I can. I just hope she'll still be there when I've done it.

"Ready to head back?" Ethan asks.

We shift and lope through the woods back to the house. The trees are thin as we approach the backyard, revealing Mallory and Daphne lounging on the patio. No sign of Valerie. That's good. When the girls notice us, Daphne wanders to the side of the house. I guess Logan will meet her there and shift? Mallory gets up and wanders into the yard toward me. Her brothers continue to the patio, and I hear her nephews cry out for their dad. Ethan and Trevor remain in their wolf forms to tussle gently with the boys. Mallory has never seen me in my cat form, so I stay as I am, trusting she'll tell me if she wants me to shift.

"Wow, you're gorgeous," she says as she approaches me.

I swish my heavy tail just to show it off before sitting on my haunches and wrapping it around my front paws like a house cat. I'm a big guy, and so is my cat. Seated like this, I'm eye to eye with Mallory.

She reaches out a hand to touch me and then stops herself, embarrassed. "I'm sorry. I was going to pet you without asking permission. I know better." Her green gaze meets mine. "May I touch you, please?"

Like she ever needs to ask. I nod my head and lean forward, welcoming her touch. She reaches out and runs her hand over the back of my head.

"Oh, you're so soft."

I give a chuff of laughter. Those are words a man never wants to hear.

"I didn't realize you'd be so big," she continues.

That's more like it. I nuzzle Mallory's shoulder, and she wraps her arms around my neck, hugging me. I close my eyes and relax into the embrace, letting out a contented purr. For all the times I've had sex with Mallory and other women, this is the most intimate encounter I've ever had.

Mallory's parents join us on the patio and ruin the mood. Mallory stiffens and steps away. If I could roar, I would. Her brothers shift back, and so do I. We walk to join the group as Daphne and Logan come from around the corner of the house, looking slightly disheveled.

Her mother smiles at the boys with their father and uncle and turns to Robert.

"I remember when you'd play with the kids like that. Those were good times," Beth says. Turning back to her sons and grandsons, she says, "I can't wait for you two to start shifting so we can do family runs through the woods."

EJ, Mallory's older nephew, shakes his head. "If Aunt Mal doesn't go, they aren't family runs. They're just runs."

"Well, EJ, you know your aunt can't shift. She couldn't go with us," Robert says.

"She could ride a four-wheeler. Family means nobody gets left behind or forgotten," the younger boy, Matt, says.

Holy crap, he's quoting that Disney movie Kennie made me watch a thousand times when we were kids.

"Exactly right, boys," Ethan says, laying a hand on each boy's shoulder.

"Or we just run as people," Trevor suggests. "Your Aunt Lory is a great runner. She runs through the woods all the time. She's probably the fastest of us on two legs."

"Really? Will you run with us tomorrow, Aunt Mal?" Matt asks, bouncing on his toes like Tigger in his eagerness.

I hear Mallory's shuddering inhale, like she's trying to control her emotions. Shaking her head, she clears her throat and says, "Not tomorrow. I need to go to work. If we don't get to it this week before you go home, we'll do it the next time you visit, okay?"

The boys run around on their own, yelling yay and doing all the little boy stuff Logan and I did as kids. I hope to have kids running around in this yard someday.

Matt runs up to us as we reach the patio and looks at me with a cocked head. "You're a cat?"

Beth tries to shush him, but I ignore her.

I nod. "Yep, I'm a cougar shifter."

"Can you roar?" EJ asks, joining us.

"No, I can't. But I can purr loudly, which lions and tigers can't do. It depends how our throats are. Some cat species can roar, and some can purr."

"Can you climb trees? Like really high? As your cougar." Matt again.

"I can. One of my favorite things to do is climb this certain tree behind my house and rest on a big branch. It's most fun in the summer when the leaves can hide me." I look over at Logan. "Did you know my cousin is an eagle shifter? He can fly super high."

The boys go over to ask Logan questions, which he happily answers. Robert and Beth go back in the house with Trevor. We sit down in the chairs Daphne and Mallory were in when we returned. The warmth from the patio heater is nice.

"You're good with kids," Mallory says, surprised.

I nod. "I like kids."

"You do?"

"Of course. Don't you?" We haven't discussed much in depth about our feelings around having and raising children since she's adamant we're just friends with benefits.

"I do. I thought about being a teacher but became a paralegal instead."

"If you were a teacher, what subject would you teach?"

"History. Pre-industrial revolution. European or US," she says.

"That's what my mom teaches!"

"Really? I knew she was a teacher, but I didn't realize the subject. I think I assumed she taught younger grades."

"Nope. High school. She was my Grammy Morgan's student

teacher for one year. That's how my parents met. Dad came by Grammy's classroom after school, and my dad fell for her like a ton of bricks." I smile, thinking about the stories I've been told.

"He asked her out, and Mom said no. She refused to have anything to do with him while she was working with Grammy. She didn't want anyone to say she got special treatment or a better grade than she earned."

"I get that," Mallory says.

I know she does. And I do too. Now.

"Once the term was over and Mom's grade finalized, he asked her out again. That time she said yes, and the rest is history." I bump her shoulder as I say the last part, and she laughs at my lame joke.

I'm probably a teenage girl for admitting this, but my heart flutters at her laughter. This is what I want. Sitting with the woman I love—and I do love Mallory—laughing over stupid things and being together. I've known she's my mate almost from the start. My cougar wouldn't shut up about it. But I love her as a man loves a woman. I love all of her—her humor, her heart, her courage, her fears. Today I found out about her past, and I'm part of her present. I hope to be part of her future.

"This is nice," Mallory says softly.

"It is," I agree. Is she thinking that we could have something like this someday? I'm afraid to ruin the moment and ask.

The door opens behind us, and we turn to find Beth standing there. Valerie is behind her, glaring at us.

"Will you be joining us for dinner?" Beth asks.

Not the warmest invitation I've ever received. I glance over at Logan, and he motions that he's ready to go.

I stand and face them. Mallory rises to stand beside me.

"Thank you, but no," I answer. "We're going to head out now."

Beth closes the door, and Valerie continues to watch us. Creepy.

I surreptitiously brush my index finger along Mallory's hand. I wish I could be overt in my actions, but under Valerie's glare, I don't dare. For Mallory's sake. I don't care who knows about us. I want the whole world to know she's mine.

"I need to catch up on some stuff for the pier project."

Mallory nods.

"I want to kiss you," I admit.

A pretty flush dusts her cheeks, but it fades when she glances at her sister.

What the hell is going on?

"Let's walk around the house," she suggests and takes the lead. Logan and Daphne have already gone that way.

"Wait. I need my phone and wallet," I remind her.

"Oh, right. I'll meet you out front." She turns and dashes back into the house, and I continue the trek around to the front.

I hear the front door close as I round the corner, and Mallory meets me in the driveway to hand me my things.

"Um, Valerie knows about us," she says.

I shrug. "Okay." I want the entire world to know.

"She's not happy about it."

I cross my arms over my chest. "I don't care."

"Liam!" she whisper-shouts.

"What? I don't care who knows about us. You're the one who wants to keep it a secret."

"You know why! You just told me about your parents. I know you know why."

I incline my head, acknowledging her point. "I know why. Doesn't mean I agree with it."

She sighs. "I'm sorry, Liam. This is the best I can do for now."

"I know, Sparky. It'll be okay," I say.

She smiles at my use of the silly nickname. It was only a few weeks ago I first used it, but it feels like a lifetime has passed.

Mallory stands on tiptoe and presses a quick kiss to my lips. She's backing away before I have a chance to grab her and kiss her the way I want to.

"I hope so," she says.

As I ride away with Logan and Daphne, I make a silent promise that it will be.

30
MALLORY

I walk back into the house, dreading the conversation I'll be having with my family. Conversation is a less scary word than confrontation.

"A cat. Really, Mallory? It's not enough you're screwing your boss. He's a cat too? You don't have any self-respect, do you?"

Valerie has me cornered in the entryway to the house. *My home.* I can smell the wine on her breath, and I want to gag. My back's against the door, the doorknob pressing into my spine. Valerie towers above me and, for the first time, I'm afraid of her.

"You're such a fool, Mallory. He doesn't care about you. You're an easy piece of ass. No one cares about you. You're useless. You're a burden to the family. Mom and Dad wish you were never born. *I* wish you were never born."

I wake with a gasp, my heart pounding and sweat pouring down my face. Looking around my room, I confirm I'm alone. I'm always alone. I'm always going to be alone. Last night with Liam can't happen again. Not if I want to have respect at work, not if I want my family to respect me. Not if I want to respect myself.

I check my phone. It's four in the morning. I wonder what Liam is doing. I wish he was beside me.

Stop it, Mallory.

It was just a dream. When I walked back into the house, no one had anything to say about our visitors. Valerie sat in stony silence at the breakfast bar, scrolling on her phone. My brothers and nephews were playing video games in the family room. Mom was cooking a lasagna with forty-five minutes left on the timer. I went upstairs to my room until dinnertime. Dinner was tense—at least it was for me. It was quiet, polite, cold. Even Matt and EJ were quiet. I went back up to my room as soon as the meal was done.

I sit on the window seat that looks out into the woods. Movement catches my eye, and a shadowy figure emerges from the trees. It's Valerie, and she's not alone. Ethan and Trevor follow her. Their wolves are beautiful. Valerie's fur is so black it almost looks blue. With her mysterious hazel eyes, she looks like she should be a cover model for shifter romance novels. Our brothers flank her like gallant knights protecting their queen. I guess that's how it's always been. The three of them have a bond that I don't share. I'll never share it. As well as I get along with Trevor, we'll never share the bond he shares with Ethan and Valerie, that he'll share with our nephews when they shift. I give a mirthless laugh. It's fitting that a pane of glass separates us. I'm always on the outside looking in. Yeah, I'm inside, but it still fits.

I hear their low murmurs as they reenter the house. Since I don't have super-duper wolf shifter hearing, I can't make out what they're saying. Probably what a good time they had and how they should do it more often.

I crawl back into my bed and manage a few more hours of fitful sleep. I wish I could call out from work for a mental health day, but being cooped up in the house with my family won't help my mental health at all.

I've been at my desk for about an hour when my phone chimes a text notification. I thought I'd silenced it, but I guess I forgot.

Liam: Hi, going to have to go out of town sooner than expected. Issues with an outlet in Washington state. Will miss New Year's. Sorry.

Me: Are you leaving today?

Liam: Yeah, on my way to the airport.

He's not even going to say goodbye in person?

Me: How long will you be gone?

Liam: Not sure. Have visits to other centers on the West Coast already scheduled. A few weeks?

Me: Okay. Safe travels.

Liam: Thanks.

I sit back in my chair and stare out the window. Was my dream a premonition? Was Liam just using me for sex while he was home, and now that he's back to traveling, he can get some wherever he goes? He obviously has sex on these trips. That's how we met in Vegas. I am so stupid. I can't believe I risked my career and my family's respect for someone who doesn't even care about me. I knew better.

31
LIAM

I CAN'T BELIEVE I FLEW HOURS ACROSS THE COUNTRY FOR A MEETING THAT'S probably going to be an hour long, only to jump back on a plane and fly back to where I was. But it's worth it to be in the same room as Mallory. Even if I can't kiss her or love her publicly like I long to, just breathing the same air is enough. For now. Soon we won't have to keep our love a secret. Everything I've been working toward will come to fruition, and there will be nothing in the way of having the future I want for us—and I know this love is mutual, even if she isn't ready to say or hear the words yet.

I park my truck in the lot for Morgan Development, pull out my phone, and hit Mallory's contact. There's no holding back the smile that spreads across my face when she answers.

"Hey, Mallory. Are you free to meet me?" I ask.

"Hi! When did you get back? I thought you were out of town until next weekend. What a wonderful surprise." I can hear the smile in her voice, and it makes my heart light.

"This morning, it's a one-day thing. In and out."

Her low, throaty chuckle makes it obvious her mind is in the same place mine is. Our time at Devil's Den and all the in and out we did.

"I'm not going to be your nooner," she teases.

Suddenly, she gasps and hangs up on me. That's okay, I'll see her in a few minutes.

There's definitely a pep in my step as I walk into the building, which is amazing considering I got up at the butt crack of dawn to fly back here. Coffee is in order. Maybe two. I wonder if I should pour one for Mallory and have it waiting for her in the conference room or if that will be weird.

I hear Janet before I see her. Ugh. She's so unpleasant. She's talking to one of her minions. Whatever. I'm just here for the coffee.

"Of course Mallory's going to be on the pier project," Janet says, venom dripping from her voice.

My blood runs cold. How does Janet know about the project and Mallory's part in it?

"Of course," her minion echoes.

"Mallory's the type of woman that will do anything to get ahead. Or anyone."

They cackle, and my stomach turns. This is what Mallory has feared, and it turns out she was right to.

"You've seen the way she bats her lashes and flirts with Will and Mike. And they're flattered enough a girl young enough to be their daughter—their daughter!—comes on to them. I swear I don't know how their wives stand for that sort of thing. She's a tramp."

The other bitch laughs. "Well, that's what women who don't have brains or respect for themselves do to get jobs they aren't qualified for. Like Daphne getting the marketing gig once she hooked up with Mike's son."

"Maybe she's fucking Liam too. Keep it all in the family," Janet says.

Her voice gets further away—they must have gone out the other door. Thank goodness. If I came face-to-face with her, I don't know if

I could hold my temper. Or my breakfast. My stomach is churning—coffee isn't going to sit in it.

Damn it. Mallory was right to worry. I can't expose her to this kind of venom. This was her worst nightmare, what her mother warned her about. And it's my fault. I have to protect her.

"Hey, Liam," Dad calls from down the hallway. "Mike's gone up to get Mallory. Let's get this meeting going."

I grab a bottle of water from the break room and take a seat in the conference room. How am I going to be able to be so close to Mallory and act like there's nothing between us? I'm going to hurt her. I know this is going to hurt me more than any car crash ever did.

32
MALLORY

I HATE JANUARY. I KNOW IT'S SUPPOSED TO BE THE SEASON OF FRESH STARTS and resolutions, but to me it's the season of crappy weather, monotony, and loneliness. Daphne is doing marketing work with her video tours of centers, so she's not in the office every day. The collection work is almost done, so I've started working on some leasing. Steve worked on some commercial transactions, so I have experience with retail leases, but not the volume that Morgan deals with. Thankfully, it's a bit like riding a bike. You don't forget how to do it.

Valerie moved in and is still giving me the cold shoulder. I try not to let it bother me; I know she's been through a lot lately, but I don't enjoy having a strained relationship with her. I don't want her to think less of me for being involved with Liam. Not that we've been involved since that night at Devil's Den. We text and FaceTime now and then, but it's not the same as it was.

I know I said this was friends with benefits, but it's not. First, there are no benefits being had at the moment, so that's a failure. Secondly, I feel more than friendship. I want more than that. He's a good man, and I like him. I could see myself falling in love with him. Honestly, I'm afraid I already have. I see what Daphne has with

Logan, and I want that too. I think we could have it. Well, I thought we could have it. I feel like Liam has been pulling away.

My phone rings. "Good morning. Morgan Development. This is Mallory. How may I help you?"

It's Liam—he's in town and wants to meet with me.

"I'm not going to be your nooner," I tease.

I hear a throat clear behind me and spin my chair around to find Mike standing in the doorway of my office. He heard what I said, and I want to hide for the next ten years. Maybe by then, the flush that's probably turning my face crimson will have faded.

"Hi, Mike." I hang up the phone without saying goodbye to Liam. "What's up?"

He gives me an embarrassed grin. He probably wants to go hide somewhere too.

"Can you come downstairs? There's a meeting we want you to be a part of."

Oh crap, the human resources department is downstairs. Do they know about me and Liam? Not that there's anything to know about. There aren't any fraternization rules either. I've checked.

"Sure. Do I need to bring anything? Laptop?" Purse, coat, personal belongings because I'm being fired and escorted out of the building?

"Just yourself," Mike assures me.

All righty then.

We take the stairs to the second floor and turn toward the conference room. To my relief, no one from human resources is there. Instead, Will, Ben, Miller, Teagan, Jake, and Liam are occupying the seats around the table. My eyes widen. When he said "meet with him," I didn't think he meant attend a meeting!

"Good, we're all here," Will says from the head of the table as I take the seat next to Ben, and Mike sits at the other side of the table, opposite Will. Teagan is directly across from me, next to Jake. Liam is down the table, next to his uncle. Unless I turn my head to look at him, I can't see him. From the glance I had when I walked in, he's wearing a navy suit. He looks so handsome. He's not wearing a tie, and the top buttons on his shirt are open, showing the spot at the base of his neck I love to kiss. Our eyes meet briefly when I glance his way again, but he looks away.

Will looks to my side of the table and starts speaking. "As you know, Morgan Development has purchased the Sand Dollar Pier and will renovate it. It will not be opening as a typical Morgan retail center. This property is going to be a mixed retail and entertainment property as a joint venture between Morgan Development and Penhall Enterprises. Representing Penhall Enterprises are Teagan Penhall, owner of the Devil's Den casino and on the board of Penhall Enterprises, and Jake Whitman, Senior Vice President of Hotel Operations at Devil's Den."

I smile across the table at Teagan and Jake. I had no idea Teagan was a Penhall. We didn't share last names at the Flyers game.

"Thanks, Will," Teagan says. "As I've discussed with Mallory previously, spaces that are a mix of retail and entertainment are the way of the future."

Will smiles at me with approval, like I passed a test. We were just chatting at a game. It wasn't a business strategy meeting!

Jake takes the reins of the conversation. "We've done research and will have an ice rink installed on the main floor of the pier. It will be a full-size sheet, capable of hosting hockey games, figure skating competitions, ice shows. It will be open for public skating and private lessons, parties, and events. There will be locker rooms, concessions, and a pro shop. We'll want additional tenants that will complement the rink. Retail, restaurants, other entertainment."

I grab a pen and pad from the center of the table and start writing notes. Ideas flood my brain of what else would work there. Batting cages, an indoor driving range, a sports bar, athletic wear stores. I realize the room is quiet except for the scratching of my pen on the pad. I look up, embarrassed.

"Sorry. Had some ideas. Can't help it," I say sheepishly.

Teagan smiles at me warmly. "That's exactly why I asked for you to be on the leasing team! I knew you'd have ideas and understand what we were trying to do."

"Oh, yeah, you three are the primary legal and leasing team," Mike says. "Miller and Mallory are just about done with collections, and Ben has excellent leasing experience. The three of you working together will be a dream team."

Ben holds up his fists so Miller and I can each bump one.

"What did you write down, Mallory?" Liam asks, his blue eyes intent on mine. I want to crawl across the table and kiss him. I've missed him.

I look down at my pad, glad I didn't write my grocery list.

"I was brainstorming what else may be good along with the rink. In terms of entertainment, we could focus on other sports with batting cages and an indoor driving range. A sports bar, as well as a family-friendly place with an arcade, like the fifties diner down Route 42. Ooh, mini golf." I add that to my list. "For retail, a sporting goods store, casual clothing, athletic wear. Book store."

"Book store?" Jake asks.

"A lot of families will have one person—adult or child—who isn't feeling like being sporty and would much rather sit somewhere and read. Parents needing something to read during a practice. Having a bookstore will cater to them. Plus, you'll draw people from the beach and boardwalk."

Everyone is smiling, so I guess my ideas made sense.

"Total dream team," Mike says, smiling down the table at us.

Liam drums his fingers on the table. Is he nervous?

"It's early days still, and we should be able to provide more details and plans in a few weeks as more pieces fall into place," Will says. "However, we wanted to bring you three in now to give you the heads up. We'll make a formal announcement upstairs when we know more. The role the three of you will have is not a secret, but it's not common knowledge yet. Any questions?"

"Are we remaining Morgan Development employees, or is the joint venture a separate entity?" Miller asks.

"Still Morgan," Will says with a smile. "You're our all-stars. We're not letting you get away!"

Jake leans in. "The joint venture is going to be a separate entity, but the leasing will remain in Morgan's purview."

"Will we get an employee discount to use the rink?" Ben asks with a laugh.

Liam turns to Teagan and Jake. "Ben has twins in pee-wee hockey and has to go to Voorhees for practices and ice time."

Teagan grins at Ben. "The three of us love hockey, and part of the reason for wanting a rink in the pier is so that we can help support and establish youth hockey here at the shore. We hope teams will make the pier their home base and cut out the commute. You'll definitely get a discount."

"Any other questions?" Mike asks. There are head shakes around the table. "I guess we're done then. Thanks for coming down," he says to us. "Thanks for coming in," he says to Teagan and Jake. We all rise, and handshakes are exchanged.

"Want to join us at Francisco's?" Teagan asks as we shake hands. Her gaze includes Ben and Miller.

I wasn't expecting that. I glance to Liam. He gives a quick lift of his brows. What the hell?

"Sure. Let me run upstairs and get my purse. I'll meet you guys there?"

"Sounds like a plan," Teagan says.

"I brought lunch, but thanks," Miller says.

"Me too, and I use my lunch break to study. I'm in law school," Ben says.

I leave the conference room behind Ben and Miller. We take the elevator upstairs, so we have a moment alone.

"Wow," Miller says, "wasn't expecting that."

"I know, so cool," Ben says. "Have you known Teagan long, Mallory?"

"No. Just a few weeks. I went to a Flyers game and sat in the Morgan box. She and Jake were there as friends of Liam's. I didn't realize she was a Penhall. We had a casual conversation about shopping centers needing to be more than just retail to stay relevant in the age of online shopping. I didn't realize this was going to come from that."

"Good job making an impression! You had some great ideas too. I'm looking forward to working together on this," Miller says.

The elevator reaches our floor, and we exit to return to our own spaces. I grab my purse and head back downstairs. Liam is waiting in the lobby.

"Want to ride together?" he asks.

I look around to see if anyone's nearby, but we're alone.

"I'm only having lunch. I meant it when I said I wasn't going to be your nooner," I warn him with a flirtatious wink.

Liam doesn't laugh. "No nooner. Just lunch. I fly right back out."

"Okay, but I'm driving." I'm teasing. I doubt he'll fit in my MINI Cooper. To my surprise, he agrees.

I can't do that to him—he'll have to fold himself like a pretzel to fit in there.

"I was just kidding. We can take your truck." I bump his biceps with my shoulder as we cross the parking lot.

He just grunts in reply as he takes the keys out of his pocket. He opens the truck door for me as he always does, but he doesn't kiss me or make a naughty suggestion. He's coldly polite. I wonder what's up. I assume he'll tell me when he's ready.

Teagan and Jake are waiting for us when we arrive at Francisco's. We decide to order a buffalo chicken pizza and settle in a booth. Jake and I slide in first on opposite sides. I expect Liam to slide in next to me, but he sits next to Jake. Teagan sits next to me and glances at Jake, who just shrugs.

"So, the three of you grew up together? How was that?" I ask to ease the awkward silence we find ourselves in.

"Ugh, horrible!" Teagan says.

"No, it wasn't. It was great," Jake insists.

"Great for the two of you, maybe," Teagan says. She leans toward me like she's going to tell me a secret. "These two had a racket where they'd work together to get girls. They'd go to the boardwalk. Jake would shift into his seagull and harass whatever girl Liam had his eye on. Liam would 'rescue' her and be her hero. Jake would shift back and hang out with her friend."

I burst out laughing. "How old were you guys?"

"Thirteen, fourteen. We were kids." Jake shrugs.

"You're a seagull shifter?" I ask. I've never known one before.

"He's a beach chicken," Teagan teases, shooting her straw wrapper at him.

"Nah, beach chicken is too cute. Seagulls are more like devil birds. No offense, Jake," I say.

"None taken. Devil birds. Huh. I like it." He looks to Liam and Teagan, who nod. I don't know what that's about, but our pizza arrives, so I don't ask.

We chat about hockey and general stuff as we eat our pizza. It's nice. I know Jake and Teagan aren't a couple, but it would be so much fun to hang out with them socially. I wonder if either of them is in a relationship. I'll have to ask Liam later.

We get back in Liam's truck, and I expect to go directly back to the office. Instead, Liam drives us to a local park and pulls in near the walking trail.

"Liam, I need to get back to the office. You know I only get an hour."

"I know. I just need to talk to you. I don't know when we'll get another chance with my crazy schedule and your crazy sister." Liam undoes his seat belt and leans against the driver's side door.

"Hey! She's not crazy. She's just going through some stuff. I swear when she's not heartbroken and bitter, she's fun."

"If you say so."

I turn toward him, expecting our lips to meet. But they don't. Liam has his arms crossed over his chest, and it feels like a brick wall is erected between us. What the hell?

"What's up?" I ask.

"I know how important your career is to you."

"It is. I'm so excited to be working on the pier project. This is what I've been hoping to do. It'll bring a lot of jobs and opportunities to the region. We'll be able to work on it together! I have so many ideas. It's going to be great."

Liam somehow seems to retreat even further away from me. The cab of his truck isn't that big, but the couple of feet between us on the bench seat may as well be the Grand Canyon. What is going on?

"Yeah. I heard from Uncle Mike how your goal was to be involved in the selection of tenants and not have 'cookie-cutter' centers. Well, you got that now."

It's almost like he's accusing me.

"It was my goal. *Is* my goal. I've never made it a secret. I want to do well at work. Why is it an issue now?"

"I'm not saying it's an issue. Just acknowledging you got what you wanted. Look, I'm going to be busy with the centers, so I won't be here that much. When I am here, I'm going to be focused on the pier. I care about my career too. We should each focus on our careers for the time being."

Where is this coming from? I know we never said anything out loud, but I thought we were something to each other. I thought our silence was only because of my reluctance to talk about it. I thought he was ready to move forward and was just waiting on me. I think I'm ready now and was hoping we could finally figure out a way we could be together. Maybe there's a way we could be a couple openly without it impacting my career. If I do a good enough job on the pier, then I'd prove I deserved the job and it wasn't just handed to me because of being with Liam.

The silence draws out. I know my heart's still beating, but I'm not sure how since it's broken in two. Liam is breaking up with me. Not that we were together, but I thought he wanted me. I thought he wanted to claim me.

Wrong again, Mallory. He wanted to fuck you, not be with you.

Not love you. I knew I wasn't enough. I've never been enough. Hell, I'm not enough for my own family. That's fine. Lesson learned.

I nod. "That sounds like a wise decision."

I make a show of checking my phone for the time. Liam takes the hint and buckles his seat belt and starts the truck. Thankfully, the park is only around the block from the office, so I just need to hold back my tears for a few minutes. As he pulls into the parking lot, I unbuckle my seat belt and grab my bag, ready to jump out the second he stops.

I turn to look at him as I reach for the door handle. His hands are gripping the steering wheel so tightly his knuckles are white. He's staring out the windshield, not even looking at me. If it wasn't for the twitching muscle in his jaw, I'd think he didn't care at all.

"Goodbye, Liam. Safe travels," I choke out past the lump in my throat as I open the door to make my escape. I don't know if he responds because the slamming of the truck door cracks like a gunshot in the cold January afternoon.

Miraculously, I'm on time returning to work. I stop in the downstairs restroom, first making sure there are no little critters around, to confirm I don't look as devastated as I feel. My eyes are bright with unshed tears, but if I stay in my office, no one should notice.

I hope.

33
LIAM

IT TAKES ALL MY SELF-CONTROL NOT TO BURN RUBBER LEAVING THE PARKING lot after dropping off Mallory. I hurt her. I hurt myself. But it's better to stop whatever there is between us before it becomes too much for us to keep quiet, before everyone knows. I can't let my desire—my love—for her keep her from achieving her goals. Uncle Mike told me about Mallory's dream to be involved in the planning and creation of new centers. She had all those great ideas at the meeting. She's meant to do this kind of work.

I wanted to vomit when I overheard Janet's vicious gossip. I knew what she and her minion were insinuating, and it was disgusting. It took everything I had not to burst out there and fire them both on the spot. But that would have added fuel to the fire and hurt my parents. Dad and Uncle Mike are honorable men. They would never cheat. I know Mallory admires both of them—it would break her heart to have gossip spread linking her to them in that manner. It would hurt Mom and Aunt Holly too. People would whisper about how when there's smoke, there's fire. I wasn't going to allow our budding relationship to be kindling. Better to break it off now before we get too deep. Maybe once the team is announced and my ties to Morgan Development are formally severed, we can try again. If she'll talk to me.

Stopped at a red light, I hit my steering wheel in frustration. My cougar is pacing inside me, restless. I wish I had time to go for a run, but I need to get to the airport ASAP to catch the flight to Oregon. I didn't need to be here for the meeting today. They could have handled it just fine without me, but I jumped on the opportunity to see Mallory again, no matter how briefly. Now I wish I hadn't. I'd give anything to go back to naively thinking this could work out and only good things would come from it. Her career would flourish, and we could work together on a project that was important to both of us. That we could build something together, literally and figuratively.

I park in the garage at the airport and text my dad where the truck is parked. Not that it doesn't stand out. Not many red-and-tan 1990 F-150s around anymore. I go through security quickly and down a whiskey at the airport bar before boarding my flight. Maybe if I stay slightly buzzed, it'll ease the pain in my chest.

It's not like I was really, truly in love with her. It was a fling. A brief infatuation. There was no future. I never thought about little redheaded girls with braids running through the woods or little boys learning to play hockey on the rink their grandmother invented. I didn't imagine Thanksgiving next year with Mallory by my side at Aunt Holly's. Nope. Never crossed my mind.

If I keep lying to myself, maybe I'll believe it. Eventually.

It's been a week since I left Mallory at the office. A week since I've seen her or spoken to her. A week since my heart has felt whole. But the pain I feel will be worth it if it gives Mallory her dream, if this success is what she needs to prove herself to her family. Show them that she's as focused and as driven as they are, that she isn't lesser because she doesn't shift.

I pick up my phone and FaceTime Logan. He'll understand.

"Hey, Liam. What's up?"

"Nothing. I'm in Idaho. Bored. Just checking in. How are you?"

"I'm fine. I figured you'd be calling Mallory, not wasting time with me."

He doesn't know. I guess Mallory didn't say anything. Why would she? It meant nothing to her.

"Yeah. We haven't been talking much. She needs to focus on her career now. So do I. Neither of us needs the distraction of a relationship or the gossip that goes along with it."

"What are you talking about?" Logan gets up from the sofa and starts walking through his house.

"Teagan picked her to be on the leasing team for the pier project, and I heard people gossiping about how Mallory will do anything to get ahead. About our dads. They meant it in the most disgusting way."

Logan drops into his desk chair heavily, the leather creaking under him. "Wait, what? Who the fuck would say something like that? I hope you fired their asses on the spot!"

I run my hand through my hair and let out a huff of frustration. I wish I had.

"No, I didn't fire them. I didn't want to even acknowledge their existence. I can't let Mallory be subjected to that kind of malicious gossip. Or the family. Since I'm out of town so much, I decided it would be best to just call things off. We had a meeting where Teagan and Dad told her she had the new pier job. She was so excited and came up with a dozen ideas right off the top of her head. She's made to do this kind of work. I can't stand in the way of that. We went to lunch with Teagan and Jake, and on the way back, I told her we should focus on our careers. I wanted to let her down easy. I could tell I hurt her, but she agreed, and then she couldn't get out of my truck fast enough. I swear she practically left a jet trail." I take a breath and refill my lungs. I had to say everything at once or else I would've never gotten it out.

Logan cocks his head. That's what he always does when he's trying to understand something. If I had the heart to laugh, I would, because he reminds me of his eagle when he does that. Trying to figure out what he's seeing.

"You broke up? Because of stupid gossip? You didn't give her any say in it?"

"We were never together to break up. Friends with benefits, remember?"

He waves his hand like he's flicking away a mosquito. "I'm not getting this. So, some busybodies gossip. It was probably that Janet chick you all can't stand."

I nod.

Logan huffs out a breath and rolls his eyes. "You throw away your relationship because of some nosy bitch. You decide to be a martyr and fall on your sword to protect your lady love. You don't tell her, or anyone—for example, our fathers, or the human resources department of Morgan Development—what's going on so they can handle it appropriately. You just throw a hand grenade into your relationship, blindside Mallory, and take off?"

He shakes his head in disgust. "Liam, you're a fucking dumbass."

"She didn't fight for us! The second I gave her an out, she took it!" My voice is shaking. With frustration. Not with anything else. Frustration is all I feel. Not hurt. "She didn't say there was no reason we couldn't have our careers and each other. She just said okay and got out of my truck!"

"Why did you give her an out if you didn't want her to take it? Why were you testing her?" Logan looks at me like I'm stupid. Why doesn't he understand this?

"I'm trying to protect her!" I yell. I'm this close to throwing my phone against the wall of this generic hotel room in Podunk, Idaho, or whatever town this is. I don't even care anymore.

"Give me that." Daphne wrestles the phone from Logan's grasp.

"What did you do, Liam? Did you break Mallory's heart? Is that why she's been quiet and withdrawn? She looks like crap, and I think she's lost weight. I assumed it was her sister, but it was you?" Daphne's face is flushed, and her narrowed brown eyes stare me down. I've never seen her like this. I've only ever seen her angry when hockey and bad calls from refs are involved.

"I didn't do anything. There's gossip at the office, and I'm shielding her from it."

Daphne's mouth falls open at my statement before she snaps it shut. She hands the phone back to Logan but leaves it facing her as she paces back and forth in front of their desk. She's muttering to herself and waving her hands around, but I can't hear what she's saying until she comes back to the phone.

"You are such a fucking dumbass!" She points at me through the screen. "Do you think dumping Mallory protects her? If anything, she's more vulnerable now because she's on her own. If people were gossiping, they'd be careful in case it was true and she had your protection. Now she doesn't, so they can be as nasty to her as they want without fearing repercussion."

Daphne resumes her pacing.

"It looks hinky that she suddenly got this plum assignment over everyone else after we started hanging out. They hired her for collections," I say.

"No, you idiot, they didn't! They hired her for leasing, and when Martha and George both announced they were retiring, she agreed to do collections to help the company and help *me* keep my job! She sacrificed her career goals for the good of the company." Daphne glares at me.

I run a finger along my collar to ease the tightness in my neck.

"She didn't have to take the switch in position. She could've been in leasing this whole time, doing what she likes and what she's good at. She didn't have to spend a year downstairs with mice and crickets and jacked-up technology. She did it because she's a team player. And this new position rewarded that loyalty and because she's damn good at her job! You threw her caring about her career back in her face. I'm ashamed of you, Liam."

I watch her stomp out of the office and feel a moment of vertigo when Logan flips the phone around to face him.

I look at my cousin, not knowing what to say.

"So that went well," Logan says, the calm tone a welcome switch from Daphne's ferocity.

"You're supposed to be on my side."

"I am on your side, Liam. Other than Daphne, you're my best friend, and I want you to be happy. I know you have this urge to protect, but it's misguided." Logan's green eyes are sympathetic. I need to look away before mine fill with tears.

"Well, I failed. I didn't protect her. I hurt her." I hate admitting that, but I have to be honest.

"And you hurt yourself. Let me know if I have this right. You two spend the night together at Devil's Den, everything is great, she runs into the biggest gossip at your office, and that makes things weird. We run at her house, her sister is bitchy, then you leave town suddenly. You come back for this meeting and tell her you want to cool things off and focus on your careers. So, for all she knows, you slept with her, got what you wanted, and dumped her because you're traveling and will sleep with other people while you're gone. Because you hook up on your trips. You hooked up with her."

"What? No! That's not how it is at all!" My protest is automatic. Then my brain kicks in, and I think over what Logan just said. I think about what Mallory has shared with me about her past. Damn it. I hurt us both.

Groaning, I lean my head back and stare at the ceiling. "I am a fucking dumbass."

"Daphne told you so. And dude, blow your nose, you got a big old booger up in there, and I did not need to see it."

For what feels like the first time in weeks, I laugh. And get a tissue.

"What do I do? How do I fix this?" I hope Logan has the answers because I sure as heck don't.

"Grovel. Hope she forgives you."

I was afraid he'd say that.

34
MALLORY

A LITTLE OVER A WEEK AFTER OUR MEETING IN THE CONFERENCE ROOM, WILL emails me, Ben, and Miller to alert us that there's a department meeting this morning to introduce Teagan, announce that the pier will be a joint venture, and that we're taking point on leasing. I can only imagine how my involvement will go over with some people. I'm newer to the leasing side of things, and no one knows that I've done this before—admittedly on a smaller scale with strip malls, but the mechanics are similar. I'll just do a good job and shut up anyone who doubts me.

Instead of having a formal announcement in the conference room, we all just gather in the open area of the third floor. I stand with Miller and Ben as Will and Teagan come off the elevator. I look around but don't see Liam or Jake. I don't know if I can hold myself together if I see Liam. I'm still raw from him dumping me last week. I have bags under my eyes and have been putting my hair in a basic ponytail. I'm neat and clean, but I haven't been making much of an effort with my appearance. What's the point? In contrast, Teagan looks coolly professional in a navy pinstripe pantsuit with a red blouse. I bet it's silk. Her blonde hair is in a chignon. If I didn't already like her, I think I'd hate her for being so perfect. She's intimidating, that's for sure. I'm glad she's on our side in this business arrangement.

The chatter in the room dies away as Teagan and Will move to stand near Mike's office. He comes out to join them.

"Hello, everyone," Will begins. "I'd like to introduce Teagan Penhall, owner of Devil's Den and part of Penhall Enterprises out of Las Vegas."

Teagan smiles and inclines her head in greeting to the assembled group in response to the murmured hellos.

"As you know, Morgan Development has purchased the Sand Dollar Pier and will renovate it. What we can now announce is that the pier will be owned as a joint venture between Morgan Development and Penhall Enterprises. It will be a departure from our typical retail center." He looks to Teagan.

She nods. "We're so excited to be partnering on this. The Sand Dollar Pier most recently has been retail, and in the past was successful as a typical mall, but as you all know, consumer tastes have changed, and Atlantic City is certainly not a typical destination."

She pauses to allow murmurs of agreement to ripple through the room. She's good at public speaking, but I guess that's expected for a person in her position.

"We're doing something different for the market and combining specialty retail with sports entertainment. The pier is being refurbished to include a full-size NHL ice rink with smaller practice rinks and locker rooms in order to host hockey tournaments, local teams, ice skating shows and competitions, private lessons, parties, and public skating."

Excited murmurs spread, and Ben grins at me.

"We're also considering other activities for families and events such as batting cages, an indoor driving range, and possibly basketball and tennis courts on the top level."

I hadn't thought of all of those sports. They could be used year-round, depending how they're set up.

"We'll have casual dining and a food court as well as retail stores for clothing and equipment to complement the attractions we offer. We'll also have non-sporty offerings, like a bookstore and coffee shop, for those who get dragged to games and practices and really just want to read their book and drink some good coffee."

I smile at the chuckles from my coworkers. I'm excited that all my ideas are being presented as fact. Miller nudges me with his shoulder and gives me a wink when I look up at him.

Will holds up his hand to quiet everyone. "In time, everyone will work on this project, but for now, our point people for the initial leasing will be Miller, Ben, and Mallory. With their backgrounds and experience, we know they'll be integral to bringing exciting and valued tenants to the property."

"Experience sleeping their way to the top," someone mutters. By someone, I mean Janet, of course.

I want to pass out.

"Who said that?" Teagan asks sharply. Will looks pissed. Mike is typing on his phone.

No one says anything, but people move away from Janet until she's on her own little island in the room. She lifts her chin defiantly but doesn't admit to being a bitch.

Teagan looks directly at Janet. "I'm the one who hand-picked each person on that team, and I assure you, I'm not sleeping with any of them. Anyway, only an idiot would make multi-million-dollar business decisions based on sex, and I am most definitely not an idiot."

Looking out over the room, Will has the air of a disappointed dad who's going to ground the hell out of someone as soon as their guest leaves.

Shaking his head, he says, "I must apologize for that outburst, Teagan, and to the three of you." He looks to where I stand shell-shocked, with Miller and Ben, who are flanking me like they're the guardians of my honor.

They aren't stupid men. They know that comment was directed at me. I'm so embarrassed. I'm pissed too. I've done nothing wrong. Hell, I've refrained from following what my heart and other vital parts wanted to avoid this type of situation. I am afraid to look around the room and see the faces of people who agree with Janet's opinion.

You know what? Screw it. I know I deserve this opportunity and the people that matter know I'm more than capable of doing this. Ben and Miller want to work with me. They don't think this is a special favor for boinking Liam. I straighten my spine and look around the room with my head held high. To my surprise, what I view are smiling and sympathetic faces. Liam is standing at the back of the gathering with Jake at his side. Jake's face is furious. I can't read Liam's expression. I look directly into Liam's blue eyes, stormy with emotion. I miss when they used to be clear blue and looking back at me with affection.

I turn my attention to Will, who's just started speaking again.

"Thank you for giving us your attention. We'll share more details on the progress of renovations and other things as they become available." Will turns to shake hands with Teagan and then walks over to Mike. They go into Mike's office and close the door. Jake and Liam approach Teagan.

"You okay?" Ben asks quietly.

"Yeah. Mortified, but I'll survive," I say.

Miller gives my shoulder a reassuring squeeze.

Teagan, Liam, and Jake join us.

"What a cow," she mutters.

Assorted coworkers offer us congratulations and well-wishes as they get coffee from the break room and head back to their desks and offices. We smile and thank them.

"I think the cow is about to be slaughtered," Miller murmurs with a chin jerk, directing us to look across the room where Janet is entering Mike's office. Mike looks our way and nods before closing his door.

"Moo," Jake intones, causing us all to laugh and garnering looks.

"You're not the first person she's pulled crap like that on, Mallory," Ben says. "But hopefully you'll be the last. She's toxic."

"And sneaky," Miller says. "She went too far this time."

I cast a worried glance toward Mike's closed door.

"It's not because she targeted you specifically," Miller reassures me. "It's that she said something like that about *anyone*."

"We shouldn't be standing here watching Mike's door like a flock of vultures," I say. "I'm going back to my desk to finish up the last few collections matters. Good seeing you, Teagan, Jake."

With my attempt at a calm, friendly smile, I turn and walk back to my office. I make it to my chair before my knees buckle. Propping my crossed arms on my desk, I rest my head on them and groan. I can't win. I tried so hard to not have whatever my relationship was with Liam be an issue in my job, and here it is, alluded to in the middle of a department-wide meeting. Great.

"Hey."

I raise my head. Liam's entered my office and is standing in front of my desk with a look of concern on his face. What I wouldn't give to be held by his powerful arms and to rest my head against his chest. I could cry, and he'd let me. Well, he would have. Before. Not now.

Daphne comes rushing in right behind him and comes to my side, bending down to give me a hug.

"Oh my God, Mallory, are you okay?" she asks as she releases me and straightens up. She leans a hip against my desk next to my chair.

Tears fill my eyes, and I blink rapidly to keep them from falling. I guess news of my humiliation made it down to the second floor already.

"No. Yes. I don't know!" I pull in a shuddering breath. "I'm embarrassed. Everyone knows Janet was talking about me and Liam, no matter how Teagan deflected it. That's what I've been trying to avoid."

From the main room, I hear Mike say, "Take your purse. We'll have your personal belongings boxed up and delivered to your home this evening."

They fired Janet? I don't think they've fired anyone in the year I've been here. Except for retirement or a change in life situation, no one leaves Morgan. It's a great company to work for, and they're loyal to their employees.

"It's been discussed before, even before recent events. She's been given multiple chances and used up her last one," Daphne says in a whisper.

I nod. The elevator doors close, chatter resumes in the office, and I let out the breath I was holding.

"She's spread similar rumors in the past. No one cares. She's like the girl who cried wolf. No pun intended." She's trying to make me laugh, bless her.

"Well, this time they're true!" I whisper-shout.

"No, they're not. Your position here has nothing to do with your position with him." Daphne shoots Liam a dirty look.

What's up with that? She's always been Liam's biggest fan.

Liam clears his throat. Other than "hey," he's had nothing to say to me. What is there to say?

"Mallory, I..." He stops, his eyes searching my face like he's looking for something. I don't know if he finds it or not. "I've got to catch my flight back out to Montana. I caught a chartered flight with Penhall executives who were coming here from out west for Devil's Den business, but I've got to get back to finish up. I'll be home next week."

He reaches out like he's going to place his palm against my cheek. As much as I'd love to close my eyes and revel in that minor contact for a moment, I pull back. Liam doesn't get to touch me like that. Not anymore.

"It's all going to be okay, Sparky. Trust me."

I want to. I used to. I won't again without a damn good reason.

"Here's to Janet finally getting what she deserves." Daphne refills my wine glass. We're having a slumber party at her house while Logan's doing a photo tour out of town.

We're clinking glasses when there's knocking at the front door. Our pizza arrived ten minutes ago, so I don't know who it could be. Daphne opens it and greets Faith and Holly, who come bearing what smells like freshly baked brownies and carrying cartons of ice cream.

"Hey, Mallory! I've missed you!" Faith puts the platter of brownies on the counter and gives me a hug. I'm stunned but hug her back.

"Hi, Faith, good to see you," I whisper. My throat suddenly feels clogged. I take a gulp of wine in hopes it moves the boulder lodged there.

Holly turns from putting the ice cream in the freezer. "So my nephew is an idiot?"

I look at Daphne with wide eyes. Am I being ambushed?

"Um..." What am I supposed to say? What do they know?

"He is," Daphne confirms.

"Make him sweat before you forgive him," Faith advises.

Not what I expect to hear from his mother.

"What else is going on? Is Liam the only reason you look so miserable?" I can't help but love Holly. She's so direct.

"I'm just tired. Haven't been sleeping great. My sister is living with me and she's...difficult."

"She's a bitch," Daphne says bluntly.

Loyalty requires me to protest, albeit weakly. "No, she's not. Valerie is going through stuff."

"Everyone goes through stuff. She treats you like crap, and you take it. I don't get it."

"She's my sister. I love her. I want her to approve of me, to be proud of me. We're supposed to be best friends."

"What kind of Hallmark horseshit is that?" Holly asks. "She's family. You love her, I get that. But why best friends?"

I'm flummoxed. We're sisters. We're supposed to be close. It's just how it is.

Faith places her hand on my arm. "Holly only has Will. She doesn't get it. No offense, Hol."

Holly looks at Daphne, who only shrugs. "I don't get it either, I guess. Only child."

Faith squeezes my arm. "I have an older sister, Lisa. We aren't as close in age as you and Valerie, but close enough. Growing up, I was always seeking her approval and wanting to be included. She always picked her friends over me. Anything I accomplished, she made sure I knew she did it first. Did it better."

She takes a sip of her wine. "She didn't understand why I was wasting time being a teacher when I could do something useful, like business. When I started dating Will, he wasn't good enough for me. He was just going to use me for sex and dump me. When we got married, our wedding was too small. Everything I did was wrong in her eyes, and it hurt me. All I wanted was for her to love me and accept me and approve of me."

Now it's my turn to comfort Faith. I place my hand over hers and give a gentle squeeze. She understands.

"Mandy, Will and Holly's mother, was my mentor. Mandy really became like a mother to me." Faith smiles at Holly.

Holly smiles back. "I lucked out big-time in the parental lottery."

"One day she saw me sniffling over a tiff with Lisa and sat me down. She asked me questions that changed my life. She asked if I would want to be friends with Lisa if she wasn't my sister. Did she have qualities I admired? Did she make me feel better about myself when I was with her? Not if I loved her. She asked if I liked her. I was dumbfounded. Of course I liked her. But then I thought about it, something I'd never really done before. Lisa's overbearing. Everything is always about her. She's judgmental. I realized that no, I wouldn't want to be friends with her. I didn't like her. I love her because we're family, but I wouldn't choose her as a friend. That realization lifted such a weight off my shoulders. I could stop trying."

Air whooshes out of my lungs like I got punched in the solar plexus. I think about Valerie. She sounds a lot like Lisa. I wouldn't pick her as a friend. At least, not as she is now.

"It's not that Lisa is a bad person. She's not. She's very generous, and she does a lot for her community. She's the first to lend a helping hand. She's admired and beloved by many. But we don't click. And it's okay. Mandy helped me see you could love your family, but you don't have to like them. Doesn't mean you wish them ill, but you kinda just stop caring. You choose yourself over their approval and acceptance."

Choose myself. Those two words cause what feels like a seismic shift in my being. What if I just choose what I want without worrying about what my family thinks or what my coworkers think? Would my world end if they disapproved or were disappointed? Would that be much of a change from how it is now?

I hug Faith and tearfully thank her. Deep in my heart, I hope she becomes my Mandy. I couldn't imagine a better mother-in-law and friend. But first, her son needs to stop being an idiot. And so do I. I spent so much time and energy worried what everyone would think that I pushed away a guy who wanted to be with me, and that I wanted to be with too. Then when he gives me the space I say I need, I'm here moping. That's not fair to either of us. I do want him. I want us to have a future. Would he be willing to give me another chance? Or start over?

35
LIAM

"We're approved! We officially own a hockey franchise!" Teagan is giddy on the FaceTime call with me and Jake.

"When is the Paranormal Hockey League making their announcement of the formation of the League and the inaugural teams?" Jake asks.

"February fourteenth," she says.

Valentine's Day. I can work with that. It's only two weeks away. If everything goes according to plan, it'll be perfect. If it doesn't... well, I'll have a hockey team as the focus of all my time and attention. We officially closed on the pier, so pulling permits and renovating has started. The few remaining tenants were agreeable to having their leases bought out, and any of their employees that were interested and qualified were offered jobs at Devil's Den, so it's worked out that we can move full steam ahead with an empty property. It's an eighteen-month timeline before the PHL starts their preseason games. It will be tight, but it's doable. We *will* do this.

We spend the following few hours discussing the next steps and working through our lists. A lot of things have been in progress secretly for months. We're excited to make them public. I can't wait to share them with Mallory. Hopefully, she wants to listen.

I check my watch. It's only just past seven in the morning, so no one should be in the building this early to see me make my special delivery. I hope this works. I sit at Daphne's desk to pen the note. I should have prepared it at home, but I returned from the Philly airport a couple hours ago, and I'm exhausted.

I read through the note one more time.

> *Dear Mallory, Happy Valentine's Day. I could have gotten you a card, but I think this may make more of a statement. I'm sorry for being an idiot. I wanted to protect you, and all I did was hurt you, and I'm sorry. I will never do it again. I hope after you see what is in the envelope, you'll agree to be my girlfriend. If you want to give this thing, and me, another chance, please be at the Leeds Ballroom at Devil's Den at 10:00 a.m. Enjoy the kiss. I have more if you want them. Yours, Liam.*

I put the sealed white envelope containing a copy of my letter of resignation from Morgan Development on Mallory's keyboard and place the note I wrote on Daphne's yellow legal pad on top. I use tape from Mallory's funky plastic unicorn tape dispenser to tape a Hershey's Kiss to it under my signature.

Today is the announcement of the formation of the Paranormal Hockey League and our team's inclusion as one of the inaugural members. One way or another, my future starts today. I hope it's everything I've been dreaming of.

"You okay, dude?" Jake asks.

We're in the ballroom at Devil's Den, and the press conference announcing the PHL and our team is about to start. Reporters train their video cameras and recorders on the dais with the video screen behind it. The league will be announced via video, and then we'll field questions about our local team.

"Yeah," I say, "just anxious. Hope this goes smoothly."

I look around the room. Mallory isn't here yet, and it's almost ten. Everything else is in place, ready for the announcement. The banner that will unfurl with the team's name and logo is hanging above the screen. My family's standing in the back with Teagan's parents and all of Jake's crazy family. Other than his Uncle Enzo, who we swore to secrecy, Jake hasn't told any of his family about our plans. His sisters would post it on Facebook and Instagram before Teagan took a breath.

Teagan looks to us to confirm we're ready, and we nod. She walks to the podium and welcomes the crowd.

"Thank you for joining us this morning. We hope you're as excited as we are for a new opportunity for Atlantic City."

The video screen comes to life. Brian Benn, the PHL Commissioner, makes the announcement of the league, calling it an important first step in professional sports. It's an important first step for a lot of things. Yada, yada, yada.

Mallory still isn't here. I guess that's it. She doesn't want this. She doesn't want me. Can't say that I blame her. She sees me as someone who would use her and casually toss her away. She doesn't know I was ripping out my own heart in order to protect her reputation and make sure she got the chance she deserved to show all that she's capable of. I'm going to have to try to keep on existing without her. Don't know how I'll survive with my heart outside my chest. Because it no longer belongs to me. It's been Mallory's from the moment we met all those months ago.

The video ends to murmurs throughout the room, and we take our place with smiles for the crowd. Mine is forced.

Teagan resumes her place at the microphone. "The PMW Group, consisting of myself, Liam Morgan..."

I incline my head and raise my hand in a lame-ass wave.

"And Jake Whitman," she continues, as Jake waves, "is proud to announce that we have been chosen to own one of the first teams of the Paranormal Hockey League. Collectively, we have a deep-seated love for the game of hockey and are looking forward to bringing professional hockey back to South Jersey. Ladies and gentlemen, I'm thrilled to present the Atlantic City Devil Birds!"

The banner unfurls and shows the team's name in a funky gothic font and our team's logo—an angry-looking seagull holding a broken hockey stick in its beak. I can hear Uncle Enzo proudly say, "That's me!" Jake and I share a laughing glance. Enzo has been dying to tell someone ever since the photoshoot we did with him holding a mini hockey stick. We're using an illustrated version of the photo, but anyone who knows Enzo knows it's him, with the ferocious gleam in his eyes and the slightly crooked beak. Enzo was a boxer in his youth, and both his human nose and his seagull beak show the damage.

Questions start, and Teagan and Jake handle them. I look over the crowd again just to torture myself, and my heart stops.

Mallory's here. Her smile is huge, and even across the room, I can see her eyes shining with tears.

She waves and mouths, "Sorry! Crazy traffic!"

I smile back. Hell, there's no holding back the smile on my face now. Daphne follows my line of sight and sees Mallory. She practically skips on her way to hug her and lead her over to the family where my parents welcome her with hugs of their own.

A reporter from one of the Philadelphia channels stands to ask a question. "Devil Birds is a unique name. I assume it plays in part to the Jersey Devil legacy Teagan Penhall is part of, and the prevalence and reputation of seagulls here at the Jersey Shore. Who came up with it?"

I step forward. "You got it exactly right, Jim. My girlfriend came up with the name, and as soon as we heard it, we knew it was perfect for the team. She didn't know she was naming a hockey team. She was teasing Jake, but sometimes things are unexpectedly perfect."

Finally being able to claim Mallory as my girlfriend is one of those unexpectedly perfect things.

We field a few more questions and hand out the media packages to wrap up the press conference. I walk over to where Mallory's standing with my family. I ignore everyone's congratulations and do what I've been longing to do for weeks. I wrap Mallory in my arms and kiss her as if my life depends on it. Because it does.

I'm sure there are hoots and catcalls and other obnoxiousness in response to our very public display of affection, but I don't care, and from the way Mallory's kissing me back, she doesn't care either.

When we finally come up for air, Mallory pulls back. "You're really resigning from Morgan Development? We aren't going to work together any longer?"

"It's time for something new. I'm hoping it's with you."

Mallory's happy nod tells me what I need to know.

I try to clear the lump in my throat. "You've officially been my girlfriend for about four minutes. Is it too soon to tell you I love you?"

No one ever told me that someone could sob with happiness, but apparently Mallory Carter can.

She grasps my face and kisses it all over while laughing.

I laugh in return. "So not too soon?" I ask.

"I love you too, Liam!"

There's a squeal of happiness to my left. I guess that proclamation got Mom's attention. If I know her and Aunt Holly, they're going to start trying to plan our wedding.

I'm okay with that.

EPILOGUE

MALLORY - EIGHTEEN MONTHS LATER

I can't believe it's the first game of preseason. Everyone's worked so hard to get us here. The Sand Dollar Pier is affectionately known as the Nest since it's the home ice of the Devil Birds. The renovation is incredible. The rink is state-of-the-art and the envy of many NHL teams. We were able to get the variety of tenants we wanted on long-term leases. Everything's perfect.

Liam's been working so hard to assemble the best team possible and have them ready for tonight's first game. This preseason game against the Salem Spellbinders won't count toward the standings, but of course we want to win our first game ever. That it's our first home game in front of friends and family makes it even more special. I can't wait to see Liam after the game to either celebrate the victory or help him forget the loss. Either option will include the special Devil Birds jersey I had made with his last name on the back acting as lingerie.

"Go, Trev!" Ethan yells.

"There's Uncle Trevor!" Matt cries out, pointing.

The teams have just entered the ice for warm-ups. My family's here in the owners' box, all wearing our Carter #24 jerseys. I'm so proud of my younger brother. Trevor graduated law school at the top of his class. I swear, as soon as he received notice he passed the bar, he negotiated his contract with the Devil Birds. He's the first-line center. It's great seeing him back on the ice competitively again.

"When do the coaches come out?" Daphne asks.

"I think after warm-ups," I say.

The team looks snazzy in their blue-and-gray jerseys. They chose the colors to reflect the Atlantic Ocean right outside our door. Looking out over the sold-out crowd, I see a lot of the jerseys being worn by the fans, and my heart swells with pride. They did it. They took this crazy dream and made it happen.

Kind of like our relationship. When we hooked up that night in Vegas a couple of years ago, I didn't think we'd ever find each other again. Thank goodness fate had other plans.

I'm standing at the front of the box, looking out over the ice, when arms wrap around my waist. The fresh scent of pine reaches my nose, and I relax against Liam's chest.

"You have a magnificent view up here," he murmurs in my ear, pressing a kiss in that spot under my ear that always makes my tummy flip.

I turn and wrap my arms around his neck.

"My view just improved," I say with a grin.

Liam steps back from my embrace and takes my hands in his. Aww, his hands are trembling slightly. He must be nervous about coaching his first game. That's so cute.

"You know how you became my girlfriend on the day they announced the team?" he asks.

"Yeah..." What's he getting at?

"I thought if I asked you another question today, with it being our first game, it would be a good balance."

What?

Liam drops to a knee, up here in the owners' suite, in a packed arena, in front of our family and friends.

I gasp. This can't be happening, can it?

"Mallory Carter, I love you. Will you make tonight the best night of my life and agree to be my wife?"

In his hand is a diamond ring. I'm sure it's gorgeous, and I'll admire it later, but for now, all I see are Liam's bright blue eyes looking up at me with so much love and hope, I swear my heart skips a beat.

"Yes! Of course I'll marry you! Oh my gosh! I love you!" I'm babbling, but I can't believe this is happening.

Liam rises to his full height and wraps me in his arms, kissing me like he has all the time in the world.

At the front of the box next to us, Jake cups his hands around his mouth and yells so loudly, the entire Nest can hear. "She said yes!"

The roar of the crowd is deafening, and it's then I realize they featured the proposal on the Jumbotron and everyone was watching with rapt attention, even the teams warming up on the ice.

Laughing, we break our kiss and wave out to the crowd and the teams, who give us stick taps in congratulations.

Teagan comes alongside us before our families and friends mob us. She hands us each a champagne flute.

"We all want to congratulate the happy couple and we will— after the game. First, our groom-to-be needs to get his newly engaged self downstairs and coach our team to victory. Let's make a toast. First, to Liam and Mallory. Congratulations. I speak for everyone here wishing you all the happiness life has to offer. Secondly, let's toast the real reason we're here." She winks. "Go, Devil Birds!"

We all raise our glasses and cheer, "Go, Devil Birds!"

Liam gulps his glass and presses a hard but too-brief kiss to my lips.

"That's my cue to get down there. Hope we give you a good game!" Liam rushes from the box back down to the locker room to meet the team when they finish their warm-ups.

Regardless of the outcome of tonight's game, I know we already won.

———

Did you enjoy Mallory and Liam's story? Want a peek into their future? Logan and Daphne too? How about Kendall, Trevor and Miranda? Start reading the Paranormal Hockey League series with Sexy Pucking Polar Bear!

Did you know a wonderful way to support authors is to leave reviews and tell your friends? I'd appreciate it if you'd review any of my stories on your favorite platform!

ALSO BY JENNY FENSHAW

KEEP IN TOUCH!

Follow Jenny now for her romantic stories, stay for her ridiculous personality.

Warning: Snort laughing possible.

If you'd like to keep in touch with Jenny Fenshaw check out Jenny's website for all the ways to connect

https://jennyfenshaw.com/
Or just scan the QR code!

ABOUT THE AUTHOR

Jenny Fenshaw is a funny, goofy, and creative author of contemporary paranormal romantic comedies who loves daydreaming about ordinary events, making them ridiculous, and including them in her stories. A native of southern New Jersey, Jenny loves to set her stories in the area she knows so well. From the Atlantic City Boardwalk to the Pine Barrens, her stories are a love letter to her hometown just as much as they are the love story of her characters.

When she's not writing, Jenny enjoys watching ice hockey (for research!) and reruns of *Murder, She Wrote*. She has been married to her cinnamon roll of a husband for over thirty years and has a grown son who has the best adventures.

f facebook.com/JennyFenshawAuthor

⬡ instagram.com/jennyfenshawauthor

BB bookbub.com/authors/jenny-fenshaw

www.ingramcontent.com/pod-product-compliance
Lightning Source LLC
Chambersburg PA
CBHW031614240626
47153CB00002B/753